I0642647

CONTAINMENT FAILURE

HARMONICS
BOOK 2

COLLIN EARL

CHRIS SNELGROVE

SILVERSTONE BOOKS

Containment Failure

Harmonics: Book Two

By Collin Earl & Chris Snelgrove

Copyright 2025, SilverStone Books. All rights reserved.

This ebook is licensed for your personal enjoyment only. This ebook may not be re-sold or given away to other people. If you would like to share this book with another person, please purchase an additional copy for each recipient. If you're reading this book and did not purchase it, or it was not purchased for your use only, then please purchase your own copy. Thank you for respecting the hard work of this author.

ISBN-13: 978-1-967473-16-8

CHAPTER 1
MY FICKLE FRIEND, FATE

Time: Current day

Scene: Undisclosed remote paramilitary facility

Dirk Garrett was screwed, yet again. If he could just get Fate to pencil in an appointment, perhaps this little tiff they had been having over the last few decades might be resolved. It wasn't like Dirk had done anything to piss Fate off. At least, nothing off the top of his head came to mind. But Fate consistently refused to take Dirk's calls, and every time he had tried to walk in, that snooty little receptionist had come up with some lame excuse about Fate being out of the office on important business. She was even less helpful with Fate's schedule. Despite Dirk pointing out that Fate carried with him that whole certainty thing, it didn't seem to matter. In the end, Dirk just felt frustrated, but more determined than ever to get on Fate's good side; at least he thought Fate had a good side.

Anything would be better than where their relationship was now.

Dirk looked around the cell that he had called home over the past weeks. While much more modern than the Jadian cell he had been in before, it still wasn't any five-star accommodation. Dirk remembered wondering if he was leaping out of the frying pan as he followed the man in black out of his cell and up the side of the hill to the waiting chopper. At the time, he was fully convinced that anything was better than transport to the Seven Cities. And it wasn't like these replacement captors were anything like the grunts that patrolled that gods-forsaken wasteland. Still, despite the improvement in the food, Dirk was not sure that he was any better off.

The first few nights were the worst. Dirk was plagued with nightmares of guards storming into his cell, dragging him through dark hallways, and then throwing him off a tall cliff. These dreams seemed to soften over the weeks, as the more recent ones were just of the man in black blowing the cell door off and taking Dirk to a large room filled with golden statues. Dirk had tried to psychoanalyze what that meant, but after making associations with golden statues and his repressed feelings of resentment towards his great-uncle Louie, he had given it up.

At one point, Dirk was convinced that the man in black could hear him, that he was just on the other side of the door. But no matter how loud Dirk yelled and how long he pleaded, he remained locked up in the cell. No exploding doors, no magic smoke, just him and his military-grade cot. Perhaps the man in black was working *for* Fate. Then again, perhaps Dirk needed to get more sleep.

Two loud knocks echoed off the metal door of Dirk's cell, followed by a squeaking hinge being slid back on the lock. Dirk tensed as he lay on his cot, staring at the ceiling. His mind raced to remember what day of the week it was. Shower day was two days ago, and exercise day was... wait, maybe shower day was three days ago. Dirk tensed a little more at the thought. The two guards came into Dirk's cell, the restraints clinking together with an ominous tinkling sound. Yep, shower day was definitely three days ago.

Dirk tried to keep his apprehension in check and fully stowed away from the guards. They always seemed to smirk more when they saw that he was nervous about the impending field trip. Dirk had stopped resisting being put in the restraints when he found out the hard way that field trips with a taser-induced headache were much worse. Now he calmly sat up and waited for his less-than-fashionable accessories.

Restraints in place, Dirk and his 'buddies' shuffled down the winding hallways. With each step, Dirk's body seemed to kick on more of his sweat glands as his skin temperature rose, an almost motion-sick feeling beginning to creep its way up his gut. Dirk had seen the inside of a number of rooms in this facility through the course of these field trips. Sometimes it was the blue room, other times the gray room. He'd even seen a red room once. But all the rooms were down the same hall-way, and it was the threshold of that hallway that Dirk seemed to have the most trouble with.

The three-man team shuffled closer to the end of the walkway. Dirk's heartbeat ratcheted up as the sinister, sterile-looking doors loomed nearer. Dirk squeezed his eyes shut, hoping the absence of visual stimuli would put a dent in his blossoming anxiety. He involuntarily flashed back to the memories of the previous trips down the hallway. He remembered the agony, the frustration, the grating on his nerves. He couldn't do it again. He wouldn't do it again. His resolve in place, Dirk forced his eyes open.

What he saw did not register immediately. His surroundings were very unfamiliar. Dirk glanced back down the hallway and saw the menacing doors retreating away from him. Wait, that wasn't right. If they weren't headed for the color rooms, then where were they going? Dirk looked around, trying to remember if he had ever seen this part of the facility. He perhaps saw down this hall a few times, but only through the swinging doors as someone exited this wing. What could possibly be down here? Dirk's mind raced through the possibilities, each as uninformed as the one before it.

The guards swung him down a narrow hallway that diverted off the main thoroughfare. There was nothing along this hall. No cameras, no signs. Nothing but blank walls. Blank walls and a small door at the very end. Dirk figured out very rapidly where today's field trip was to end up. His mind was so conflicted, flip-flopping between curiosity and sheer panic of the unknown.

The small door opened just as the three arrived, and Dirk was ushered into a very dark room. He could not see the edges of it, nor the ceiling. The floor looked very clean and sterile, almost like an operating room. Dirk's eyes adjusted to the dim lighting as he saw the chair that he could only guess would be his for the next however long. The lights around the chair grew brighter as they approached. Dirk could now see that it was no ordinary chair. Strange wires and metal instruments protruded out at every angle.

His feet started to apply more friction to the medical-grade white floor, yet found little purchase. Dirk's mind had stopped its vacillating and was now stuck squarely, securely, and determinedly on sheer panic. Dirk heard the small door swing shut behind him with a finality-ringing thud.

CHAPTER 2
AN UNEXPECTED HERO

Time: Late afternoon

Scene: Academy 676

All thoughts of screaming or crying melted away as the voice came. The words echoed in her mind.

"Big Daddy to Doughboy. Permission granted. Protect package at all costs. Bravo weapons use only. Engage tangos at will. I repeat, engage tangos at will."

Slow motion, the everlasting cliché from so many stories and Vii theater experiences, commandeered her cognitive function. She could hear and see everything as the bloody mess unfolded.

Richard's lips moved in a slight whisper. "Bravo weapons, huh? About brickin' time."

Richard's head tilted skyward to meet the gaze of the Móguǐ soldier trying to skewer him with a wicked-looking knife. Richard smiled a half-smile as the soldier's eyes went wide in surprise. Sharp movements so fast Sam could barely make them out, and the unmistakable cracking of bone replaced the echo of the crackling voice in her head. The soldier's scream of pain was abruptly cut off by an odd gurgle.

Next thing Sam knew, Richard was standing tall and undaunted, while the soldier was on the ground, his arm horribly disfigured and obviously broken in several places. Blood flowed across the scarred tile, coating the space with red. The soldier's lifeless eyes distracted from the gaping hole in his throat. Sam took an involuntary step back. Icy indifference rolled out from Richard in cascading waves of cold.

Richard was saturated with blood. Sam could see it soaked into his clothes and running from his gut. She knew he was hurt. How could he not be hurt after a blade to the stomach?

Light shivs stretched to their full length as the reality of the Móguǐ's downed leader set in. Murderous eyes fixed themselves on Richard as the Jadian unit fanned out.

"Sam."

He said her name, but she didn't recognize the voice. Sam couldn't answer him.

"Sam!"

Sam gulped, "Yeah, Richard."

He looked over his shoulder at her as he flicked the switch of a light shiv. Now where did he get that?

"Get behind me."

It was a command. No room for dissent or argument. Sam didn't think to argue.

Just as she retreated behind him, the first soldier attacked. A fast cross-body blow aimed directly at Richard's neck swiped out but struck nothing. Richard didn't block; he didn't even try. He simply leaned back, avoiding the tip of the light shiv by centimeters or less. Richard's counter was a quick spin and slash from hip to shoulder that ended with Richard facing Sam. It was like Richard was trying to give the man a piggyback ride. Sam instinctively found the man's face. It was lifeless.

Richard ripped the dead soldier's light shiv from his hand and dumped the body just as the other soldiers leveled strikes from the left and right. With a reverse and fore grip on the shivs, Richard blocked both blows, put an elbow to the nose of one soldier, and delivered a quick snap kick to the gut of the other. He finished the two men with thrusts to the heart. Four men lay dead at Richard's feet. Blood was everywhere: Richard's, the soldier's, and probably Sam's, though she couldn't remember getting hurt. She didn't know anymore. Conscious thought had all but deserted her.

The rest of the soldiers met similarly gruesome fates. They fought and died in a heaping gory mess. Richard dealt with them with speed and violence that Sam did not think possible. She was dreaming. She had to be dreaming. Richard had been stabbed. He was bleeding. He should be dead. *She* should be dead. Had they had their way with her? Used her and thrown her aside? Had they killed her?

Sam fell to her knees and retched violently, spewing up bile and the lunch she had barely eaten. Lunch... she had just been sitting in the lunchroom with Richard, worrying about a mysterious savior and the object of her budding affection, and now... now she sat crumpled on the floor, barely able to stand. It all just felt wrong, so very wrong. Richard was at her side. She couldn't remember him moving there. He held her hair out of her face and her sick on the floor. Instinctively, she buried her face in the side of his neck. His skin was *still* cold to the touch. She felt him stiffen.

"Sam, we can't stay here. We've got to move."

Tears formed at the corners of her eyes and rolled down the side of her face. "What are you, Richard?"

Richard pulled Sam away from him, moving a healthy distance from her. He stared at her with heavy, piercing eyes. Her blood slowed to molasses.

Who was this person?

Richard stood and pulled her to her feet. "We need to move. There are still Móguǐ, school security, Republicans, and MESA."

He looked at his timepiece. "I think it's safe to say that MESA has called both Containment and S&D. If we don't move, we're dead. Bravo weapons aren't going to take down those monsters. Same for the Móguǐ Heavy Ops. We could have a real fight on our hands."

Sam wanted to argue. She wanted to run. Her fear was consuming her loyalty and sense of friendship. Richard. Fat, genius, sarcastic Richard, had just slaughtered those men, butchered them without hesitation or remorse. Could she really go with him?

A terrible thought struck Sam.

It wasn't *could she* go with him, but would he *allow* her to leave? Would he let her go?

Sam inched her way along the hall, away from Richard. Richard's eyes narrowed as she did. Quick and graceful, far more graceful than his pudgy frame should have allowed, Richard moved in front of her, blocking her escape. Sam sucked in a deep breath. He wasn't going to let her go.

"Who are you, Richard? Why are you here?"

Screaming voices and the sound of gunfire echoed in the distance, close enough to be heard but not close enough to cause immediate concern. Nevertheless, others were coming. Friend, foe, classmate; at this point, it didn't matter. They had only a few moments, and they both knew it.

Richard's eyes didn't leave Sam. "I've always thought you were more intelligent than this, Sam. I would have thought the reason I'm here is obvious."

His eyes remained passive. Too passive, as if... as if he wasn't trying to look somewhere. The gears in her head dislodged themselves, a single thought forced its way in.

The box. He has to be after the box.

Suddenly, Richard's eyes fixed on something above her

head. He flicked on the light shivs and dashed toward her with unnatural speed. Sam felt her eyes clamp down, and her arms reflexively shield her face and body. Why was he charging her? Was he going to kill her? Did he know where the box was after all? Perhaps he didn't need her anymore.

Sam felt a *whoosh* as ionized plasma scorched the air overhead. A thumping noise to either side of her body forced her eyes back open. Sam looked into his eyes and felt... felt... fear. Their faces were centimeters apart as he held light shivs to either side of her body.

She had difficulty looking away from his eyes. They were cold and dead. No eyes should look like that. She glanced to the side and saw clumps of tiled ceiling. She understood. Richard had rushed her to keep the falling ceiling debris from crushing her head. She suddenly felt stupid for thinking he was going to kill her. After all, if he wanted her dead, he could have done that ages ago.

Richard grabbed her hand. "Come on. We need to leave now."

"But—but what about your wounds? Aren't you going to—?"

Richard pulled on Sam, and they set off back down the hall, Richard's pace not slowing in spite of his injury. They continued to backtrack, making a couple of turns before exiting the school hallways into the Academy City 676 central courtyard, a massive central yard that divided the different education levels. They made their way to the elementary level buildings where the youngest of the Academy City 676 citizens did their learning.

Sam and Richard ran, but hadn't moved more than a few meters when the sounds of fighting erupted once more. MESA, some of the rag-tag bunch of fighters, and the Mógǔ were on each other. To make matters worse, the school's defenses were finally kicking in, blasting just about anything that moved.

A concentrated blast of heat fried a patch of grass right in front of Richard and Sam, cooking it completely. Richard pulled Sam behind a row of unique trees, a cross between pine and oak. They rounded the edge of the tree line just as another group of Mógǔ soldiers came dashing from the other side of the tree line. Light shivs flickered to full length, and hands went for their waistbands. Each of the soldiers touched a large blue button, and a slight blue haze enveloped them. Sam knew instantly they were in trouble.

Richard hesitated, but Sam didn't know for what. Was he scared? That seemed unlikely, but he wasn't doing anything. He wasn't firing up his shivs or taking a fighting stance. Nothing.

Then Richard attacked himself.

Sam watched in horror as Richard extended his two stolen light shivs to quarter length and proceeded to shear off his own skin. Richard's actions were so jolting that the soldiers stopped just short of their attack. They stared at Richard in disbelief. Sam just screamed.

"Richard, what in the hell are you doing?!"

Richard's skin fell off in long strips, the light shivs slicing through it like butter. Sam's head went fuzzy, her upchuck reflex reacting once again. For a second time, she fell to the ground, throwing up. She simply couldn't stand the sight of any more blood.

Her vision was blurry, but she picked up on Richard also hitting the ground. This made more sense than any of the events transpiring around her today. He had lost so much blood, yet he still sheared large chunks of his skin right off his body. It was like he was peeling an apple, a fleshy human apple. Perhaps he had lost it and was committing suicide. In the wake of all that had happened, *that* at least she could get.

The soldiers advanced, apparently recovering from their dismay at watching a man filet himself. The one closest took two steps forward and—

Crack, Crack, Crack.

Cracking sounds filled the air one after the other. The noise was beyond forceful and made Sam's ears hurt. Sam struggled to find the source but could only focus on the lead soldier. His blue hazy field flickered. He took two steps back, then dropped to the ground. The soldier's neck flopped to the side, allowing Sam a clear view of his face.

A 2-centimeter hole sat directly in the middle of the soldier's head. Life fluid trickled from the wound. Again, Sam felt queasy. The cracking commenced again, the sound repeating over and over as the remaining soldiers fell in the same pattern as their leader, each accompanied by a fluctuating blue haze and a hole in their head.

Sam searched their immediate area and found that she and Richard were alone. Once more, all the soldiers near them were dead.

Richard was suddenly in front of her, attempting to help her up. He was too slippery, and she didn't know why. Nothing about the situation was making sense.

Richard swore. "I can't get a grip on you. I need to get this thing off first." Immediately, Richard began removing parts of his body, shedding his girth like clothing.

Like a lightning strike to the brain, abruptly it clicked. Everything clicked. Sam finally got it. His cold skin, his healthy diet with no change in physique, his reluctance to get in the water, his disproportionate strength and speed. With Richard, there truly was more than met the eye.

"Okay, get up. We need to leave."

Richard was, once again, back at her side, picking her up. This wasn't her Richard, though. He stood tall, muscled, and ruggedly handsome. The fat from his face was gone, his hair color different, and he handled Sam with forceful strength and surety. Sam looked him up and down but quickly whipped her head skyward. Her face went beet red. Richard was bare butt naked save a black bag in his hand.

For all that was holy, he was naked! She tried not to look, but she couldn't help but watch him. He had scars on his body. Healed wounds from the looks of it. His skin was tanner than it should have been and warm. His body was incredibly warm.

A short distance away, the fat Richard, or parts of him, were stacked in a heap on the ground, burning like pig fat. Far from just a costume, Sam could see intricate biomechanical infrastructure, wires, leads, and other devices all meeting the same fiery fate as the fake skin. Sam was at a complete loss. She didn't know what to do anymore. Sam looked back and forth from the burning pile of artificial flesh to his body as they retreated back into the hallway.

Richard surveyed the area, looking for any hostiles. Sam allowed herself to be led. Satisfied she wouldn't run, Richard let go of her and proceeded to put on clothes, which he pulled out of the black bag.

Richard quickly dressed in a plain black shirt, pants, and boots. He then placed several pieces of equipment on his person. They were weapons she had never seen before, at least in real life. She had seen these guns on the classic 2D movie channel, but she didn't know any of them still existed.

The sounds of fighting could still be heard off in the distance.

"Richard, you're so skinny."

Richard didn't look at her as he checked his weapons. "Yes, sixty kilos of biomechanical weight tends to make you look chubby. How observant of you."

Without warning, Richard pulled two pistols up to eye level and pointed the guns in her direction. Sam reacted, trying to move out of the way, but Richard was too fast; more gunfire ripped through the air.

"Sam, stop moving." Richard pushed forward and shot his arms out to each side of her head. The guns were loud and echoed off the enclosed space, deafening her.

The figurative dust settled, and Sam turned to see what Richard had fired at. She saw three downed individuals at the end of the corridor. Once again, Sam's breath caught in her throat. She tried to look back at Richard but was having difficulty.

Smoke trailed up from Richard's guns. His thumbs touched the side of each weapon, causing metal columns to fall out. Richard popped two more back into the bottom and pulled the tops of the guns backward. He placed the weapons in holsters on his thighs.

Richard turned his attention back to Sam. "Listen closely, because I am only going to ask you this once. Do you want to live through this little experience?"

Despite Richard's voice sounding like it was trying to escape from a thick blanket, Sam nodded.

"Good. If you want to live, then you need to do exactly as I say and stop flinching every time I get near you."

Sam felt her skin go hot. "If you don't want me to flinch, then stop pointing guns at me. Anyone would flinch in that situation. And who says I need you to stay alive?"

Richard laughed. It was cold. It made her skin prickle.

"You think you can survive this? Fine, go on, I'll leave on my own."

Sam froze. He couldn't be serious, could he?

He was. Richard walked away, again displaying a grace and smoothness she would have never thought possible from him.

"Wait," she called out, attempting to be heard but not overdo it. They were still in danger, after all.

He stopped but didn't turn to face her. He merely looked over his shoulder.

"Yes."

"Please."

"Please, what?"

"Please don't leave me alone."

Richard returned to her side. "Remember you said that. Now follow and stay behind me. If I move, you move. That's it. Do you understand?"

Sam nodded.

"Then move."

They wasted no time returning to the courtyard. The smoldering wreckage of Richard's artificial body was little more than ash. Richard stalked past, not sparing it a glance. Sam used all her willpower not to throw up; she couldn't help looking. They approached the tree line more cautiously this time. Richard led, a pistol in each hand, the guns sweeping the area. Once clear, they moved from cover to cover as they crossed the courtyard.

Sam snuck a glance at Richard. No hint of expression, no acknowledgment of her existence. He came off calm, cold, and calculating. Scary. She was scared to be with him. Then again, right now, she was scared to be without him. Maybe she could ditch him once they made it to safety. *If* they made it to safety.

She and Richard entered one of the side doors on the far side of the courtyard. They were in the eastern wing now, hopefully far away from anyone else. Suddenly, the report of gunfire rattled her. Flashes of bright light, the sudden starts and stops of screams, and then silence. She found the courage to open her eyes. Four more soldiers lay dead in front of her, all with gunshots to the head. Richard was reloading. He reholstered them and gestured to her.

"Come here, Sam," he said, walking over to one of the dead soldiers. "I want you to put this on."

He removed a belt from one of the dead men. It was of the same make and model as the dead soldier's out in the courtyard. He wrapped it around Sam's waist and clicked it into place. His hands touched her exposed skin just above the line of her skirt. She became abruptly aware that her shirt was cut open, exposing her bra to Richard.

"What are you doing?" she said, sounding more embarrassed than she would have liked.

Richard glared at her but didn't answer.

Sam rolled her eyes, exasperated. "Okay, so I know you're the new super-Richard, but if you ignore me, I'm going to continue to ask you questions until you kill me or answer me. Would it be that much harder to answer me than kill me?"

Richard cracked his neck. "Yes."

"Yes? Yes what?"

"Yes, it would be more difficult to answer your questions than to kill you."

He took a deep breath, apparently calming himself.

"This is a Jadian Oscillation Shield. The Jadians pride themselves on their martial talents, so most of their weapons and tactics highlight those particular values. The Plasma Scimitars I was using earlier are a prime example of this. What I'm putting on you now is standard issue defensive equipment for Jadian Special Ops. The belt is like a force field that uses energy to absorb, displace, or flat-out block projectiles. It does have some—"

Sam interrupted him. "You mean like body armor? That doesn't make any sense. How can energy be used as armor?"

"Sam, energy and matter are all made of the same thing. If harnessed in the right way, energy can be just as effective as a plate of carbonized steel."

Richard engaged the belt. "This will keep you safe. The belt can withstand most low-velocity energy weaponry with near impunity. It will even take a strike or two from a plasma scimitar. Just be careful and watch the gauge."

He slapped a sort of wristwatch on her. "100%" appeared on the screen of the watch.

"Keep a close eye on this gauge. If the number goes down

to zero, then take cover immediately." He pointed to the watch. "Any center-mass hits after that, and you're dead."

She still didn't really understand, but she figured she really didn't have a choice. They proceeded on their way.

———

Skinny Richard was like no one Sam had ever met. A personality and person so unique it was borderline exquisite. Ironically enough, this was exactly the same feeling he had cultivated the first time Sam met him so many years ago. Fat Richard had been so different in personality and action he couldn't help but stand out. Skinny Richard was more of the same, but in different ways. Incredibly different ways. Violence, aggression, and the single-minded certainty he displayed burned at her nerves and inflamed her fight or flight response. He intrigued her even while he instilled the fear of God in her. Yet she followed him without hesitation. She did not know why.

This whole escape experience was surreal. If she didn't know any better, she could have sworn they were in an espe-cially intense game of Combat Tag. This feeling was only exacerbated when Sam actually saw weapons of similar make and model to the ones used at the combat range. The weapons didn't act the same, though; there were no minus-cule doses of incapacitating energy or subdued prickling feel-ings after the light blue balls of semi-solid energy hit. No, these weapons used by these soldiers, these... invaders, were just as their title indicated. These were weapons; equipment designed to kill, and they fulfilled their purpose enthusiastically.

Soldiers continued to appear, only to be cut down by Richard with his archaic weapons. It was miraculous on every plane of reality, imaginary or otherwise, and it seemed every encounter would end the same. A gunshot wound to the head. Sometimes Richard fired once, sometimes as many as four times. Regardless of who stood before him, they fell like bricks.

It felt like hours had passed when they finally made it to the large underground building made to house personal transportation modules for those students privileged enough to have a personal vehicle. Richard hopped on a two-person open-hatch rocket with the name—

"Dyson?" said Sam, scandalized. "You're going to steal his bike?"

Richard nodded and put on a helmet. He threw a second helmet to Sam. "He owes me for not killing him."

"Kill him? Why would you—" Comprehension dropkicked Sam in the head, closely followed by anger, then rage. She punched at Richard, who dodged her hastily thrown fist.

"You jerk!" she shouted. "That's why Dyson never actually hurt you, isn't it? ISN'T IT? Do you know how worried I was? How I thought—"

Richard was upon her, his hand over her mouth. Again he

immobilized her. She thought that he had drugged her again, but she didn't feel any sort of poke or injection. How was he doing this?

"We don't have time for this," he whispered in a deathly voice. "This is your last chance, Sam. Do you want to stay with me and live or stay here and die? Your choice. Make it."

She tried to take a deep breath, but even that was hard. Richard seemed to feel and understand this. He released her.

"Sorry," she said. "I will be good from now on."

"Good," was all that Richard replied. "Now get on."

Richard and Sam climbed on the bike and sped away from the main building of Academy 676.

———

I could feel the rumble at the back of my knees and in my thighs as we roared down the road. The power of the turbocharged hydrogen engine screamed as he throttled the bike, the whine of the gears pitching higher and higher as the speed increased. 50, 100, 150 kilometers per hour. I didn't know how fast he could go, but I could barely catch my breath as we pushed forward into the darkness. I held him tight, feeling muscle so taut it couldn't be real. My body and mind were like the aftermath of a warzone. I was hot. I was sweaty. I had bruises on my arms and shoulders from the grip of the soldiers. The soldiers who had tried... who had tried to... I could not say it. I would not say it. Saying it would make it all the more real. I buried my face in his back.

I did feel comforted. Those soldiers wouldn't be after me, not anymore. They wouldn't be after anyone anymore. I felt tears form at the corner of my eyes, tears that were instantly swept away into the night, lost to the wind and road. Lost like me.

My body shivered from the churn of rushing air pouring over my sweaty skin. My shirt was split, whipping up behind my back and exposing my skin to the torrent of the artificial tempest. The violence blocked my senses. I couldn't feel anymore. I was numb; at least that's what I tried to tell myself. Actually, I was scared. I was scared of what might be following us up the road.

How many were dead? How many were gone? The faces of my friends played over and over in my mind. Cammie. Oh, Cammie, you were so good to me even though I was from Partial Palace. Coda, dirty-minded Coda, how will things develop in the future with you and Lacey? Are you in love? Are you ever going to realize Cammie's feelings for you? Are you even alive? Mother, oh my poor lonely mother, for some reason I can't— remember your face.

The bike coasted, coming to the crest of the highest of the hills that circled the valley. We slowed unexpectedly to a stop at a place where I could see the valley we had just traversed. The lights of the city and the twinkling of the stars fought to hold my attention. Both of them, the stars in the sky and the lights of the city on the ground, sparkled in their respective element. Beautiful.

More tears formed on my face. I longed to speak. I longed to ask the question and finally found the courage to do so.

"We can't ever go back, can we?"

He didn't say anything. He just turned to look at me, the faint glare of the bike's headlights barely illuminating his face. We sat there staring until he opened his mouth and said a single word.

"No."

He spun the bike around and ripped down the backside of the hilltop to the inter-way. Once again, my breath was lost to the wind. We tore our way along the backcountry, whipping along the road faster and faster. My worry seemed lost to exhaustion, fear, relief, and then sadness. I didn't know anymore. I didn't care anymore. I let my hands go from his waist, feeling them catch the air as it rushed past. I felt the urge to let go completely. I just wanted to be free from all of this. Without warning, the bike skipped and skidded. I opened my eyes as I screamed and felt myself lifting from the seat as we tumbled over the steep cliffside.

CHAPTER 3
NIGHTMARES

Scene: A dreary one
Place: Mountain facility

Samantha sat bolt upright and screamed, long, hard, and without throwing her hands up to shield herself from an imaginary crashing landing. She let her hands fall to her side when she understood that no impact was imminent. She breathed deeply in and exhaled in a haggard fashion. A dream. A dream of the day that she and Richard fled Academy City 676, though the last part was a recent addition. Crashing and falling off the cliff probably meant something; some sort of projection of her inner thoughts or feelings, or manifestation of her inner fears. Whatever the explanation, the nightmares were becoming more vivid, more real, and oh how they scared her.

Sam swept the back of her hand across her forehead, wiping off the sweat. Her face felt hot, and her pulse was racing. She slowed her breathing and slowly felt the tension drain from her body. She fell back onto her bed and sighed. It was getting really old waking up to her flight or fight response.

Sam got out of bed. From experience, she knew that any further attempt at sleep would be fruitless. Her feet touched colored decorative tile, which was freaking freezing. She half-ran, half-skipped to her bathroom, stripping immediately once she passed the door's threshold. She showered, taking much longer than she would have normally, her mind rolling back to the same tired topics.

This "safe house," a phrase coined by Richard, featured a seemingly endless hot water supply. It took a lot to clean water nowadays with all the fallout from the Great War, and while heating water was relatively easy topside because of the solar cells, Sam had difficulty seeing how that helped here. The Rocky Mountains kept a few secrets close to the chest, it appeared. Not that she was inherently wasteful. She knew what the basic necessities cost, but seeing as she was being held in this place against her will, the jack-hole, Richard, could eat the cost for all she cared.

Sam jumped out of the shower, toweled off, ignoring the help droid that was ever ready to assist her, and threw something on from the mountain of clothes located in her room's walk-in closet. Clean and dressed, Sam took a series of passages from her quarters into a side room just off the main hallway of the underground complex. The side room was quite familiar, a place of discernment and reflection. A place she used for meditation where she steeled herself to continue. Sam took a deep breath. She really hated this part.

The main tunnel of the underground complex (tunnel is a better word than pathway) stretched for hundreds of yards, creating a scene and atmosphere straight out of the horror virtual theater experience. Poor lighting and unexplained noises played off each other, feeding relentlessly into Sam's own paranoia. The eerie feeling of being watched and the clip-clap of her shoes on the hard floor unnerved Sam, and without fail, she ended up running a portion of the massively large tunnel. At a dead sprint, before long, she was passing intersection after intersection of other tunnels, other pathways which led to the recesses of who knew where deep under the mountain.

Sam only stopped after she reached her destination. A well-lit, nicely furnished area of the underground complex that served as a sort of unofficial common room for the base's only two occupants. Sam turned a corner into the main corridor of the common area. Richard was just leaving the mess hall, a cafeteria-sized room that at one point probably fed hundreds of people at a given time. Sam ran up to Richard.

"Done already?"

Richard barely looked at her as he passed.

"Come on, Rich, I know you're the new mysterious type, but couldn't you at least sit with me? You're forgiven for lying. Please? Seriously, I want you to. I like the new and improved Richard."

Again, nothing. Apparently, he didn't care if he had been forgiven.

"You're not still mad about me trying to escape, are you? I promise you I won't do it again. So please just come and eat with me. Please."

She watched him until he turned a corner at the end of the hall. He disappeared from her view into a section of the complex that she wasn't allowed in. She kicked the door as she went into the mess hall. Richard wasn't still mad about her little escape attempt, was he? That was weeks ago. Sam felt her teeth grind and wrung her hands in frustration.

"It looks like we're going to be held up here for a while," Richard told her a few hours after they arrived at their underground safehouse. "So we need to set some ground rules."

Sam remembered protesting. "Wait, why are we going to be held up here for a while? I don't want to live under a mountain in the middle of nowhere. What am I, a Hobbit?"

Richard glared at her. "First, hobbits don't live underground, and second, please try not to do that annoying thing."

"What annoying thing?"

"Talking."

At the time, Sam glared a glare that was potent enough to put down a tiger, if they weren't extinct, of course.

"Back to the ground rules, most of what you need to know is in this booklet," Richard handed her a rather thick packet. "I only make mention of one rule in particular; you can go anywhere within the complex except for the western access tunnels. Just stay clear of there, for your own good, do you understand?"

She had nodded, though really she had only taken in a few of his words.

"Good," he said, "welcome to the Cheyenne Mountain Site."

If she had known to what she was agreeing, there was no way she'd willingly have said yes. Richard appeared to live in the western access tunnels and spent the majority of his time there. He emerged from time to time, mostly when she least expected it, to accomplish whatever happened to be on his agenda at the time, usually to eat and then disappear again, without a word. Not a single, sinking word. Sometimes she would go days without seeing him, without seeing anyone, and thus was left to her own thoughts and internal brooding. It was an extremely lonely existence. A few weeks ago, she had had enough and tried to escape. Well, trying was a bit of an exaggeration. The word implied that she actually did something. Really, she simply walked down the main tunnel out the main entrance. Little did she know that she was in the middle of the Rocky Mountains without a single person as far as the eye could see. Being on the top of the mountain, she saw really far. Richard was sitting on a rock just watching her. He was not happy with her.

Sam entered the kitchen area of the mess hall and made herself some food. Unenthusiastically, she sat down to eat. The food tasted bland, like her existence. She wished there was a window down here; some natural light would be appreciated. Wishful thinking. That wasn't going to happen, not in the belly of the mountain. But the dream of it was a welcome change.

It should have been a surprise, this underground base; it should have come as a shock, but alas, Sam found herself nodding as Richard pulled Dice Danni Dyson's motorcycle into the ridiculously long tunnel that preceded the entrance. She should have been even more surprised when the tunnel opened into a huge cavern and not some sort of path or forgotten highway through the mountains, the Rocky Mountains, one of the few names that was not changed after the war, probably because barely anyone lived in this part of the country.

It didn't surprise her that Richard had a secret retreat; that seemed like something he would do, whether he be fat Richard or new super Richard, but the sheer size, complexity —shoot, the existence of this elaborate hideout seemed a bit much, even for Richard. Suffice to say that the huge underground complex was a shock.

Sam wasn't given the chance to protest the new digs.

Richard simply moved in without hesitation like this was normal, an everyday thing. She wished she knew then what she knew now. If she did, her stay here would have been short-lived. She did not know, and she did not run away, however, and now, because of that ignorance, she was living deep within the mountain, and the only thing Richard said to her with any amount of regularity was "stay away from the western access tunnels." Big fat jerk.

Still, while she was inclined to disobey him, super Richard could be downright scary, so she didn't dare do this. Richard was—and she never thought of saying this aloud, especially about Richard—dangerous. It perked her interest and had her wondering. What was he doing down there?

Probably looking at porn. She giggled but found that she really didn't find that thought all that comforting. Still, the memory brought back to mind a conversation with Coda and Cammie and Coda's book, *Pervert 101: How to Get Caught in Voyeurism.* Not his title, one of Sam's own creations, but the book fit. That was the day that her hell really started, the day she found the box; everything in her life went ape-crap crazy. She didn't find that she dwelt on it, though, as what she really remembered from that day, from that time, was Adam. Sam found that she was thinking about Adam a lot lately. Adam was just as mysterious as Richard, but Richard didn't like Adam, did not trust Adam. At the time, she dismissed it as simple jealousy. That obviously wasn't the case. But if not jealousy, then what? Perhaps it was because Adam had known all along what Richard was, and Richard didn't want his little ploy broken up. That would explain some things.

That answer didn't make a ton of sense. It figured. Richard *being* "super Richard" didn't make a lot of sense. Why was he at the school? Why did he bring her with him? Why not just kill her, take the box, and be done with it? That would have been the easy way out. Beyond none of the answers to these questions having any sort of logical line of fact, analysis, and conclusion, there was a more fundamental problem. In reality, none of the questions really made sense.

Sam pushed her hair out of her face and found streaks of wetness. She banished all of it—the questions, the concerns, the hurt feelings—away from the forefront. The last thing she wanted to think about was home, her mom, Cammie, Coda... Adam. It was too painful, too lonely. It also made her painfully aware of the seriousness and extent of her current predicament. Instead of being with the people she loved, she was terrorized by the reality of a fake Richard, locked up in some fate-forsaken mountain, functionally alone and losing her mind. Truthfully, she didn't even know how long she had been gone. Was it days? Weeks? Months? Sam wasn't sure, and Richard made it clear that V-space was off-limits; no contact with her friends and family, no leaving. That's all he said. No explanation, no comfort, no time frame—no nothing. It cut her deep. She thought she was going to die, and he simply did not care. The tears on her face thickened. She wanted things to go back to normal.

Normal. She thought, *If only I could go back to being "normal."* Sam knew that things could never go back to how they were. Not so long as she had the box. The stupid metal curse had given her nothing but trouble from the moment she touched the dumb thing back in the lake. What was more frustrating than knowing that the box was responsible for all the hullabaloo she was currently experiencing was the box's persistent tendency to hide anything about its origin or purpose. Sam knew it was special; of that much she was cognizant. The physical and emotional effects the box invoked left a lasting effect on her. The first time the box acted up, really manifested the incredible, was right after the slavers attacked she and Cammie. Sam still remembered the strange pull, like her hands were metal and the box a giant magnet, weeks after the incident. After the bizarre circumstance of awakening in her bed with PJs and all; the box called to her, it weighed heavily on her mind since. Sam shuddered involuntarily; more stuff she did not want to think about.

The downtime in Richard's underground lair/prison gave her an awful lot of time to think, and this was one of the subjects her mind invariably settled on. Time made things clear for her. Things that remained hidden suddenly became obvious, though they did not give her the whole picture. They helped.

Time allowed Sam to recognize, to understand that the strange mental stress she experienced in full force the night of the slavers' attack was a sensation that she had been experiencing for more than a year. The revelation was bittersweet as all the knowledge did was create more questions, questions that stood unanswered and would remain so without more information. Fortunately, she knew someone could probably answer all her inquiries and more; it was just getting him to talk.

Sam wiped away some of the lingering tears at the corners of her eyes. It was time for her to start taking her life into her own hands, and starting today, she intended to do just that.

Adversity can do different things to people. Some buckle under the pressure of whatever storm they are attempting to weather; some traverse the darkened clouds until the end just to be broken in some ironic twist of fate. Some still overcome all adversity and become wise. In Sam's case of adversity, the verdict was still out on what she was willing to do in the face of her tribulation, and it was about time she found out.

Sam picked up her plate, rocking the bits of half-eaten food, scraped them, cleaned them, and put them away. Once the kitchenware was safely stored, she walked to the back of an old walk-in freezer, one that wasn't functioning, and picked up a backpack. She placed the bag on her back and threw on a ball cap. Sam walked back out of the kitchen and turned off the lights to the dining hall. The place went black briefly before a group of ground-level floodlights flickered and doused the edges of the walls with soft luminescence. Sam tiptoed to the hallway and peeked her head out. She was alone. She called out just to make sure.

"Hello?"

Her voice echoed; the only sound was the reverb of her own tones. She spoke again, this time a little louder.

"Richard... are you there?"

Again, no answer; Sam closed her eyes and took a deep breath. It was time. She took a step and then another and then a third. She took two more and stopped. Still nothing. No Richard, no sound, no nothing. Sam took off this time at a brisk pace, heading for the western access tunnels and hopefully, some answers.

———

Finding Richard's little hiding spot was easier than she anticipated. The western access tunnels were just as large as her living area but far less confusing. In contrast to where Sam slept, the western tunnels made up several large caverns instead of many rooms. Sam imagined that at some point this area of the underground complex was used for a variety of purposes, like storage and whatnot. There was no way to know for sure, however. This was exactly what Richard was using these spaces for, so it made sense.

The first room was part mechanic shop and part garage. There were dozens of vehicles there; many Sam recognized, many she did not. She hurried past it, trying not to make any noise—still no sign of Richard.

The second room had weapons, and lots of them, and again some familiar and others foreign. Sam recognized a couple of disassembled pulse pistols, unloaded rapid discharge plasma launchers, arm-mounted flak cannons, and to Sam's distaste, an assortment of Jadian light shivs; the list went on. Like the initial garage with all the vehicles, there were also many weapons that Sam didn't recognize but could guess. Suffice to say that there were many guns, explosives, and launchers from another time and era.

The armory transitioned into the strangest of obstacle courses. By far the biggest of the caverns yet seen, this room was a sort of odd nature preserve abound with heaps of rocks, piles of sand, giant trees surrounding a fairly convincing artificial river whose current led deeper into the mountain and out of sight. This room baffled Sam mostly because she couldn't for the life of her understand what this room was for, as each explanation felt just as unlikely as the one before it. Was it here for the scenery? That seemed doubtful; if his actions were any indication, new Richard was hardly the nature worshiper. A newfangled power supply of some kind? Improbable as well, though that explanation answered at least one of the burning questions and resolved one of the mysteries of the underground facility; namely, where the heck did this place get its power? It was feasible that Richard was using these materials in some sort of experiment as well.

That sounded like something old fat Richard would do, but alas, new Richard was altogether a different beast; who knew what he did in his free time?

A resounding *click* right behind her head made her freeze. She was not alone. She fought the impulse to spin on her heel. She waited.

His voice came in a whisper.

"I've seen intoxicated elephants move quieter than you."

Sam didn't turn around. "Elephants are extinct; shouldn't you know that, or was you being a genius a lie too? And isn't the expression 'more quiet' not 'quieter'?"

"I assure you I'm every bit the genius you think I am. And as a general rule, no, adjectives with three or more syllables use 'more' and 'most' instead of the more popular '-er' and '-est.' Now what are you doing here? And be careful of your answer, or I might just shoot you."

Sam felt her patience break. He just threatened to shoot her! Stupid jerk-off! Sam turned to face Richard. "Then shoot me."

Richard glared at her, but thankfully he didn't shoot.

"You heard me, shoot me. Come on, Rich, where is all your bravado now?"

Still, Richard said nothing, though Sam could feel his irritation. "You know, when you were fat Richard, you were a lot better at controlling your emotions."

Sam saw the muscles on Richard's hand tighten momentarily and then release. He lowered his gun.

"Now that's better, *super* Richard. I know you're not going to shoot anyone; you can't do anything without permission. Isn't that right, Doughboy?"

Richard's face remained passive, but Sam knew she was still driving him crazy. This was more a feeling than anything else, but she was just as sure. The use of his call sign surprised him—he was even a little impressed.

Richard again didn't say anything but twisted in the opposite direction and proceeded to walk away. His abrupt action startled her, but Sam strived to not let it show. Richard stopped a few feet away.

"Leave, Sam, now."

"No, I'm not going anywhere."

"I'm serious, Sam, do as I ask, or do you not remember the number one rule I told you?"

"Oh no, I remember; I'm just ignoring it."

"Why are you being so difficult?"

"Me difficult? Oh, I'm *soooo* sorry. Did I interrupt your quiet time? Forget that I was stolen away from my home, I'm unable to check on my mom, and all my friends might be dead, and the added bonus is the best friend I've ever had is a total and complete fabrication. All I want is some companionship, you jerk? Even if it's you. IS that really so much to ask?"

Richard resumed his retreat, but Sam wasn't going to let it go that easily. She followed him.

"You can't be here, Sam; you need to leave."

"I already told you that I'm not going—"

"The stuff you asked for arrived."

Sam's mouth clamped shut. "What do you mean, the stuff that asked for?"

"I mean the items you asked for; they are upstairs if you put your mind to it—"

Sam wasn't listening but was already sprinting back toward the way she came.

CHAPTER 4
TRAITOR

Scene: MESA
Time: Midday

Orlando Creed sat staring at the updated reports flowing down his screen. The amount of data streaming out of the Harmonics lab was astonishing. He had to admit that when Kingston and Jameson had suggested that the time was right to acquire Thurman, Creed had his doubts about what could be accomplished with the old man. Those doubts had all dissipated now. The man seriously knew his stuff and seemed to have an uncanny knack for pushing his research in just the right direction. Creed had been in research for what seemed like a lifetime, and had never before seen someone with that level of intuition in their chosen field of study. If Creed had believed in destiny or fate, it would have been a little creepy.

Creed finished reviewing the updates and pulled up his production-load client. He scanned through his personnel resources, searching for a team with some open cycles. It seemed that all of the teams were already strained, sifting through the copious amounts of data that he had already assigned. He scrolled to the bottom of the list. Only one name was open: Sally. Creed let out a small, subdued sigh. He double-checked the roster, hoping that he had overlooked someone. Nope. The sigh came back a little more heavily.

Creed stood from his desk and walked through his office toward the lab floor. The constant humming of servers and the relative quiet of people crunching the latest break-throughs in physics was a small comfort as he made his way to the back of the lab. The brightly decorated workstation seemed to pop as he approached, and with every step, his weariness about the woman ebbed upwards.

It wasn't that Sally was a terrible worker or that she was inefficient. Her performance metrics actually showed the complete opposite: efficient, concise, prompt with reports, punctual to meetings, inquisitive. It was this last attribute, however, that consistently wiggled underneath Creed's skin and made him hesitant about keeping her in the lab. Sally had good intuition and wanted to dig deeper into the assignments she was tasked with. Unfortunately, she didn't know when to stop asking questions. Creed had some serious security clear-ance around MESA, and even he didn't know the answers to some of the questions she had raised. It wasn't until recently that she finally got the hint to keep most, if not all, of those questions to herself.

Sally looked up from her work as Creed approached. She gave him a sickly sweet smile.

"Good afternoon, Mr. Creed. All ready for the weekend?" she asked.

"Hi, Sally. Uh, yes I am. Thanks for asking." Creed concentrated on keeping his tone pleasant and light. "Before you head out, I need you to log these updates onto your work list for next week." With a swipe of his fingers, Creed transferred the updates from his interface to hers. "Thanks, Sally. Hope you have a good weekend as well."

Creed turned to leave, proud that his interaction had been polite, but also grateful that he hadn't given her any time to ask—

"Excuse me, Mr. Creed?"

Creed stopped, closed his eyes, and mentally counted to five. So much for her getting the hint. "Yes, Sally," he asked in a forced polite tone as he turned around.

"I just had...well I mean..." Sally looked down at her hands, fidgeting with them. She took a deep breath, then started speaking very rapidly, as if she didn't get it out fast enough, it would never come out. "I just wanted to know where all this data came from since none of the teams here at the Interface lab have devoted any cycles to this type of work.

I mean, if it's not coming from our lab, then it has to be from another lab. I guess I was just curious as to what they are working on." Her eyes sheepishly raised from her hands to Creed's face. She instantly knew that this was probably one of the questions she should have kept to herself.

"Sally, you and I have discussed how your natural curiosity is a valued asset when it is applied to the tasks that you are assigned. We also have discussed that there are many things that you will be tasked with which are small pieces to a very large puzzle. These pieces, while important, are tasked in such a way to best serve the project as a whole. So while I do appreciate your inquisitive spirit, I must ask you..." Creed's polite expression faltered a bit, "again...to apply that 'gift' to your assignments." Creed smiled, nodded, then turned to leave.

"But...Mr. Creed, sir?" It took Creed until ten this time before he could turn around. "Sally, unless this is about me having a wonderful weekend, I don't want to hear about it." Creed stared at the woman, watching the internal conflict play across her face. Her common sense won out, and she waved at Creed and then started logging the updates into the work queue.

Creed turned once again and proceeded back to his office. There had to be someone else in MESA's resources that could take Sally's place in the lab. Creed was done with her. Absolutely done.

He reached Jameson's office and knocked twice before entering. "Jameson, we need to talk."

Jameson quickly looked up from his desk with a slightly hurried look on his face. It almost instantly changed when he saw Creed in his doorway. "Oh, Orlando, it's you. Yes, what is it?"

"It's Sally. We need to talk about Sally." Creed stepped over and sat down in front of Jameson. "She needs to be replaced. I suggest you input the request before you leave today. We should be able to have a replacement up to speed by early next week, which won't adversely affect the production schedule."

Jameson looked a little confused. "Orlando, Sally's work has been impeccable. She is one of the brightest team members in the lab. I understand that you don't particularly like her, but she is a valuable asset."

"This goes beyond my personal feelings, Jameson. She is asking too many questions. The others just do the work we assign them. She is constantly poking around where she shouldn't. It's become a security concern, and she needs to go."

Jameson shot Creed a doubtful smile. "Orlando, I don't believe for one instant that Sally's curiosity is a security concern. We've successfully insulated the Harmonics lab's activities from the entire staff. Most of them have been too busy to even care where all this data has come from. One person is not going to change that."

"Look, Jameson," Creed started, "I understand the protocols we set in place, and I for one think that for the most part, the insulation has worked brilliantly. I just don't want to see that tarnished by one overly curious set of legs that can't understand how things work around here."

Jameson nodded slowly. "So this is just about the protocols and has nothing to do with a certain previous 'set of legs' from your past? Is that what I'm hearing, Orlando? Sally is a valued member of the team. She does good work, and in all honesty, I don't believe we can afford to be short-staffed right now. I hear your concern, but Sally stays."

Creed looked very concerned. "Why are you defending her so adamantly, Jameson? She's just a staff member, nothing more."

"So, now she's been upgraded to a staff member?" Jameson looked away from Creed and back to his work. "Orlando, I appreciate your concern; I just..." Jameson broke off. Creed stared at him, wondering what was going on in his mind. Jameson was normally very decisive, very sure about everything. This was not like him at all.

"Do you really think she is a concern?" Jameson asked defeatedly without looking at Creed.

Creed hesitated for just a moment before answering. This was not like Jameson at all. "She just asked me which lab produced the data since none of the Interface teams had devoted any cycles to its production. Yes, Jameson, I think she is more than a concern. If left unchecked, she's a risk. We should do the right thing and get rid of her."

Jameson looked like he was going to argue again, but then looked up at Creed. "Okay, Orlando. Go ahead and request the staffing adjustment, but I insist that we are not short-staffed. Sally can be exit-processed as soon as her replacement is up and running, not a day sooner." Jameson paused, hesitated, and then returned to his work.

Creed nodded, then stood and exited the office. He could have notified security from his office terminal; he even could have used any one of the terminals down the many hallways as he passed them. But he didn't. Creed exited the wing, passed through three security and bio checkpoints, entered the elevator, and exited just as the initial business finished in the boardroom.

"Ah, Creed. Good of you to join us," the old man said without a hint of politeness. "We were just getting to your update from the Interface Lab."

"Sorry, sir. I have my update ready if you would like me to proceed," replied Creed.

"By all means, go right ahead. We're all waiting with bated breath," the old man retorted.

Creed shifted uncomfortably on his feet and then cleared his throat. "Well, as I said, my update on our progress in the Interface Lab is...well it's..." Creed stalled out, a concerned look dominating his face.

"Something wrong, Creed?" asked Kingston from the back of the room.

Creed shifted his eyes from the old man to Kingston, then back again. "Actually, there is. It's about...well, it's about Jameson, sir."

"What about Jameson?" inquired the old man. "Did he finally lose at chess?"

"No, sir. But he has been a little off lately. Well, more than off, actually. You see, part of my update is a small staffing change that I just requested. Sally Hammond is a team lead in the lab, and I requested that she be terminated from the project."

"Mr. Creed," started Kingston with a very serious tone, "I trust you are aware of the importance of the work you are processing within the lab and consequently how that work might be negatively impacted by a staffing change. I also trust that you discussed this with Jameson?"

"Of course I discussed it. That's part of the problem." Creed shifted his feet again. "Sally was on warning about making inquiries regarding the data she and her team were processing. Just before I came up here, she asked which of the other labs had produced the data since it was obvious that the Interface lab did not have a hand in it. Add that to the numerous other inquiries that flitted around what the data was, who was running it, among other things, and I felt that she had become a concern. A serious security risk." The old man looked impatient. Creed shifted his weight yet again. "I brought this to Jameson, asking for a staffing change. That's when I noticed that something was different."

"What was different, Mr. Creed?" asked Kingston.

He hesitated. "I asked him to get rid of her, and he hesitated. And not just like he didn't hear me. We had a long, drawn-out conversation about her. He kept bringing up the fact that we needed her in the lab, that she was an important part of the team. All valid points, but in my mind, nowhere near the weight needed to offset the security concerns."

"What are you getting at, Creed? We're all adults here; come out with it," the old man said softly.

"It's just...well, I've known Jameson for years. He has always been the definition of determined and full of purpose. This wasn't like him. It was almost as if..." Creed hesitated. "It was almost as if he wanted to keep her here despite the risks."

The boardroom was quiet. All eyes slowly moved from Creed up the cherrywood table and rested on the old man.

The old man's fingers slowly drummed on the table as he stared down its length. Creed determined to not back down, resisting the urge to move his feet. The visual standoff seemed to go on for eternities by Creed's clock. Yet the old man just sat there drumming. Creed's anxiety won out, and he shifted his feet.

"So, let me make sure I am clear about this," started the old man. "What you are saying is that Charles Jameson, the man who rebuilt the Interface Lab, the man who tirelessly has given himself to this company without question, the man who for almost the last decade has worked to bring Eli Thurman into MESA, that man...that Charles Jameson—hesitated about dismissing an employee who you believe poses a security risk to the project. Does that about sum up your update, Mr. Creed?"

"Sir, this wasn't the first time." Creed stammered, "I understand that it sounds like I am making a big deal out of something small, but—"

"No, Mr. Creed," said the old man. "I understand that you are making a big deal about an isolated occurrence over a staff member involving a man facing more stress than when he was asked to rebuild the entire Interface lab from scratch almost ten years ago is something small indeed. Jameson has more than purchased the right to be worried that a staffing reduction might negatively impact his consistent pursuit of greatness that we have all come to expect from him. I am willing to give the man a little pass on this one, and I strongly suggest you do the same, Mr. Creed."

His last name seemed to echo a little off the ceiling of the boardroom, unimpeded by any other noise from any other person. Creed knew he had gone too far. He should have kept his mouth shut and found some other solution. Once again, he shifted uncomfortably. "I will, sir, thank you. As for the remainder of my update, things are going along quite well. Each team is on or ahead of schedule. If you have nothing further for me, I'll get working on the staffing adjustment right away."

The old man continued to stare down at Creed, his fingers still drumming out a steady cadence. Kingston spoke up. "Thank you, Orlando." Creed gave a slight nod, then exited the room.

The uncomfortableness seemed to follow him out as the boardroom business continued. "Sapan, where are we in the data-mining break-in?" barked the old man. A dark-skinned man on a monitor perked up, the old man's tone indicating how quickly this update should be given.

"Our final analysis shows that since the break-in and subsequent attempt to reacquire MESA's property at Academy 676, there have been a number of investigations into the break-in itself and the complications with the reacquisition op." Sapan spoke clearly but with a hint of haste in his voice. "Security feeds and presence data were all wiped at the site, and remote backups failed due to the introduction of a highly sophisticated rage worm that tunneled through our Stormwall servers."

The old man's fingers came to a silent stop at this last remark. His eyes slowly raised to the monitor.

Sapan continued. "While we were able to successfully launch the op at 676 based on data gleaned from the leftover pieces, the completion of the op was hindered by unforeseen complications."

"Mr. Bhat...please spare me all the analyst-speak and spit

it out. Please tell me that you have an idea why our government liaison division has been working around the clock trying to explain why MESA ordered a Containment team and S&D to an academy city filled with students."

"Sir, factions of what we now believe to be a domestic terrorist network named the Republicans, and members of the Jade Empire's elite strike unit and possibly a Jadian secondary support unit were present during the op. From our operational data streams, we are 85% sure that these other units were working off indirect intel. They appeared to be reacting to our presence rather than acting on independently confirmed data."

Sapan thought he saw a glimmer of relief cross the old man's face. "And tell me, Mr. Bhat, have you been able to determine how they were alerted to our presence?"

Sapan looked down at something off-screen and then back to the boardroom. "We have some probability results on possible causes, but nothing definiti—"

"What's at the top of the list, Mr. Bhat?" asked Kingston.

Sapan looked a little panicked. "Sir, I would suggest that perhaps a review of the possible causes would be prudent prior to reviewing them with the entire board."

"I don't think that will be necess—" started Kingston. Sapan cut him off. "Sir, I think it is quite necessary." Sapan looked intently at Kingston. They both seemed to share a silent communication.

Kingston turned to the members seated at the long table.

"That will conclude today's updates." Monitors faded out into spinning MESA logos, and suits and lab coats alike stood and shuffled to the elevator. Upon the doors closing, Kingston turned back to the single remaining face on the row of monitors. "Sapan, why did you just ask me to have everyone leave?"

Sapan cleared his throat. "Sir, I believe...I believe we may have a high-level security breach."

CHAPTER 5
LINGERING FAMILIARITY

Scene: A much happier one

Place: Mess Hall, Cheyenne Mountain Site

"I know just how to whisper and I know just how to cry. I know just where to find the answer and I know just how to lie."

Sam did a little swaying booty shake as she chopped garlic and onions. Music blared out of an ancient electronic device called a CD player. Two feet across, ten inches tall, with a width of around six inches, it took Sam a while to figure out that this antiquated oversized paperweight was actually a music player of some kind. She came to that conclusion by mere happenstance when she tried to turn it on. A small rotary on the top of the box spun noisily. Connected to that rotary was a small plastic removable disc. She was trying to make sense of it all when she noticed a "power" and "play" button. It was unexpected and probably a little out of character for her, but next thing she knew—

"But I don't know how to leave you, how to never let you fall. And I don't know how you do it making love... out of nothing at all."

The song crescendoed sharply, and Sam couldn't help it; she let loose. She grabbed the broom on the other side of the table and started to spin and sing at the top of her lungs. She knew the song by heart now.

It was a perfect moment, or would have been if she hadn't tripped over a mop bucket. Water splashed about, the mop handle went flying when Sam's flailing arms knocked it with the broom handle she had been holding. Then, Sam fell on her butt. Hard.

"Ouch," she said as she rubbed at her backside. "Well, it's official; the universe has spoken. I can't make love out of nothing at all after all."

"I hate to be the one who points this out, but that doesn't make any sense."

The voice startled Sam to the point where she tripped again. Luckily, Richard caught her before she went very far. Sam felt her breath catch as strong, steady hands propped her gently, setting her upright before he released her and retreated. He watched for a second, then resumed what he had apparently come to do, going to a cabinet where he kept his "food." Sam looked at the clock. 6:30 already. Time really flew when she was cooking.

Richard went on to prepare himself a plate of preserved enhanced soy protein, vitamin supplements, and a powdered carbohydrate shake that smelled like stinky man feet. Sam spied Richard's plate, a meal about as unappealing as they came. The thought of eating it made Sam want to vomit.

Richard prepared his food quickly and quietly. He sat down and commenced the complete devastation of the meal.

This behavior was new to Sam. He was barely chewing before swallowing. She wanted to ask why he was eating like that but was hesitant. She didn't want him to leave; it had been weeks since she had last seen him. Not since the day she had ventured into the western access tunnels and he had told her about the care package. She didn't want him to leave, but she wanted to talk, so maybe a different question wouldn't upset him.

"What were you talking about? What doesn't make any sense?"

Richard didn't answer.

She sighed and resigned herself to cleaning up the mess she had made. It was okay; she didn't need him. She could always flip back on the music, and her lasagna was almost complete as well. The smell was just strong enough to permeate the room.

"I said your conclusion didn't make any sense."

Sam froze. Richard just spoke to her. New super Richard just willingly answered one of her questions. Again, this was new ground. She wasn't sure what she should do.

Sam figured it was okay to follow up his answer with a point of clarification. "I heard what you said. I'm just not sure what you meant."

Richard took an unusually deep breath. "You said, right after your embarrassing display of ill-coordination, that it was official, that the universe had spoken and you could not, and I quote, 'make love out of nothing at all.'"

Sam's jaw dropped—whether figuratively or literally, she wasn't sure. Now this was a bizarre conversation.

"So are you saying that you believe that I can make love out of nothing at all?"

Richard rolled his eyes. "The idea of romantic love is an ill-adapted and completely irrational relationship construct, which I remind you, adds nothing of value to human relationships."

Sam's jaw dropped even lower. Without thinking, she rushed forward and centered a beady eye upon him. "That is something that Fat Richard would say; is he another personality? Can you bring him back? Or did you just eat him or something and you're burping up the aftereffects?"

Richard glowered. "Your infatuation with my cover identity simply goes to show that I did my job in an uncannily brilliant fashion."

Sam slouched. "So you're not him? You were just 'being' him."

"Not exactly accurate, but for our pretense and purpose, I suppose it works; irrelevant, however, as that was not what I was attempting to articulate to you. What I *was*—what I *am* telling you is that I am a genius; I can *be* anyone you want me to *be*."

"Could you *be* a nice person?"

Richard started to get up.

"Wait, come on, Richard. Stay. You can't be satisfied with the food you just ate. Have some Italian food with me. I've been cooking and eating up here by myself for weeks. I know you've got this macho thing going on now. But please, for old times' sake. Just sit with me."

Richard was already standing and just about to leave, but then stopped suddenly as a message icon flashed across his tablet. Holy crap. She hadn't even noticed the thing. Richard glanced at the tablet, and Sam saw his eyes darken. She took an uneasy step back.

"Listen, Richard, I—"

Richard sat back down. "I will sit, but no talking."

A crazy turn of events? Yes, but Sam would take the win.

She regretted thinking that 20 minutes later as Richard, true to his word, did not say another word to her. She thought that she would give it a try.

"So you got all these ingredients for me, right?"

Richard shot her a withering look.

Sam exhaled exasperatedly. "Did you really think I wasn't going to talk? That we were just going to sit in silence? I'm a girl, Rich; you should know better."

Richard's countenance softened. "Yes, that is true; the

female Homo sapiens do have a strange proclivity towards constant, unending chatter."

"See, it's in our DMV, you should just accept that, being the science-type person that you are."

"Samantha, DNA stands for deoxyribonucleic acid. Basic building blocks of life; DMV is an acronym from the early 20th century. It stood for Department of Motor Vehicles. Sam, I swear; I wonder about you sometimes."

"So you think about me?"

"That's what you took from that statement?"

"What can I say? Selective hearing."

Richard put a hand to his forehead and rubbed it in a frustrated manner. Sam changed the gearbox of their conversational car.

"Why can't I get on V-Space?"

Richard continued to rub his head. "I've already explained this to you. You can't get on V-Space. It's dangerous."

Sam rolled her eyes. "Yeah, you mentioned that part. But that's not what I asked. I asked why. You've told me I can't, but you haven't actually told me why."

"Sam, with the right software, we can easily be tracked, which would be completely counterproductive to us hiding. If you access the cloud, we might as well put up a giant fluorescent sign that says, 'Hi, Richard and Samantha are here; send everyone to kill them.'"

She didn't mean to, she tried not to, but in spite of herself, Sam smiled.

"You sounded like Fat Richard there. Do you think you could put the fat suit back on so I can give you a hug?"

"You're hilarious."

"So I've been told, but seriously, Rich. I'm really worried about my mom. I would really like—"

"Not going to happen, Sam. I'm sure your mother is fine, but trying to find out would only put her in danger."

"I remember you being nicer; that's always how it happens, though. I should have guessed. You see it with girls all the time. A sweet, ugly duckling suddenly turns into a beastly beautiful swan, and they get nasty. I really think you should put the bio-mechanical weight back on; it might aid you in removing that stick from your butt."

"I think we're done here." He rose.

"Sit down, Richard," said Sam as she herself stood up and moved towards the kitchen. "You haven't even eaten. Well, you haven't eaten real food. I was only kidding. That's what you get for leaving me to my thoughts for two weeks. Geez, are all spy types always this PMS-y?"

Richard glowered. "That's an interesting question; what makes you think I'm a spy?"

Sam shrugged. "What else could you be? We've been friends for what, a couple of years now, and then all of a sudden you shed, like a snake mind you, 60 kilos of fat suit and can take out laser sword-wielding, energy shield-wearing members of a Jadian death squad like you're punishing a group of precocious three-year-olds. If you're not a spy, then I've got bigger problems here than getting you to talk to me."

Sam placed a steaming pan of lasagna, plates, silverware, and a bowl of greens in front of Richard. "And yes, I used the word precocious; I'm not as dumb as you think."

She returned to the kitchen and came back with a pitcher of water and some glasses. She also placed these in front of Richard. Her eyes locked onto his. She spoke again, choosing her words very carefully.

"What I don't understand—I mean, what continues to elude me is the 'why.' Why would you pretend to be Fat Richard, stay in Academy City 676, and live as a normal primary education student when clearly, you're not?"

Richard's eyes remained mostly passive, though they narrowed ever so slightly. "That's not quite an accurate assessment, Samantha. You're 'dumb' all right, but only when it seems to suit your purposes. I'm a wheel in the cog, Samantha. A simple soldier that goes where his general tells him."

"I noticed," said Sam, her voice going louder than necessary. "But you didn't answer my question, Richard."

"I see that you're not going to let this go. So allow me to answer your question with one of my own. I want you to think hard on this, Sam, and answer me. Why do you ask the question when really, you already know the answer? I can tell it's written all over your face."

Sam broke eye contact, her mind reeling. So it was the box. It was all about the box. "So now everything is out in the open; now what?"

Richard shook his head. "Nothing. I told you. Just a simple soldier, Sam; there are far more important people involved here. I just do what I'm told."

Richard stood abruptly and, without warning, moved swiftly without saying anything.

"Wait, Richard. I thought we were going to eat—"

Her sentence trailed off. Richard stopped probably a few feet from the door. "Just so you know, I've had confirmation that your mother is okay. She is in Partial Place. She is looking for you desperately, but she is okay."

Sam felt like she just got punched in the gut. "Richard, how do you—how do you know this?"

No answer. He was already gone.

Sam felt like screaming at the top of her lungs. He just left, again. He gives enigmatic clues and then leaves??? Who the hell does stuff like that? Maybe it wouldn't be so bad to let him kill her if she was allowed a good pop to his face. Were all boys this frustrating?

She attempted to put it aside as other things commanded her attention. On a good note, her mother was fine. Apparently back in Academy City 676, alive and probably heartbroken. No doubt her mom saw the breaking story on the attack, probably heard eyewitness accounts of the battle that went on between MESA and the others. She was probably worried sick about Sam and Richard. No doubt "they" told her—"they" being some genetic and random person from the school, though not the principal because he was dead. They probably told Sam's mother that she and Richard were dead. But her mom, bless her heart, wouldn't lose hope. There weren't any bodies, and she would refuse to believe that her baby was gone. Sam's mother insisted on believing that there was hope. That's what Sam's mom would be thinking. She just knew it. Sam had to figure out a way to get out of here.

And still, that damn box pulled at her thoughts. What could all those organizations possibly want with that stupid box? What did the box do to cause MESA, a Jadian death squad, and the Republicans to attack Academy City 676 for it? And what about Richard? What kind of spy stays under-cover for that long? Was Richard looking for the box the entire time? Something about that scenario rang true to Sam, but the idea of Richard, especially this new Richard, spending that much time attempting to accomplish—well, anything!—was completely foreign to her. Richard had proven himself resourceful beyond the ordinary person, and if he had difficulty finding it, then maybe—perhaps only a certain type of person could find the box. That circumstance might explain MESA and the other groups' sudden appearance.

Sam mulled that particular point over a bit more.

The idea actually made sense and served to clarify some of the more unexplainable events from that day at the school. MESA was obviously trying to find something at the school; the scientists, the tests, the gathering of all the students in one place at one time testified to that. As a matter of fact, they had wanted... they had wanted the girls, 16 years and older. Something about them undressing. What were they looking for? Did the box show some outward sign of use? As far as Sam knew, she didn't have any unexplained marks or anything like that. But she wasn't looking for any sign either. This mark, whatever it was, may be something subtle or a mark only detectable with special equipment or something entirely different. Sam pushed her hand through her hair in frustration. She had no idea what MESA was looking for with all their crazy demands, and really, there was no way of knowing or finding out without more information.

Okay, she had no chance of figuring out why finding the box was so difficult without more information. There was also no way of determining the reason for MESA's visit to Academy City 676. What about what the box actually did, what its purpose was? Was there a conclusion to be sought there?

Sam thought about that particular morsel for a span. It was obvious that the box was special; that much she knew, but what did it actually do? She thought back on her own experiences with the box, the way that it drew her mind back to it in that constant yet subtle manner. How the emotions, strong ones, seemed to plow over her own sense of self in such an overpowering and commandeering way, and then there was the most disconcerting of all: the few times, the very few times, that the box captured control over her physical body. Like the box had a mind of its own and wanted to use Sam for its own purposes. Was that the box's ability? Mind control or some other way of forcing your will onto another person? That could be it. A weapon like that, being able to forcibly enact your will on another, would enable such a stifling collection of power. It was scary.

The fact that the box played tricks on the brain also brought her a considerable distance in explaining her strange mental sensations that had been happening over the past year. If the box was in the lake that whole time... maybe it had been affecting her the whole time, and her picking it up accelerated the effects. Sam shuddered. That was not a pleasant thought. But again, there was really no way of knowing without more information.

Sam picked up the plate sitting in front of her, scooped out a heaping helping of salad and lasagna, and placed it on her plate. She started to eat, chewing thoughtfully and coming to a conclusion as she did. If she couldn't figure anything out with more information, then the logical answer naturally dictated that she gather more information. There really wasn't any way around it.

Sam cleaned her plate quickly and placed the leftovers in

the cooling unit. She smiled as a rare thrust of giddiness surfaced; she made her decision. If gathering information was the only way to reach a point of understanding, then that was exactly what she was going to do—starting with her former fatty of a friend.

CHAPTER 6
DANCE WITH THE FIREFLY

Scene: A deceptive one.
Place: Mess Hall, Cheyenne Mountain Site

Sam strived to steady her breathing. If Richard found her hiding here, a sudden and unexpected meeting with Death might occur; very little got past him, so she had to be extra careful.

Richard stood in the middle of a large padded area, wearing a simple sleeveless shirt and shorts—an experience in and of itself. During the course of their friendship, as unknowing Samantha and fat Richard, he had never worn shorts. At least now, some of those more subtle nuances made sense. She had been watching him for more than two hours. He was like a machine. First were the free weights, flexibility training, and cardiovascular work in the form of running and jump rope. Next, he moved on to stretching and balance exercises, tightrope walking, and structure-free running, which had to be one of the most idiotic things that Sam had ever seen. Free running was basically using any and all standing structures as one's personal jungle gym. Richard was literally running sideways along walls, flipping off random pieces of construction several stories high, and scaling building-like erections as if he were some sort of superhero. It was spooky and more dangerous. There were a couple of times when Richard was moving from structure to structure in the massive training area that she thought he was going to find her. He didn't, but there were a couple of close misses. And it wasn't because of her brilliance in picking her hiding spot either; she sensed that he was preoccupied—something kept his attention.

His free running finished, and after returning safely to the ground, Richard took a short break. He drank a bit of water, did some breathing exercises, and stretched occasionally. The silence was eerie. It was so quiet down here without any of the natural noise that accompanies life: no wind, rain, animals, or the like. She had been saying it since they moved in. She hated living within the mountain. She didn't know how Richard could stand it.

With his few minutes of break lapsed, he changed gears, moving to the middle of the training area and centering himself under the main light, sitting cross-legged. Richard's eyes were closed, swinging his hands in a deliberate fashion—some movements sharp and thrusting, others sweeping and flowing, but all in a somber, connected rhyme. The motions were hypnotic.

Richard gradually rose to his feet, the gesture following in a continual and calculated fashion. Hand flow, which looked like a painter with an imaginary canvas, was soon accompanied by footwork. His steps drifted from place to place in a primal example of grace, his feet lightly touching the ground, gliding as if on pockets of air. Richard was sweating profusely, another of those things that, up until now, Sam had rarely seen. His movements increased and became more vigorous.

Sam looked at Richard as he floated under the various spotlights of the underground lair. Richard's body was far from perfect. He had much in the way of scar tissue sporadically strewn across what could be seen of his frame—a fact she gleaned as he peeled off a sweat-covered shirt. She stared at him in a mix of fascination, horror, curiosity, and fear. Many of the scars, the ones that were clearly seen on his chest and back, were older and healed completely, but at one time were probably quite serious. The conclusion was obvious; Richard had seen much in the way of combat. Not that this detail was anything to be dazzled about; Richard's prowess was proof enough of his experience. No matter how much he was a genius, you don't learn to shoot and fight like him without some serious training. Genius or not, he had practice and probably an incredibly patient teacher.

Sam's face went red as the image of his naked body popped into her head. She pushed it away.

The idea of Richard being taught by somebody—anybody—was laughable. Sam already knew Richard to be the world's most frustrating student. Many a teacher at Academy City 676 tried in vain to teach Richard. He simply knew more about their subject than they did. Most stopped trying altogether. The idea of Richard having a teacher was one to push aside; it was too unbelievable.

After some days of spying on him, Sam gleaned very little information. Richard spent most of his time training in one fashion or another: shooting, martial arts, free running, weight training, and even studying. He read about physics, chemistry, biology, physiology—all sorts of subjects. He read through book after book for hours at a time. He was preparing for something; she just didn't know what. He was a well-read, highly trained operative who had been undercover for years, but why? What was he playing at? Trying to make sense of all that she knew was depressing. There simply wasn't a picture to be found with the puzzle pieces presented.

She found it hard to concentrate as her thoughts and questions were pulled in another direction. An idea slammed into her like a ton of bricks.

It was a question that was now so unbelievably obvious that she contemplated why she failed to consider it until this very moment. It pricked at her, and she wondered—how long had Richard been fighting? Those scars on his back looked really old. That question intrigued her; it was so simple that she almost felt stupid for not seeing it sooner.

Yet, a fresh revelation, a second propositioned inquiry eclipsed the first.

The second was more important of the two. The first question riddled: how long had Richard been fighting? And the second, and much more important inquiry asked: what was Richard fighting for?

She was so stupid. She plotted and schemed in an attempt to learn about him without starting with the most fundamental inquiry. How did she not ask the simple question of: what was his purpose? For what reason was he fighting? It was so simple. If she figured out what Richard was fighting for—his overall goal—then she should be able to work backward from that goal. It all seemed so simple.

Sam ducked her head. He started moving again, and much in the way of noise rang out—the noises she now recognized. It was the unmistakable patter of gunfire, 20th-century gunfire. Sam slid back from her perch of a hiding place and was just about to slip away when—

"Doughboy, report."

The jarring, booming voice filled the space, further setting Sam's teeth on edge and nearly causing her to slip and fall. The voice filled the entirety of the training room.

Richard sounded annoyed when he answered.

"I hate that call sign."

"Yes, I am well aware, but we can't go changing call signs very often. It might confuse the mission protocol."

"Protocol? Don't feed me a line, *Big Daddy*," he said, the

call sign dripping with derision. "Are you or are you not in charge?"

"You're awfully mouthy today, soldier. Can I assume that things aren't going well?"

"That's the understatement of the year."

"It's good for you."

"Like hell it is! When can we execute mission protocol and get on with things? I'd like for this nightmare to be over as soon as possible."

"Soon, Doughboy. And like I said, it's good for you. You've been under deep cover too long; it will be good for you to stretch your wings, so to speak. Get out of your comfort zone. The situation is ripe for experimentation."

The voice paused. "Just not *too* much experimentation."

Richard's answer dripped with sarcasm. "Please."

"Like I said, it will be good for you. Besides, I'm still trying to figure out how much they know. I can't do much from where I am because of the constraints I am under. So for the time being, I need you to stay put. Once I know, you'll know, and then we'll execute the extraction."

This was not what Richard wanted to hear. "I'm the only one that can handle this, and you know it. I can get close and finish before they know what's going on. Why do we have to know anyway? Let's just pull the weed up by the root. Who cares what the weed's purpose is? If you'll just let me come in—"

"Negative. If they get their hands on the package, we

could all be in danger. You've been on this assignment longer than anyone; you know what's at stake. I don't know how much longer the preventative measures I put in place will last. And we don't know what abilities will manifest once the suppression wears off. Until we can test it, we are all in danger. You know this. We aren't going to let our guard down until we understand better what we're up against."

"You don't know what we're up against? How can that—"

The voice cut him off but sounded either concerned or upset. "The latest addition—you know of whom I discuss— he's a game changer. We need to be prepared in case the time-line improves. Remember to upload your alpha weapons protocol algorithm to my server so the locks are automatic. We don't want a repeat of what happened at Academy City 676, now do we?"

"No, sir, but won't you reconsider my request for—"

"I know what you're going to say, Doughboy, and you know the answer. You let me handle things on my end, and you get some well-deserved rest. Am I understood?"

"Yes, sir."

"Good. Now I suggest that you escort the young lady hiding on your artificial mountain and eavesdropping back upstairs before your guests arrive."

———

Richard was really, *really* mad!

"Samantha, what the hell do you think you were doing?"

Sam shrugged. "Just what the mysterious voice on the intercom said. I was eavesdropping."

"Your overwhelming ability to recount the obvious is breathtaking. I understand that you were eavesdropping when I explicitly told you not to come down here and bother me. Now my question is why. And answer carefully, Samantha, or I may choose to kill you and throw you in the lake."

Sam smiled widely. "You sounded like fat Richard just then. Can I hug you?"

"Samantha!"

"Okay, okay, don't get your nick-nats in a twist, jeez."

They went silent. Richard put his hand out impatiently. "Well?"

Sam smiled again. "Well, what?"

"Oh my George W. Bush, woman, if you don't start—"

Richard paused, a look of surprise splashed across his face. "I can't believe I just said that."

Sam patted his arm and then turned to walk away. "See? Our time together wasn't all pretend. At least you're not an alien robot like I thought. I'm hungry; I'm going upstairs."

She didn't wait for an answer. Richard called after her.

"Sam, I'm not done talking to you yet."

"Well, you'll know where I will—"

Sam came to a dead stop. Richard was back in front of her as if he had been standing off in the distance, simply waiting for her to come to him. She looked at him, the bewilderment evident on her face, though she attempted not to show her surprise. She *hated* it when he did crap like that. How did he move that fast?

"Answer my question, Samantha," said Richard in a condescending tone. "Why were you spying on me? What's your goal?"

Sam felt a flush of anger boil up; the emotion ran headlong into her already growing frustration. "What's my goal? Seriously? Are you retarded, Richard? My goal, my only goal since we moved into this freaking mountain, was to figure out what the hell is going on. Oh, and get out!"

Richard attempted to speak, but Sam wasn't done yet. "What's my goal? Honestly, what a stupid question! What did you expect to happen, Richard? You ignore me for weeks at a time after lying to me about being my chubby best friend, and then don't allow me on the V-Space to check in with my mom, Cammy, or Coda. You won't let me leave, so I am just stuck here, emotionally by myself with only the fungus to talk to."

"Actually, fungus can be fascinating if you—"

Sam didn't know what came over her, but something inside her cracked, and anger bled out. She was so mad, so frustrated, so worried...so scared. She did the only thing she could think of that might make her feel better. She took a swing at Richard, the second time she had tried to do so. He had dodged that punch thrown at his head back in the parking garage of Academy City 676, and just like the first of

Sam's outbursts, he dodged this strike, stepping out of the way with ease. Sam tried again, this time aiming at his midsection with a similar result. She tried a third time but changed tactics, attempting a kick aimed at his head. Not only did she miss, but she lost her balance and fell over herself. She lay on the ground panting.

"You know, Sam, Albert Einstein once stated that the very definition of insanity was doing the same thing over and over again and expecting different results. I think we can safely say that you're insane."

Sam righted herself, still breathing hard, and glared at Richard. "Only a crazy person does the same thing over and over again and expects different results, huh? Well then, I guess I need to do something different."

Sam started walking towards Richard slowly. Richard rolled his eyes. "Sam, even if you get close to me, there is no way that you're going to be able to hit me."

Sam ignored him, advancing forward like a soldier on a death march. She didn't halt until she stood right in front of him.

"Before we continue, Richard, can I ask you a question?"

Richard's face looked slightly amused. "If you must."

"How confident are you?"

Richard's eyebrow rose. "What exactly are you referring to, Samantha?"

"Are you confident enough in your ability to stand before a *crazy person* like me and close your eyes?"

Richard's expression soured. "That's your plan? You're going to ask me to close my eyes, and then what, Sam? Try and hit me?"

"Well?"

Richard closed his eyes. "Your childish baiting does not affect me, Sam, but I will humor you just to show you how pointless this exercise is."

"Ugh! Were you always this arrogant?" Sam threw the punch at his head a half a second later. Richard caught the punch at the length of its extension.

"Are we done yet?" Richard sighed, his eyes still closed. "Can you go now?"

The beating of Sam's heart filled her ears while settled, calculating emotion washed over her. Sam felt an unparalleled calm as she encroached on Richard. She whispered in a voice that was deep and dry. It didn't sound like her. "The unmovable, impenetrable object is a façade; everything moves eventually."

Sam moved closer, ever closer. She was right in front of him. "Given enough time, Richard, everything will move... even you."

Sam moved in slowly, deliberately getting closer and closer. She closed her eyes.

Sam kissed him softly on the lips. The kiss held for a span —one second, two seconds, three seconds, four...

Richard took a step back, and for the first time in his life, he appeared absolutely dumbfounded, so much so that he didn't see the right crossover streaming toward his head. Sam hit Richard with all the strength she possessed.

Sam turned on her heel and sped off, calling over her shoulder, "Well, Richard, how's that for crazy?"

———

Sam went immediately to the kitchen to ice her hand, still fuming, not believing Richard's arrogance. How could he treat her that way? How could he act like he didn't know her? She threw a piece of glass across the room. That wasn't right; he did *know*—he knew her incredibly well, too well. It wasn't that he didn't know; he just didn't care.

It was a piercing revelation. Richard, her Richard, simply didn't care about her. Sam flipped on the faucet and, with her good hand, threw in a couple of cups of ice. She waited for it to fill.

Had their relationship, their friendship, been all part of his cover? It had to be the case; there was no other reason for him to befriend her. She suddenly felt extremely stupid. She also felt the dregs of embarrassment slowly filter up. That was her first kiss! What kind of girl does that?

Sam plunged her hand into the icy water and felt pain and a certain amount of relief. She mused momentarily on how fighters didn't break their hands every time they fought. It felt like she had broken hers. The bruises were already forming on her knuckles. Sam half-expected Richard to come after her, yell at her, hit her—something. But no, he didn't follow her, so she was left to her own devices, nursing a bruised hand and heart.

She couldn't deny it. Something within her chest hurt, and she was pretty sure it didn't have anything to do with something physical. Sam had heard the phrase "heartbroken" before. She remembered laughing at the idea of being so emotionally involved with someone as to have physical pains. The idea was laughable. She found herself regretting that laughter now as her chest felt like it was going to explode.

Sam clenched at her chest. The pain was increasing, but that didn't make any sense. There wasn't any reason for the pain in her chest to increase. Her logic didn't match up with reality. The pain in her chest was increasing and spreading. Sam felt a rushing need to run, to run to her room and hide.

She did just that.

Each step was agony to her body. The pain that started in her chest moved so that every part, every nerve ending lit up with fire. It was as if she were burning from the inside out.

This way, hurry! We've got to get in before they pick up our trail!

The voice sounded thoroughly shocking to her. She touched her ears; the voice sounded as if someone were whispering right next to her. She was less prepared for the new voice that sounded.

Hurry up, Teddy, we've got to go!

Shut up, Rice, I'm flipping hurt here!

Sam tripped and fell as astonishment took over. She called out to whoever was talking, trying desperately to understand what was happening. More than one voice? Who could be speaking? Was she losing her mind? Sam got back to her feet and ran.

The voices continued to buzz in her ears like flies; Sam attempted to swat them. She ran faster, recklessly down the halls until she came to the main entrance that would lead her down her tunnel to her room. She stopped when a group of gun-wielding individuals came into view.

Sam blanched. They had found them; they were here. Sam started to cry.

CHAPTER 7
INFORMATION GATHERING

Time: Some weeks ago
Place: Somewhere in the South Pacific

The echo of boots clunking along the metal walkway fills the small enclosed space as a technician makes his way to the rig's main deck. The smell of salty air lingers in the otherwise stuffy interior as the rectangular portholes show the glimmer of pre-dawn light. As the technician exits the bowels of the offshore rig, he glances toward the islands in the distance. He quickly navigates the PV-cell-covered walkways that lead to the cloud farms. Below him, he can hear the hum of the osmotic and tidal-powered generators give way to the quieter thrum of the heat exchangers that keep the massive farm cool.

As he nears the main deck, he ducks his head, being sure not to hit his hard hat on the low hatch entrance. At this early hour, only a skeleton crew is up and about. Just a few members of the maintenance crew and janitorial workers are finishing up their nightly cleaning and service. He exchanges brief pleasantries with those he passes, always keeping them to nods and smiles in line with the hour of the day. No one gives him a second look. No one recognizes him as more than one of the hundreds of technicians that regularly work throughout the rig. He wastes no time navigating the walkways, as he has a very short time before the main shift begins.

Drawing on the blueprints in his mind, the technician weaves his way to a central elevator, never hesitating at a turn or intersection. He codes in at the elevator and waits for the massive transport to reach the deck. As the doors open, he sees another employee caressing a mug of strong coffee. The acidic smell of dark roasted beans is heavy as he notices the employee's holo-badge and recognizes him as a fellow technician. They both nod a sleepy hello as the technician steps forward and selects his destination.

"Main server farm, eh?" asks the man as he sips his steaming mug. "That right there is the start of a bad day if you have to be there *this* early."

"Tell me about it," replies the technician, not missing a beat in the conversation.

"The only thing good about that place is that new sweet piece of intern tail they got working the sub-sys support logs. You seen her yet?"

The technician smiles a knowing smile. "Why do you think this maintenance request sucks double? Her shift doesn't start for another hour or so. That's the only thing I look forward to on these req's. She hasn't given me the time of day yet, but I'm working her."

The other man chuckles, sharing in the technician's lament. "I feel ya, man. Well, this is me." The employee moves forward as the elevator slows and the doors open. "Maybe you could stretch this req out and catch her on your way back up."

"I'll try that," replies the technician as the doors close. Alone, the casual smile fades from his face. He reaches into his pocket and puts on reading glasses as he checks the work req on his interface.

The elevator reaches the farm deck, and the technician exits, walking confidently toward the security desk. The man sitting at the desk is obviously from the nearby islands. He looks up at the technician as he approaches. The technician yawns as he walks past the desk and through the security terminal. The red light of the security terminal does not change as he walks through it, nor does the accompanying chime of "cleared" from the terminal sound. The technician sighs in frustration, turns, and pulls his holo-badge from his uniform, holding it closer to the RFID scanner. He waves it up and down, back and forth across the plate. Just as the guard is about to stand up, the technician touches the badge to the plate, and the light changes green, flashing his credentials across the security terminal.

The technician rolls his eyes at the badge, shrugging at

the guard. He turns and starts walking away just as the guard calls out to him. "Excuse me. Everything okay?"

The technician turns to look confidently at the guard. "Except for this defective badge giving me problems and me having to answer a maintenance req at this gods-forsaken hour, ya—just peachy."

"Maintenance req? I don't see any maintenance request scheduled. Where did the req come from?" asks the guard inquisitively.

"What a surprise," replies the technician, his voice a little perturbed. "No offense, but I don't get paid enough to fulfill a *scheduled* req this early. But a priority, non-version update, off-sched req comes in, so I get outta my warm bunk and head over here. That's how it works."

The guard gives the man an unsympathetic glare. "No req in the schedule, no access. *That's* how it works."

The technician comes back through the security terminal toward the guard, already scrolling through his interface. "Look, I have it right here." The technician raises the interface to show the guard. Without the guard seeing, the technician thumbs an execute command on the back of his interface, remotely sending a command to the desk. A small script begins to run behind the apps on the desk as the guard stares at the interface. The script works quickly and inserts a small line of code to trigger a new alert regarding the maint req. "Check again, man, 'cause if I don't have to be here, I'm going back to bed."

The guard looks up from the interface to the technician and then back to the desk terminal. The technician remotely kills the script, and it fades silently into the temp files. The guard refreshes the schedule, reviews the alert, checks it against the technician's interface, and reluctantly stands. The technician sees that the guard is trying to remain placid, but underneath his exterior, he does not completely believe the technician. "Fine. This better not take long. I'll escort you to the platform."

The two men walk through the security terminal and start down the walkway toward the farms. The technician feels the air around him grow cooler as the frigid water from deep beneath the offshore rig flows freely through the condenser coils throughout the farm network. The technician walks confidently toward the last half of the farm and stops at a door on the south side of the rig. He retrieves small earplugs from his pocket and fits them in his ears. He offers a pair to the guard, who shakes his head. "No, I'll stay out here. Just make it quick."

The technician shrugs and unlocks the coded door. As the clear partitions slide open, the deafening drone of the server blades spills out onto the walkway, and the guard winces until the technician enters the room and the partitions slide closed. The technician checks his interface and proceeds to find the server listed on the req as the guard watches him through the partitions. The technician wanders down the rows of servers and eventually makes his way out of the line of sight from the guard.

The technician drops down to his knee in front of a rack and removes his glasses. He detaches a thin clear wire and one of the arms from the frame. He folds the arm along predefined folds in the metal into a small rectangular cube and attaches the clear wire to a tiny port at the corner. He slides the hollow rectangular cube into a port on the side of the server blade and affixes the other end of the clear wire into a small port on the glasses. The lenses of the glasses light up and start running scripts and terminal commands. The technician's interface lights up as the data stream is wirelessly mirrored on its screen. The scripts make fast work of the security protocols, and in a few short seconds, the technician launches a number of spyders to search for the intel he is after.

He checks his timepiece as the spyders crawl through the vast landscape of files. While they relay their surroundings, the technician modifies their search perimeters. Coupled with their own near-SI capabilities, the spyders narrow their search grid from peta to tera, finally locating the sections that match with their search criteria.

The technician accesses the identified remote servers through an impersonation app on his interface. The remotes validate his credentials, acknowledge that the request is from a darknet protocol, and subsequently pause all logging activity. The technician checks his timepiece again, realizing that the spyder search took longer than expected. He rapidly scans through the hierarchy of the region files. Finding too much information to sort through, he hastily makes a decision to copy the entire stream. The fiber optic cable connecting the glasses to the server lights up as the high-capacity I/O channel pours the data into the crystal drives that make up both lenses.

Mere moments later, blueprints, sat recon photos, financial data, interrogation reports, and recon vids flow freely onto the massive crystal drives. The technician checks his timepiece as the last remaining bytes flow across the connection. Once complete, he launches two more packets to erase his tracks, signs off of the remote servers, instructing them to resume logging activities at the next picosecond in their records, thus leaving no interruption of activity. He disconnects the wire, refolds the frame, and tucks his glasses in his coverall's front pocket. He launches similar scrubbing commands on his interface, along with an additional maintenance req for the next shift, and then stands to leave. As he rounds the row of servers, the guard startles him.

"What were you doing back there?" asks the guard in a loud voice. The technician looks at him confused and points to his earplugs. The guard motions for the technician to follow him. They exit the noisy server room and continue back up the walkway to the main security desk. An additional guard is sitting at the terminal, scanning the screen. He looks up at the guard with a scowl on his face.

"Is this him?" asks the guard curtly.

"Yes, sir," replies the first guard in a somewhat timid voice.

The guard behind the desk shifts to look at the technician. He stares at him intently. "What were you doing in there? There are no scheduled reqs until later this week."

"Just running through the maintenance req that came down," replies the technician matter-of-factly. "Looks like an SSD module went bad. I put in an order for the next shift to come down and replace it."

The guard eyes him with skepticism. "Why don't you just fix it?"

The technician laughs but quickly stops as he sees that the guard is not amused. "I can't fix it. Don't have the replacement part, and even if I did, I'm not rated for hardware maintenance."

"So if you couldn't fix it, why did you even come down here? And further, why would they send an unrated technician to fix the server?" asks the guard accusingly.

"Look, man, the maintenance routines ran very early this morning and couldn't locate the issue, so they called me—a low-level first-line tech. The module is on a redundancy server that backs up a critical app net. Protocol requires that any issues with redundancy servers be identified as priority one." The guard's skepticism didn't seem to be lessening. "Come on, man, you know there's no way those rated guys start work before nine. That's why they dragged my butt outta bed at this ungodly hour."

The guard still looks unconvinced. "This is highly irregular." He looks at the other guard. "Search him."

The timid-looking guard haltingly steps toward the technician and holds his hand out for his interface. The technician shrugs and hands it over. The guard sets it down in front of the seated guard, who begins to sort through its most recent activity. The technician lifts his arms out to the side as the guard starts to sweep a gloved hand over the technician's coveralls. The glove emits a chirp as it passes over the holo-badge but remains silent down both legs. The only other chirp comes at the technician's pocket. Surprised and confused, the technician looks at the guard. The confusion only holds for a moment, then his face relaxes, and he reaches in and pulls out his glasses. The guard at the desk holds his hand out for the spectacles.

"Why would you need these?" asks the guard.

"All that fine motor work on wire diagrams and flow paths gives me a headache," comments the technician nonchalantly. "I'm on the waitlist for an oc adjustment at medbay, but they said it would be at least another six months or so."

The guard turns the glasses over in his hands. He waves his gloved hand over them, and it produces the same chirp as before. He scrutinizes them for a minute more and then sets them on the desk with the technician's interface. "Next time,

I expect maintenance to send a qualified tech with the needed replacement parts. Understood?"

The technician gathers his glasses and interface. "Look, man, I just go where they tell me to go. But I'll be sure to drop that suggestion off."

The technician tucks his glasses in his coverall pocket, turns from the security desk, and proceeds back up the walkway to the elevator, all while the two guards watch him leave. When he reaches the elevator, he hits the button to return to the upper platform. But two levels up, he stops at a sub-level and exits the elevator. He walks across the main walkway, looking around for other workers. Upon seeing no one, he enters a door off to the side, closing it softly behind him.

Three walkways and four doors later, he is in an older section of the rig. He makes his way through rusted-out walkways until he reaches a room adjoining the outer wall of the rig. He peers in the small peephole to check on the man and woman lying tied up on the floor.

———

Benji's head was pounding. His whole arm was asleep, his shoulder was stiff like someone had punched it, and he was freezing. His blurry vision was improving, but still, it must have been one helluva night. He rubbed at the spot on his arm that the pain seemed to be coming from. The last thing he remembered was seeing that new intern, Misa, at the onshore bar flirting with a couple of security officers. She hadn't given him or his buddies the time of day, even though they all made excuses to visit her part of the rig. He must have checked that sub-sys log at least 15 times over the past two weeks. He tried to remember what else happened at the bar. After copious amounts of alcohol, he and his fellow technicians started taking bets on who should go talk to her. He had decided the money was too good to pass up, so he headed over in her direction. He faintly remembered bumping into a few people, obviously a result of the alcohol. Perhaps that was why his shoulder hurt so bad. Then...well, then he...honestly, he had no idea what happened then.

Benji started to sit up. His head pounded a little harder as the blood rushed to it. A small noise to his left jarred his thoughts. He shook his head, trying to clear his blurry vision. He could see the fuzzy object next to him move, but it wasn't until a few more moments passed that his mind was able to piece together what it was; or rather who it was.

Benji stared wide-eyed at the curvy, tanned, soft, supple skin of Misa, the intern. In fact, that was all that Benji saw since Misa was completely naked. It was then that Benji realized he was naked too. Despite feeling cold just a few moments ago, Benji's face now felt hot. He looked around the room and found his technician coveralls, T-shirt, and briefs in a pile next to his toolbox and boots. Misa's clothes were haphazardly scattered around the room, apparently landing where they had been flung. Benji looked at the other side of the room. Where were they? He stood up off the soft blanket and staggered toward the circular porthole on the outer wall. He wiped off the grime and peered out at the early morning dawn. The only thing he could make out was the small wake of a boat just fading into the sunlight. Silhouetted against the rising sun, the single passenger appeared to be dressed in all black as the craft faded out of sight.

Benji heard a firm and resolute clearing of a female throat behind him. He closed his eyes, preparing for the worst.

CHAPTER 8

JOHN ADAMS IS A STUPID, DRUG-ADDLED GANGA.

Time: Present Day
Scene: He doesn't bricking know.

Instead of Dirk and Fate becoming fast friends, Dirk had the pleasure of making friends with The Chair. He thought about giving The Chair a better name—something like Billy or Rustafus—but in the end, The Chair suited it just fine. At first, its metal probes and snaking wires had scared Dirk almost out of his mind. Now, Dirk just tried to ignore them, despite the difficulty of doing so when they were hooked up to almost every part of his body. While the guards hadn't expressly educated Dirk on the purpose of The Chair's accessories, he had seen enough classic vids to come up with all sorts of uses, most of which he tried immediately to push out of his mind. Although nowhere near the current medical technology of rapid brain scans and non-intrusive PETs, they still accomplished one of their designs: namely, intimidation. And for weeks, Dirk had been putting them through their paces.

It only took Dirk a few days in The Chair to realize that the leads were somehow monitoring him. He wasn't sure exactly how this worked, but he was confident at least in that assumption. He was asked to look at photos, listen to sounds, and watch vids. Sometimes these were interlaced with a guard asking him questions about an unrelated topic, and other times he was left alone with the images and sounds. Dirk's nature was to automatically disrupt whatever plans these goons had for collecting information. But since none of the images, voices, or documents were familiar, Dirk struggled to decide on what to do. He decided that he would try to fake recognition of some of the items he saw. Trouble was that as soon as he decided on that course of action, the items became even stranger. They shifted from normal-looking text to odd symbols and patterns. The voices ceased speaking languages that Dirk could at least identify and started in on complete gibberish.

Fortunately, these odd strings of stimuli were short-lived. For the last few sessions, it had just been Dirk, The Chair, and some old-looking doctor guy. Dirk would be strapped in, and old man stuffy-pants would stroll in and ask how Dirk was doing. Dirk would reply with something like The Chair and he were just discussing how a softer shade of blue uphol-stery would do wonders for the decor of the room. To this, Dr. Stuffy-pants would smile and nod, jot something down in his interface, and then proceed to ask Dirk questions with no assumption that Dirk was crazy for talking to The Chair, let alone assuming blue would do anything to soften the room's ambiance.

The questions were benign at first: his age, where he had grown up, what places he had most recently visited. But then things turned weird. The doc would hold up his interface for Dirk to look at. Some crazy-looking symbol would appear on the screen, and he would ask Dirk if he had ever seen it. Dirk, of course, would say that he had, and that he and The Chair were actually just discussing yesterday how lovely that would look framed above the equipment bay on the other side of the room. Stuffy-pants would nod and smile, jot something down, and then show Dirk another symbol. This had gone on so long that Dirk was worried he was running out of crazy things to reply with.

As Dirk sat wired in the dark room, he tried to come up with something original. He had already exhausted deco-rating ideas that he and The Chair had shared, their opposing political views, his complaints about how The Chair never seemed to change and was stuck in its ways, and how The Chair had hurt him by cheating with the generator and that they were now in a trial separation. He figured he could take this a little further since he was forced to see The Chair on a regular basis even though they weren't speaking until it apologized. But seriously, after that, Dirk was tapped out. Plus, he started to actually care about The Chair, which told him that he may have taken the whole thing a little too far.

Doc Stuffy-pants strolled into the room and took his normal seat across from Dirk. Dirk organized his ramblings, preparing for more symbol matching.

Dirk was just about to share his feelings of anxiety about being forced to sit in The Chair during their tiff when the doc said something that threw Dirk's game way off. "Dirk, you have been very helpful over the past few weeks," commented the doc.

Dirk had not been expecting that. He was sure the doc was just about ready to rant about Dirk's lack of cooperation and his insane statements about inanimate objects. Dirk was prepared for yelling and screaming. This whole helpful garbage caught him off guard.

"In fact," continued the doc, "your responses have been so helpful that the man I work for has decided it's time to speak with you. Dirk Garrett, meet John Adams."

Dirk sat there dumbfounded at what was happening. He thought for sure he had been doing all that he could to not answer any of their questions and, in fact, had made immense strides in providing nothing but unrelated babble. As Dirk was mulling this change of pace over in his mind, a large vid screen behind the doc illuminated. It took Dirk a minute or so to figure out where he had seen the man that was staring back at him. He had a familiar face, but Dirk, for the life of him, could not place it.

"Good morning, Mr. Garrett. My name is John Adams. It's nice to finally meet you," said the man.

Was he a politician that Dirk saw on the feeds? Maybe a high-ranking official that had been present at one of his trials?

"Doctor Rosenthal reports that you have been most helpful in our investigation," the man continued.

Vid theater star? No... The man was too old to be an athlete. Where had Dirk seen him?

"Mr. Garrett, I wanted to talk with you about some very important topics. I apologize for the cryptic living conditions over the past little while, but they were necessary to determine if you were a threat or not."

Animal rights activist? Historical preservationist? Dirk simply could not shake the feeling that he had seen this man somewhere.

"Mr. Garrett? Mr. Garrett, I know this may be a shock, but are you all right?" inquired the man.

"Who are you?" Dirk asked. "I mean, where do I know you fr—" Then it hit him. When the doc said John Adams, he literally meant John Adams. Dirk saw the man who was the second president of the former United States. Except this man was alive and talking to Dirk. "You're John Adams? *The* John Adams?"

The man on the screen chuckled. "Well, let's just say that

my friends call me John. As I was about to explain to you, I represent a very covert underground movement that seeks to preserve freedom in this world. For many reasons, including security, you see me now in costume as the man my handle is named after. But I assure you that we haven't reanimated the dead. It's merely precautionary."

Dirk realized then that no matter what this man said, he could not be trusted. Someone hiding that much of their identity obviously had a lot to lose if they were discovered. "So, John. What exactly is it that I helped with, since all I remember doing was having some fun with the doc over here? And for that matter, why did you guys spring me just to lock me up again? Whose side are you on?"

"Mr. Garrett, we are not on anyone's side... per se." Adams paused, looking thoughtful. "It would be easier if I started with why you were in that Jadian prison to begin with."

Dirk rolled his eyes. "Well, if you are as well-connected as you say you are, then you know that I may have a few outstanding warrants here and there."

John Adams smiled as if he were about to explain something to a five-year-old. "Mr. Garrett, common criminals with outstanding warrants are not transported from the outer edges of the Empire to the Seven Cities. They are simply left to rot or are executed. You, Mr. Garrett, are obviously no common criminal." Dirk wasn't sure if that was meant as a compliment. "Further, it seems it's not just the Empire that has it in for you. In addition to your most recent incarceration and a close encounter with a Jadian enforcer in the Burning Plains a few years back, the UWC also has had you on their radar."

"Like I said, warrants. Misunderstandings would really be a better description," Dirk replied.

"Yes, well, if it were just warrants, we wouldn't have gone to all the expense of, as you said, springing you from your predicament," retorted Adams. "So let's just assume that these governments are interested in more than just executing you as a criminal. Tell me, Mr. Garrett, why would the highest levels of politicians and ambassadors have your name in their files? Why would they invest so much time, effort, and credits to procure a relic hunter such as yourself? Do you perhaps have something of value remaining in your possession?"

Dirk was silent. Partly because most people he met had no idea what he did for a living, and partly because Dirk's skin had prickled when Adams mentioned that Dirk's name was in a bunch of files. Something about that seemed right, and that scared Dirk. He realized that if these covert underground people, whoever they were, knew about his warrants, his relic hunting, and a number of other things about him, there was very little they didn't already know. Conclusion: this Adams guy was testing him for Dirk's cooperation. Well, if they wanted to play, Dirk was game. Ha. He just made a funny.

"I don't have anything of value left. Everything was sold to private collectors or confiscated upon my arrests. I doubt if they are after anything that I *borrowed*."

"I see. Well, let's try something else." Dirk involuntarily tensed. "No, Mr. Garrett, nothing like that." Dirk cocked his head to the side in confusion. How did Adams know he flinched? There was no way he could have picked up on that just through the vid feed. Then it dawned on him. The leads. All those pictures and vids, the audio clips. Dirk didn't need to concoct the insane story about his relationship with The Chair because they had been interested in the reactions that Dirk couldn't control: heart rate, blood pressure, brain activity. With all these leads hooked up to him, he had been read like an open book. No wonder Doctor Stuffy-pants never seemed to get annoyed by Dirk's blatant lack of cooperation. Dirk was cooperating beautifully as he emanated copious amounts of involuntary information. Dirk's respect and anxiety concerning his new captors clicked up a few notches.

"I'm going to show you some pictures of high-profile agents from both the UWC and the Empire. You tell me if you recognize any of them."

Sure, I'll tell you, thought Dirk. He didn't have to say a word, and he would tell Adams if he knew any of them. As the images rolled by on the screen, Dirk tried to remain calm and focused. But in reality, he didn't know any of the images. Dozens of photos later, and Dirk still had not seen a familiar face.

"Well, that was a long shot, but we had to try anyway," commented Adams. "Just one more person, okay, Mr. Garrett?" Dirk found it amusing that Adams asked him as if Dirk had any control over what was happening. The image of an older-looking man popped onto the screen. "This is Dr. Eli Thurman, a theoretical physicist. Are you familiar with him or his work?"

Dirk laughed. "I failed physics. Don't need it much in my line of work."

The image faded, and Adams was once again on screen. "Well, again that was a long shot. Forgive me, Mr. Garrett, but we are running out of theories as to why these parties are so interested in you. You say that you no longer are in possession of any of the items you, ah, *borrowed*."

"That's right," replied Dirk.

"Perhaps we can get some additional information about some of those pieces of history." Adams tapped a few commands on his desk, and more images scrolled onto the screen. Dirk recognized these immediately. He also was a little frightened at their appearance. The relics he had procured flowed across the screen in near chronological order, but that wasn't all. There was historical information, legends created around the relics, and even a list of supposed owners or other treasure hunters who sought after the prized items. The information was astounding. Who was this man that he had access to such obscure information? What enabled him to catalog every find Dirk had ever made?

Dirk continued to watch as pictures and information streamed down the screen. As he came out of his discomfort at discovering his captors knew way too much about him, his skin prickled again. Dirk focused on the images, responding to what his skin was trying to tell him. At first, he didn't see it, but then it hit him. Each of these relics was accompanied by those strange symbols that Doctor Stuffy-pants was showing him over the last few sessions. Dirk hadn't made the connection then, but now there was definitely something off about them.

Suddenly, the images halted. "Do you recognize something, Mr. Garrett?" asked Adams. Despite being unnerved that Adams continued to ask questions he already knew the answer to, Dirk answered the question.

"These are the symbols that the doc was showing me earlier, right?" Dirk asked.

"Yes, Dr. Rosenthal isolated these symbols and showed them to you one at a time. He didn't mention that you recognized any of them," stated Adams.

You mean your little sensors didn't mention that I recognized them, Dirk corrected Adams in his mind. "Right. I didn't put together what they were because I've only seen them in groups. But different than what you have on the images of the relics."

Adams looked down at his interface and then back at Dirk. "Explain what you mean by different. These images and symbols were taken from reliable sources: various texts and archive feeds. What's different?"

"Well, you can dump whatever reliable sources you paid for, 'cause those symbols are in the wrong order. I know 'cause I was there. The one on the end there," Dirk pointed to a symbol that resembled an inverted wave

, "it means gold. At most of the finds that I dug, those symbols were strewn across walls and ceilings. I never paid them much attention, you know, with all the other things that I was interested in. But now that you're showing me these, the symbols I saw were in a different order. Same ones, just arranged differently."

Adams looked at Dirk intently. "One minute, Mr. Garrett." Adams tapped on his desk, and the screen faded to a light gray background. Dirk, on the other hand, had little choice but to remain seated in The Chair. Moments later, the screen brightened again.

"Mr. Garrett, you are saying that these symbols were present in the areas where your finds were located? Is that true for all of them?" Adams looked like he was genuinely interested in Dirk's response. Perhaps Dirk could use that to his advantage.

"Not all of them, but certainly the most valuable." Dirk started to continue, but Adams cut him off.

"Forgive me, Mr. Garrett," interrupted Adams, "what I meant was, these symbols were present in both UWC and Empire finds?"

"And Burning Plains. There were a few Ganga relics that had those symbols." Dirk's skin started to perk up. Something was about to happen; his skin got a faint tingling sensation.

"Mr. Garrett, in your line of work, is there anyone else that has a more extensive catalog of historical items?" Dirk forgot all about his plans to take advantage. His pride was on the line now.

"Not a chance. And anyone who says different doesn't have the stones to back it up. I've been all around this rock and seen more gold and silver than a room full of archaeologists," Dirk finished with a tone of pride.

"Mr. Garrett, I believe that is our answer," said Adams matter-of-factly. "Doctor Rosenthal, I think we can extricate Mr. Garrett from those recorders now."

Doctor Stuffy-pants waddled over to Dirk and began removing the leads from various parts of his body. Dirk was confused. What just happened? "Hey John, what's going on? Why are the UWC and Jade Empire after me? What do I have of theirs?"

Adams smiled a knowing smile. "It's not what you have, Mr. Garrett. It's what you've seen. Please, sit down, and I will explain the whole thing to you."

The doc held out his hand to help Dirk up from The Chair. Another guard then brought over a comfortable chair and placed it directly in front of the large screen. Dirk looked at the comfortable chair, back at the doc, then to Adams, then back to the doc. He was just waiting for something else to happen. This was all too strange. Doctor Stuffy-pants indicated for Dirk to have a seat. Tentatively, he did. He turned back to the screen as Adams spoke.

"Tell me, Mr. Garrett. Have you ever heard of Harmonicum?"

Dirk's skin prickled yet again.

CHAPTER 9
A FAMILIAR FACE

Scene: A dire one

Place: Main Tunnel, the Cheyenne Mountain Site

Sam sniffed at her tears and fought the urge to blow her nose. She refused to fall apart now, not after all she had been through, all she had survived, and definitely not before these intruders figured out they were not alone. The advantage was hers at the moment; she just needed to use it. Sam took an uneasy step, hoping her legs wouldn't give out; they were already knocking against each other in fear.

Sam scanned her surroundings, searching for somewhere to hide. It was pretty dark in the tunnel, with only the occasional ceiling light to lead the way down the underground passage. This blackness would give her some time to hide, but not long. She needed to move. Sam pressed herself against the wall in an attempt to keep herself out of sight, using a pillar that protruded several feet from the rock as cover.

Think, Samantha! Think!

She had noticed them, *knew* they were coming, before the bad guys became cognizant of her. She was lucky— stupidly lucky. The actual entrance to her and Richard's common area was well lit and clearly marked. There wasn't any reason they shouldn't have seen her, especially when Sam busted into this main tunnel.

Trying to get back to her room at the time seemed like a good idea; at least she wasn't feeling that weird pain anymore. Still, running around wildly like that was a mistake; it was a miracle they didn't see her. They weren't *that* far away; there was always the possibility that these soldiers were just that good.

It was good fortune that was quickly coming to a head. In moments, they would be right on top of her, and then she would be screwed.

Sam pushed away a mental image of the Jadian soldiers and a wicked ripple knife they used to split her shirt. She felt the fear rising and panic starting to overwhelm her. Sam felt her lips mouthing *Richard* without having meant to.

Sam gripped her fists tightly, feeling her nails dig into her hands. She wasn't going down like this.

If she didn't do something right now, the option was going to be ripped from her. She acted, doing her utmost to suppress the fear.

Sam spied a hiding place maybe two meters from the door. She threw herself in that direction and ducked behind some large, rust-covered barrels. Sam struggled to steady her breathing as they moved closer to her position.

"Man, I am starving. I hope this joint has some food. I could eat a horse, a live one at that."

Another voice, this one female, giggled; the laugh sounded vaguely familiar. "I wouldn't put it past you. I've seen him eat Gangain BBQ, and we all know they don't use beef."

"Hey, pissants," said a third gruff voice, this one distinctly older, "why don't you keep it down? We don't know what kind of hostiles are here."

"Come on, Coolidge," answered the female voice, "this site has been abandoned for dozens of years, with the majority of the tree line overgrown."

A fourth voice, this one much younger, chimed in, "I still can't believe that they tunneled out a base in the middle of a mountain. Why didn't they just use displacement shields? It offers much better protection than the rock ever could. Just look at the seven cities."

Another voice, whether new or one previously heard, spoke up, "Come on, Rice, this thing was built in like 1950, even before the Third Great War and the rise of the UWC. They didn't have displacement shields then—just giant missiles armed with thermonuclear warheads. Russia and the United States were constantly threatening to blow themselves and everyone to Taurus and back. Digging out the mountain for some semblance of protection probably seemed like a good idea at the time. Lucky for us, the UWC doesn't even know about it because they burned all those pre-war records. Chancellor Himms is such an idiot."

"Thanks for the history lesson, Palin; if you're done with your lecture, form up. We are going to sweep the upper levels before we let our guard down and hunker down."

Unable to see what happened next, Sam could only assume they did as they were told and "formed up," whatever that meant.

Eventually, the footsteps faded, and Sam was alone. She wasn't sure what to do; staying behind these stupid barrels wasn't exactly an option—not with potential bad guys lurking about. She wasn't exactly safe, but she wasn't exactly in danger either. What to do now?

Her first thought was of Richard, which was weird. She knew that Richard could take care of himself; just look at what he did to the soldiers back at school. Trained, ruthless killers, he dealt them a significant amount of death, dropping one after another like they were flies on a wall. There was no way he would go down so easily. She needed to worry about herself for the moment.

Sam crept out from her hiding place and looked down the long pathway comprising the main tunnel of the underground facility. A thought was formulating in her head—a plan, and one that might work. She glanced back towards the entrance through which the soldiers had just passed and then back towards the dimly lit tunnel. Sam knew that hundreds of meters down this main tunnel, an exit awaited. This was where she and Richard had come in; she had been dreaming of that day for weeks, maybe months now. She had gone over it again and again in her head—how she should have stayed in Academy City 676, how she should have refused to come here. How she was worried about her mom, Cammie, Coda, and Adam. How she just wanted to go back to how things used to be.

While her regret was formidable and her imprisonment less than pleasant, she had not thought about attempting— well, *seriously* attempting—to escape. Mainly her fear of the unknown and, to a lesser extent, fear of Richard kept her from pursuing an escape plan. She didn't know where she was, didn't know where to go or how to get there, and if Richard was to be believed, then there were people trying to kill her. Ignoring the fact that there wasn't any reason for people to be trying to kill her, and that particular piece of the puzzle didn't make sense, it was perfectly logical to try to stay here. At least before now, it did. Does it now? The lights that led to the end of the tunnel flickered a beckoning call. Did she want to go and see if the intruders forgot to lock the door?

Sam again returned her attention to the door to her and Richard's common room. Richard would probably be safe, she told herself. No reason to go, no reason to try to warn him.

On the other hand, these intruders had the element of

surprise. He might be seriously hurt if they got the drop on him. If they got the drop on him...he might die. The question was: was she okay with that? Was she okay with Richard dying?

No, no, she wasn't.

As much as she didn't want to admit it, she didn't like the thought of Richard getting hurt. Call it lingering affection, call it relationship nostalgia, call it simple human compassion—call it whatever you wanted, because whatever you called it, the truth was, Sam cared about Richard, whether he was fat Richard or super Richard. She didn't want to see him hurt, and so she needed to try to keep him safe.

Sam sealed away her fear—or pretended to—and followed on tiptoes back into the common area after a group of blaster-yielding soldiers.

———

This was stupid. She was stupid. *He* was stupid! Where the blazes was Richard when she needed him? The soldiers' sweep found much, and it took them less than two minutes to realize someone had been here recently. Lucky for Sam, she had used up most of the fresh food staples, so there was no immediate outward sign that she and Richard were actively using the space—only lingering remnants of their occupancy. It was only a matter of time until they found Richard's tunnels, however. If she didn't do something soon, all hell was gonna break loose.

The secret was safe for the moment. The majority of the soldiers were holed up in the mess hall, eating everything in sight. Sam thought about sneaking past and finding a hiding place while they were all in there but decided against it, as hiding wasn't going to help her figure out who these people were or what they were doing in the mountain hideout. She wanted to obtain a visual, and then she might be able to make a plan. It was fortuitous that she was in earshot of them and able to make out some of what was discussed. Her fear must be helping her concentration.

"Palin, could you help Rice find a bathroom in this joint?"

Palin's answer was muffled. Sam couldn't make it out.

"I don't care if you haven't eaten in two days. Help Rice find the bathroom now."

Sam put her head against one of the mess hall doors. Loud noises, like someone kicking a table, some grumbling, and again conversation that was impossible to make out—most likely by design—and then footsteps coming right at her: two sets, one heavy and one significantly lighter...a child—an adult and a child. Sam swore and shot down the hallway, albeit as quietly as possible.

She ran to the one functioning bathroom. She was taking a risk, but she had to gain access to additional information if she was to act. Sam ripped open the large metal door of the lavatory and continued her dash. Intel gathering was advantageous in a place like the bathroom. It was long, large, and echoed like a 19th-century music hall—the unfortunate side effect of living a mile beneath a giant mountain. Sam didn't like using this restroom. She found it spooky at the best of times, much preferring the more private individual stalls located closer to her quarters. This fit her purposes, however, as she could listen to whoever was coming while hiding in the very last stall and still be able to hear them with ease. Hopefully, if she listened carefully, ascertaining the intent and objective of the intruders would be easy. Sam was just able to shut the door to the last stall when she heard the door to the bath open.

"Okay, *Rice*," said a female voice, uttering the name like it was some sort of insult. "Pick a stall and hurry; I need to eat and find a bed. I'm exhausted."

The child answered, sounding pouty. "You want me to go and pick one myself?"

"Unless for some silly reason you want me to pick for you."

"Why are you so upset?"

"I'm not upset."

"You sound upset."

"I told you; I'm not upset."

"Are things not going well with Teddy? Come on, Palin, you can tell me."

"I'm not having this conversation with you, Rice."

"Why not? I am his sister, after all."

"That's exactly why I'm not telling you anything."

"Come on, I think I can help. I heard you guys had to play happy couple. What was that about?"

"Rice, how did you know that?"

"I'm young, not stupid, Palin; and there was a *reason* that MESA came to 679."

Palin's sneer was audible. "And you're saying that was about you?"

Rice ignored her. "So back to Teddy, why don't you tell him how you feel?"

"Impossible. You know what happened in that last battle; he lost some very dear friends, one of which I'm pretty sure he had a thing for, though he would never admit it."

"Why is that?"

"Teddy works deep cover, Rice; you're not allowed to get emotionally involved. You can't. Up until his last assignment, he was cold as ice, partly because of his own arrogance, but mostly because of the training. Your brother has endured a lot because of you, did you know that?"

"Yes," agreed Rice, sounding much closer than she should. "I know he's doing this mostly for me."

"I'm glad you recognize that." Sam heard the stall door right next to her open. She continued to slow her breathing. "Anyway, I was called in on the last job because Teddy got a little funky. He was drawn to this friend of his—strangely attracted to her. He was acting really funny, so General Washington, in strict confidence mind you, contacted me.

Teddy is one of his favorites, and he didn't like the idea that Teddy being emotional might compromise the mission or, worse, his own life. The General was quite concerned."

"That's when he called you."

"Yes."

"So when did you fall in love with my brother?"

"Shut up, Rice."

Slap.

Sam swore but had the good sense to do so silently. She was so caught up in Palin's story that she forgot to pay attention to her footing. Sitting high on a toilet is harder than one might think. Because of her inattention, her foot slipped, and she just knocked her head against the wall.

"Rice, did you hear that?"

"Yeah, it sounded like...."

The voice trailed off.

Sam instinctively knew what was coming next. Slowly, the small doorknob-like latch on her stall turned, and—Sam busted out of the door, pushing forward like a raging rhino. The person who had the misfortune of being in front of her— she assumed it was Palin—took the edge of a metal stall in the chest. Palin flew back, the rubber mask she was wearing flipping to a funny angle, and the small plasma pistol in her hand going loose. Palin fell to the ground as Sam spirited the length of the bathroom.

Ka-boom!

The discharged weapon sent a conglomerated ball of red-orange energy in her direction. The ball missed Sam by a considerable margin but impeded her escape when it struck the wall of the bathroom. The shot geysered from the point of impact, splashing lava-like ooze all over the place. Sam didn't break stride, trying to get to the door before Palin had the good sense to fire another shot. She stepped lightly on the places less affected by the ooze. Miraculously, she navigated the space, flung open the bathroom door, and shut it, the fevered sound of footsteps following aggressively behind her.

Sam took a step back, her mind working feverishly. There was no way the other soldiers missed the discharge of that plasma pistol, which meant she had only seconds before they were upon her. She needed a weapon to defend herself. Only one alternative came to mind.

Sam pressed her body right outside the door of the bathroom. She was only going to get one shot at this. One shot—success or dead; those were the options. Palin had already shot at her once. She wouldn't miss again.

Half a second later, the door to the bathroom creaked, pulling in and clinging louder and louder at the strength with which it was swung open. Mask still slightly askew, Palin stuck her head and hand holding the gun out first. Once the gun and Palin's wrist cleared the threshold, Sam bounced on her.

Sam struck at the hand holding the gun first. Balling her hand into a fist, Sam struck hard at the base of Palin's wrist. The maneuver, while sloppy, accomplished its intended effect. The gun fell from Palin's hand. Sam followed the blow with a spinning back kick, merely completing the motion already set in her body from the full-force blow of her punch. The kick, meant for Palin's head, was sloppy and connected with her shoulder instead. Still, there was enough force to send Palin to the ground again.

Sam picked up the gun. She aimed it right at Palin. The glowing feeling of success was short-lived, however, as something dug sharply into the back of her shoulders.

Sam froze where she stood as a towering presence encroached upon her.

"All right, darling, that's quite enough of that. Palin over there is my pretend girlfriend, and I wouldn't be much of a boyfriend if I let you shoot her."

Sam felt her hand go slack, but not from fear, anger, or frustration; none of these emotions assaulted her. The only emotion she felt was astonishment as...as she recognized the voice of the speaker. Sam turned to face him.

She pointed her own weapon at the mask-wearing individual standing in front of her. "Coda, what are you doing here?"

CHAPTER 10
OCCAM'S RAZOR

Time: Early morning
Scene: Harmonics Lab

Dr. Eli Thurman sat at his desk as the early hours of the morning ticked by. He did his best thinking during this time of the day when all of the staff had yet to arrive, especially when Warrick wasn't around. The Professor relied on Warrick's enthusiasm and youthful energy as he buzzed around the lab, but lately, he had been showing a little too much interest in the Professor's thoughts. It seemed like he was constantly asking about what the Professor was thinking or planning for the next cycle of trials. This went far beyond procedural and administrative responsibility; it was bordering on harassment. Perhaps that's why the Professor treasured these early mornings—the quiet, the uninterrupted lengths of thought and pondering. After all, he had an extra-large helping of things to ponder. He sat staring at an old leather-bound book that was open on his desk. He had made a habit of journal writing ever since graduate school. Some may have considered it an eccentric practice, if not an archaic one, but he had always used pencil-to-paper for collecting his most important thoughts on his research.

He returned to his journal.

"I am continually bombarded by the stream of data that comes from the lab. I never thought that I could learn so much in such a short amount of time. While I hate to side with the private sector over my home turf of academia, almost unlimited resources can accomplish great things. Since my arrival at MESA, I have learned more about Harmonicum than in my combined decades of prior research. In fact, the sole factor in my ability to learn is the seemingly limitless supply of Harmonicum to which MESA has access. While still very much relative to the known supply among the population, it is almost like they are able to grow it somehow. My questions to Mr. Kingston were met with simple yet firm brush-offs. I was told that my job was to figure out what to do with Harmonicum and let them worry about how to get more of it into my lab. This, of course, led me to entertain thoughts of a synthetic —a most troubling possibility. I have also noticed that the scope of my research is gently being pushed in a certain direction—a direction that Warrick seems to support rather

adamantly. And this specific orientation is always accompanied by their dodging or even outright denying my requests to branch off with other MESA departments."

The Professor looked up from his notes and out at the empty lab. *Where does all that Harmonicum come from?* he thought. He began writing again.

"Of course, my next challenge was the composition of the Harmonicum. How could I validate my data if I didn't know if the Harmonicum was synthetic? Aside from the colossal implications that synthetically produced Harmonicum would bring, scrutiny and integrity demanded that I prove MESA's Harmonicum was the same Harmonicum that I used at the University."

The Professor thought back to those late nights analyzing MESA's Harmonicum samples against the notes he had brought from the University. Without the ability to smuggle in some Harmonicum from his former lab, he had to rely on his best educated guess. He remembered how shocked he was at the results. He flipped back a few pages in his journal and reread his notes from a few weeks ago.

"After determining that MESA's supply is indeed not synthetic, I know now that what I believe about Harmonicum will change on an almost daily basis from this time forward. If it is not a rare element as I and my colleagues believe, and it is not synthetically produced, then where are these vast deposits of it? Who is mining and refining it? What technology are they

using to discover it, and if such technology exists, could I have access to it? What does the technology use as a base—atomic structure, mass, radiation, or something else entirely? What else of my original assumptions about this mysterious material are only partially correct? Which parts are flat-out wrong?"

The Professor came out of his reverie and looked at his timepiece. He only had a short time before his peace would be interrupted by his staff beginning the day's tasks, and he wanted to get as many of his thoughts down on paper as he could. While the practice was second nature to him in his old age, it was his experiences with Jameson when he first came on board that solidified its use here in the lab. The fact that MESA was deliberately keeping him from interacting with such a keen mind screamed that MESA was trying to prevent him from recognizing the whole picture. Couple that with the plentiful supply of Harmonicum, Warrick's overeagerness, and MESA's narrow focus on where they wanted him to take his research, the Professor knew he had to keep his private notes. Acting the part of an eccentric old man seemed to help dispel any suspicion, and for now, going with the flow at MESA was definitely the most prudent course of action. But he had to utilize all of the resources at his disposal to unravel what Harmonicum was, as something about the business did not seem right. Time. It would all take time. He flipped the pages and turned to a blank page.

"Despite my prior convictions, I must admit that almost all of what I believed Harmonicum to be is proving childish

and inconsequential to what this mysterious element truly is. In fact, calling it an element is part of the ignorance that I have perpetuated. In light of MESA's ability to provide what seems to be a limitless supply, my first assumption of Harmonicum's rarity is incorrect. Where they are harvesting such quantities remains unknown to me. As a result of this supply, the more data I review, the more I am certain that Harmonicum does not act like an element but rather has all the outward characteristics of an element. This is what led us to assume its elemental nature in the beginning. Ruling out the possibility of Harmonicum being elemental, yet accounting for its atomic composition that, while different from any other substance known in the scientific community, is still only made up of subatomic particles, I can only surmise that it is perhaps a super-element. There seems to be something locked away in its structure that eludes me from grasping its true nature. Perhaps it will be able to show the effects of elusive particles that have been theorized but never proven. I suppose only time will tell. Still, I cannot shake the feeling that Harmonicum is deeper than I could have ever imagined. My life-long goals established at the University were mostly fulfilled in the first few weeks here at MESA. This has caused me to reorder all of my priorities regarding my research. Indeed, at this accelerated pace, I am constantly revising my expectations of what we will learn next."

The Professor picked up his interface and scrolled through the latest numbers from yesterday's trial cycle. He grimaced at the results, which were yet another repeat of last week's and the weeks before. Despite his best efforts, all of the trials at this point were being hampered by the same problem. He could not get the energy absorption and dissipation equations to balance. No matter how he manipulated the figures, changed the protocols, and recalibrated the instruments, the equation did not balance. Something was interfering with it; he just couldn't see what that was.

"As of late, we have replaced all the testing equipment, rotated the testing bays, and recalibrated all of the instruments. Yet the same results continue to come in from that cycle of trials. Without an accurate reading, I cannot complete the data set on energy absorption and entropic radiation. I have requested Mr. Kingston to load the staff with some additional physicists for a while. I am not beyond missing something very obvious, and perhaps these additional minds can see what I cannot. A review of the data shows that this imbalance is most perceptible when the electromagnetic oscillators approach certain hertz levels. What these specific frequencies are remains unknown, and discovering them will take additional time, as I do not want MESA to learn of this tangent of my research. Thus, I can only quantify the data that is available to me as a result of the normal testing cycles. Still, I feel that I am missing something very crucial, yet I am unable to see in which direction I should go to find it. The implications of some of the theories I have entertained range from the mundane to the earth-shaking. Occam's razor dictates that it is the testing

equipment or a similar issue that we have overlooked. However, what if it is not? In which direction do I take my research, both the data MESA sees and my own personal notes, so that I can find the answers? While this has the possibility of catapulting science centuries ahead, it is probable that those gems may be farther off than I had hoped, despite the resources MESA has at its disposal. I fear that I may be at an impasse in my understanding, and I am eager to share my theories or at least selfishly use a sounding board."

The Professor looked up and turned his head to stare longingly for a moment at the massive lab door.

"Of course, if MESA would just allow me access to CJ, I am sure the two of us could come up with a solution in no time. This only exacerbates my frustration about our forced distant relationship. He is literally down the hall and might as well be in an alternate dimension. It is not as if I do not find stimulating conversation with my staff here in the lab; it's rather that I find no equal with which to share deeper theories. I do not mean to sound boastful, but most of the staff here are very good at what they do, yet none of them seem to be schooled in theoretical application—merely extraordinary experts in their own fields of practical application, data-mining, and so on. So I will press on without CJ, and hopefully, the answer will present itself."

The Professor set down his pencil and once again stared at the lab door. The reality is he had no idea how CJ would react to his theories. If the Professor was kept from his lab, perhaps the converse was true as well. He would take great risk in divulging information that MESA was not privy to. But in his heart, he knew that would be a risk he was willing to take. Deciding that he should not let his frustrations get the best of him, he picked up his latest set of notes and thumbed through the pages. If he couldn't talk to CJ, at least he might be able to help him with his efforts...if the time ever presented itself to do so. Pencil again in hand, the Professor started adding to the documents.

"Of late, my mind has been engaged in imagining the vast possibilities of Harmonicum and its potential application to impact human lives. Ever since I arrived here at MESA and witnessed CJ's work in the Interface Lab, my views about how to use Harmonicum's abilities have expanded. What intrigues me so much about his work is the potential for a seamless interface between man and machine. The users I saw manipulating objects with merely their thoughts sparked something in my own musings about Harmonicum. Obviously, without the details that CJ could provide in a face-to-face conversation, I can only guess the CHIs he is using for his trials. But what if, at some future point, those CHIs could be augmented with Harmonicum? What if this super-element really could give the blind sight or the deaf hearing? What of those who are paralyzed? Could not a Harmonicum-based CHI provide a greater capacity to mimic those parts of the body that are diseased or were never there to begin with? The scope of this endeavor would be

daunting. Just the identification of a host that would be able to incorporate both Harmonicum and a CHI would take years. Then it would be iterations upon iterations to find the right components and—"

The Professor stopped mid-sentence. A thought struck him—something that was way beyond a mere CHI-based model. This was leaving science fact behind and definitely venturing into science fiction. Hastily, he started to put his thoughts on paper.

"If Harmonicum can mimic any elements around it, does it have the ability to mimic complex closed systems? Could it, for example, be manipulated to replicate a silicon circuit or a semiconductive nano-lens? If the possibility for replication of such a complex system as these may be possible at some future point, what about the replication of bio-based systems? Could Harmonicum mimic plants or simple-celled organisms? What would be the extent of its abilities? Could there ever be a Harmonicum-based cloning effort?"

This last thought seemed to jar the Professor. While he was a man of science, he was also very much aware of the dangers of fully adapted SI. Add to an almost limitless mind an advanced Harmonics-based CHI, and that became a frightening doomsday scenario.

"Well, enough of this thought experiment. I do hope that one day—"

"Good morning, Professor."

The Professor looked up and saw Warrick standing in his

doorway. He set down his pencil and gave him a congenial smile.

"Good morning, Warrick. You're here quite early. Ready to get a jump on today's trials, I see," said the Professor warmly.

"Early nothing. Looks like you have been quite the busy bee yourself. Whatcha working on?" asked Warrick.

The Professor looked down at his journal and thumbed a few pages around. "Oh, you know, completing mindless fancies. Trying to solve the questions of the universe."

Warrick came closer to the desk and watched as the Professor flipped the pages of the old book. Page after page of doodles, random shapes, drawings of abstract and symmetrical designs, simple equations and theorems, and stick figures with poorly drawn faces fell one at a time as the Professor casually looked through his journal.

Warrick smiled at him. "Well, let me know when you get them solved. I'll start prepping the bays for today's tasking." He turned and exited the office. The Professor sat at his desk, a knowing smile drawn on his face.

———

Warrick began the calibration sequences for the three sets of bays they were using for their current trials. As he launched the third set, a small, innocuous icon faded into the background of his interface. Warrick glanced at the symbol, dismissed it with a finger swipe, and went back to the Professor's office.

"I'm going to run and get some wakeup juice," Warrick said as he popped his head into the office. "You want anything?"

The Professor looked up from his desk interface. "No, thank you. I'm all right for now."

Warrick smiled and headed out of the lab. He walked down the corridor and caught a perpendicular hallway. He exited through a secured door and proceeded down the gauntlet of security checks and desks. Soon he was alone in the elevator heading to MESA's boardroom. As he sat in silence, he thought he had better expel his frustrations in the small space rather than in the larger boardroom.

Warrick was sure Kingston and the old man upstairs were losing it. He had suffered through another briefing just yesterday about their paranoia that the Professor was somehow keeping information from them. Seriously? Could they be that dense? All of his work was logged into the system; Warrick and a team of agents constantly monitored his communications with anyone, anywhere. They had hyper-feeds installed on his home line and personal comm, as well as the long-range RFID tag that Ms. Green had wired him with. The man couldn't relieve himself without someone at MESA hearing every drop. And yet, Warrick was forced to play spy and figure out if the Professor was keeping anything from them. *Well*, he thought, *I guess I already am spying on him.*

The door opened, and Warrick stepped out. Instead of the normally filled room, Warrick only saw Kingston and the old man. *Great*, he thought, *more conspiracy theories.*

"Ah, Warrick. Thank you for coming so quickly," the old man commented. "Kingston and I just wanted to talk with you for a moment."

"Absolutely. What did you want to discuss?" replied Warrick in an even tone.

Kingston cleared his throat. "Warrick, I know we have had discussions prior to this morning about the possibility of Thurman keeping research from us." Warrick resisted the urge to roll his eyes. "This morning, Thurman sat at his desk playing with that journal of his for well over two hours. He's not writing his memoirs, so what is he doing?"

Warrick calmed himself as he spoke. "Sometimes they're doodles. Sometimes they are rough sketches of a person or a face. Others are basic math equations that any secondary-schooler would know. Yet others are simple or abstract designs and shapes. I saw a 3D sketch of an icosahedron on one of the pages. Had to ask him what the weird-looking thing was. I've had the tech guys pull image renditions from every vid we have of them and analyze them for patterns or codes. There is simply nothing to them."

Warrick took a breath. "I even asked him about them once, offhandedly of course. He told me it helped him organize his thoughts—something about having his brain occupied by a meaningless task. He said he simply draws or doodles whatever pops into his brain for a while. Maybe it's a cathartic response to having so much junk rolling around up there. Frankly, I think the old man is losing his marbles."

By the stern look from the old man sitting at the other end of the table, he did not seem to share Warrick's evaluation of marble depletion. "So you're telling me that even though he is drawing his thoughts, none of these doodles have anything to do with the lab or anything else related to his work?"

"Unless you call random bits of thought work-related, then no," Warrick replied. "Look, I think the guy is just a bit eccentric. Tech proves that theory with no results from their analysis. I'll keep looking for information, sir, but in my opinion, this is very benign."

This last statement of continued support of their paranoid delusions seemed to get him off the hook—at least for now. The old man glanced at Kingston, then back at Warrick. "Very well. Keep up the good work. We'll see you for your board briefing later on this week."

Warrick nodded, then turned to exit through the elevator. Once out of the secured hallway, Warrick took a few more calming breaths. Sometimes those two just really got under his skin. Warrick turned and started walking back to the Harmonics Lab. Snapping his fingers and turning around, he went back down the main corridor to the employee cafeteria. Hopefully, they had that Sumatra roast again. He loved that one. Just as he turned the corner and entered the wing reserved for the Interface Lab, Warrick's ears popped painfully as a rippling shockwave of compressed heated air tunneled down the corridor. No sooner had it engulfed him than Warrick heard the deafening blast rush past him as smoke, debris, and a large fireball plumed out of the lab's door.

CHAPTER 11

THE WORLD'S GREATEST RELIC HUNTER

Scene: Interrogation Room
Time: What time was it again?

Dirk sat alone in his cell, passing the time with the only avenue available to him: thinking. He had much to think about. Harmonicum— from the moment he heard the word, Dirk knew that his life would never be the same. His skin hadn't just prickled at it; it stood up and played the Gangan national anthem. He knew then and there it was on like donkey bong. But nothing—literally for days—he was left completely to his own devices. He remained alone in his cell: no field trips, no restraints, and no freedom either.

Then today happened. Dirk once again made his trek with his 'buddies' down the hall, past the colored rooms, and into what was now more of a vid conference room than the antiseptic evaluation room that Dirk had first come to know.

As he entered, Adams was there on the wall, smiling brightly, while Doc Stuffy-Pants stood at attention over by a table. After Dirk's buddies exited the room, it was just the three of them.

"Good afternoon, Mr. Garrett," Adams said in a warm tone. "I apologize for not being able to meet with you sooner. Duty calls, as they say."

Dirk wasn't sure what he was feeling. The hunter part of him was curious beyond reason to discover why so many people were interested in him. Yet the self-preservationist that had served him so well over the years was definitely making persuasive arguments about Dirk keeping his trap shut. He decided to play it middle of the road.

"Heya, John. No problem. I'm sure there's some revolution you're trying to quell or start or whatever," Dirk said sarcastically.

Adams smiled. "Mr. Garrett, I'll get right to it. Last time we spoke, I mentioned Harmonicum. You indicated that you had never heard of it, which I expected. But just to be sure, I have a sample of it here. Have you ever seen anything like this?"

Doc Stuffy-Pants walked over with a small rock-shaped object in a glass cylinder. Dirk took the case and brought it up to eye level, rotating it around. The rock-like object was very strange. It reflected the overhead lights almost as if it had an oily sheen, with purples, greens, and blues shifting and glimmering as Dirk moved the container. The substance itself was dark, almost metal-like but not quite. It was an unfamiliar ore, of course, and a weird one at that.

"That's a mighty fine rock you have here, John," mused Dirk. "But I can't say whether I've held one like it; it is just a rock after all."

Adams nodded as Dirk continued to examine the sample. "Mr. Garrett, what you are holding is believed to be the rarest element in the known universe. In fact, the amount contained within that sample is priceless in every sense of the word."

Dirk eyed the plain-looking rock with considerably more interest. "And why, perchance, is this rock so valuable? I can't think of anyone that would want it, and I've dealt with valuables all my life. It's not even shiny."

Dirk was only half-joking.

Adams smiled warmly. "You're probably correct in that no one you know would purchase this. However, from our early conversation, I believe the UWC and the Empire are searching after you because of that hunk of stone."

Doc Stuffy-Pants walked over and carefully took the sample from Dirk, returning it to its place on the table. Almost unconsciously, Dirk followed the short path to the table with his eyes.

"Do you remember me asking you about this man?" Dirk broke from his trance and glanced at the vid wall. A picture that Dirk remembered from the last time he spoke with Adams hung in front of him.

"Thurman, a super smart doctor of some kind," Dirk replied.

"Yes, this is Dr. Eli Thurman. He is considered to be the world's expert on Harmonicum. Until just recently, Dr. Thurman worked at a university research lab trying to lay the foundation for the science behind utilizing Harmonicum."

"What's he doing now?" asked Dirk.

"Now he works for a company called MESA Labs. They are primarily a defense contractor but have their sticky fingers in a vast array of other projects and pursuits."

"World domination? I think I've seen his virtual theater experience, Adams. Not terribly original."

Adams ignored him. "Thurman is MESA's best hope at weaponizing Harmonicum in some fashion."

Dirk sat staring at the image with a baffled look on his face. "No offense, but if this stuff is so rare, how exactly would you weaponize it?"

"Depends on the method of weaponization, Mr. Garrett, but ignore that for a moment. Remember what I just said: I *believe* that Harmonicum is the rarest element in the world. However, the actions of the UWC, the Empire, and more importantly, MESA, have led me to believe that this is just a farce being fed to the public. Not that the public knows much about Harmonicum anyway. But this charade brings us back to our original inquiry: why would the UWC and Jade Empire be interested in you when we have proven that you don't know a thing about Harmonicum? You're not a geological expert or physicist. So why you?"

That was a good question. Dirk somehow believed Adams about both governments coming after him. It explained so many coincidences, especially the most recent of his missed trip to the Seven Cities.

"If there is more Harmonicum than the public is aware of," Adams continued, "wouldn't both governments do all they could to find as much of it as possible?"

Again, the perplexed look crossed Dirk's face. "Um, not really. Forgive my ignorance, but unless that rock is more powerful than a disassembled warhead, I'm not sure why anyone would want it."

Adams looked resigned. "Indeed, Mr. Garrett. Please forgive me. Let's start with what Harmonicum is, then you'll see why someone would want it."

Dirk's skin sat up a little.

"Harmonicum is unlike any other element that we know of in the known universe. Attempts to categorize it among the known atomic elements prove difficult, as the atomic structure of Harmonicum seems to expand beyond conventional atomic models and most of the theoretical ones. Even after years of research, conclusive evidence about its nature is elusive."

Adams shifted in his chair onscreen as Dirk sat watching

the vid. "Quite by accident, Dr. Thurman was the one who discovered an inkling of Harmonicum's potential. During some of his experiments, he noticed that the element seemed to shift in the presence of electromagnetic energy. After looking through his early papers, one could surmise that Thurman believed the element to be radioactive in some way. He couldn't have been more wrong."

Dirk and his skin were sitting in perfect attention now.

"Through a series of controlled experiments, Thurman was able to prove that Harmonicum has the ability to, for lack of a better word, *mimic* elements that are near it. After coupling these results with Thurman's own interest in string theory, he hypothesized that Harmonicum could act as a sort of physical incarnation of universal DNA."

Despite the furrowed brow of confusion, Dirk's skin kicked up a notch or two. "DNA like genes?" he asked.

"Universal DNA—like the stuff that makes up all of the stuff. Every element, energy source, dark matter, anti-matter —whatever it is, it is made up of something. Thurman believes that Harmonicum is the key to unlocking the genome of the universe, if you will. Literally discovering the absolute original building blocks of everything."

Dirk vaguely recalled a biology class from his primary education, and he definitely remembered the hot teaching assistant from his secondary astronomy class, but this was a little over his head. Regardless, Dirk's skin obviously had been paying attention as it crackled with excitement. "So how do the UWC and the Empire fit into all this?" Dirk asked.

"If Thurman is correct," replied Adams, "then Harmonicum, harnessed the right way, would be the ultimate weapon. Whoever wielded it would have the kind of control that old myths and legends only assigned to the gods."

This was big. Really big.

"So you see, this probably answers more than a few questions for you. Power like that in the hands of anyone is dangerous. So when we caught wind of both the Collective and the Empire seeking after you, we had no other choice but to take you out of play. If they have somehow confirmed that this is not as rare an element as they have led the public to believe, then they are searching for more of it. And that's where we believe you come in."

Dirk smiled sardonically. "So what is it that I can do for you, John? It's not like I'm going anywhere anytime soon."

Adams put a variety of things on the screen: pictures of dig sites, a rolling catalog of precious items, clips of news stories from around the world, and a variety of strange symbols. The revolving symbols were especially interesting. At the bottom of the small window, the symbols were rolling in and out of a graph while in real time; a strange shorthand was filled in across from the stacks of symbols. It was very odd. "I assume you recognize all this?"

Dirk groaned inwardly. He wasn't entirely serious about

offering his help. Still, his curious nature drew him to look at the images.

Dirk watched as the information fell into different categories and the symbols/short-hand notes scrolled across the screen. Dirk narrowed in on the symbols, his skin tingling.

"Hey, John, let me ask you a question?"

Adams nodded. "I can't promise that I will answer, but go ahead."

"Where did you compile all this data?"

Adams smiled. "I didn't. I am hacking the Empire's Dragon Net in real time."

"Do you have copies of all this info?"

"I can look as much as I want. We start to get problems when I try to copy any of the data. Pulling the data, but slow enough to wipe our tracks as we do. The second layer of the Dragon is a real beast; I have to make constant adjustments to avoid getting caught."

Dirk's skin perked up. "Impressive, but isn't that program supposed to be impossible to hack?"

Was Adams from the Jade Empire?

Adams laughed. "Yes and no, Dirk. No, if you're the one that wrote the program; yes, if you are everyone else."

"And no, I am not from the Jade Empire," added Adams.

Dirk stared at the different windows, the group of site, relic lovers, and friends—all that seemed to make sense. But what really caught Dirk's eye was the window with the symbols. Dirk watched as those symbols fell into different columns and the shorthand increased. "Adams, what is that program doing? What are they looking for?"

Adams looked down at a tablet. "Patterns, I assume; something connected to you."

Something tugged at the back of his mind, something that Dirk wasn't seeing. Dirk glanced to his left and got an idea. "Hey, John, you have copies of those symbols, right?"

Dirk pointed to the bottom half of the board.

Adams nodded. "Sure."

Dirk grinned. "Can you send that to the holo-board?"

Adams glanced at Dr. Rosenthal, who merely shrugged. "Sure. It will take a minute or two to send over a secure line." Adams got busy tapping out commands on his display. Moments later, the backlights of the bluish glass lit up as thumbnails of the images started arranging themselves across the board. Dirk walked up to the holo-board and started to float the images out around him. "John, send me those pics from the sites too." Images from the relic sites grouped at the bottom of the board. Dirk floated these out as well. Using his hands and fingers, he enlarged the images and rotated the 3D pics to see every angle of the site. Dirk's skin started to get that familiar feeling of impending accomplishment.

———

An hour later, Dirk finished moving the last of the symbols underneath images of the relic sites that were now strewn around him in a holo-induced halo. Dirk selected all of the groupings and floated them a little farther away from the center of the circle, then proceeded to walk around, looking at each of them intently. He stopped here and there, pausing for a moment and then sending a group across the ring or shifting it over three or four slots to reside next to another group. Adams and Rosenthal sat back and watched Dirk work. For the entire hour, they had not uttered a word.

Dirk continued to shuffle the groups around and then finally stepped into the center of the halo. He slowly spun around, checking that the groups were in the order that he wanted. Adams spoke up.

"Well, Mr. Garrett, that is certainly an interesting collage you have there. Any particular reason you arranged them like that?"

Without turning to face Adams, Dirk held up a finger and then returned to studying the halo. It was many more moments of silence before he replied to Adams.

"Those symbols don't have anything to do with good old Dirk, John."

Adams sat back and crossed his arms. "How do you know this?"

"Because I've never been able to properly cite these particular symbols. I've got no idea where they come from. Do you have guys looking into all this information?"

John tapped out a couple of commands. "We have experts reviewing all this information. Same for all the data we borrowed from the UWC. I've got an analyst or two looking into the symbols specifically, but nothing conclusive or even interesting about those symbols."

Dirk continued to stare at the rotating symbols.

"What's going through that head of yours, Dirk?"

"Something about this just ain't right." Dirk blew up a third of the halo with a wave of his arms. "These sites and items represent all of my work in the Collective arranged in order of their presumed civilization—ancient to modern."

He swung his hand across his body, and the ring spun to the next third of images. "These are the Empire sites and..." one more swipe brought the last third around. "These are the Gangan and other various sites." Dirk shrank the ring back down. "This is information you could get if you had access to my data interface at Wells Fairgo, the International Bank, etc. If you were trying to gain information about my friends, family, lovers, or my habits—my most likely hunting spots and favorite types of treasure—and you were doing this to come up with some sort of predictive doohickey to try to catch me in the act. This information..."

Dirk grouped the stories, cities, and other general information into a group. "...is about all you'd need."

Adams rubbed at his chin. "I think I know where you are going with this."

Dirk pulled up the symbols. "So a couple of things here. First—and this part doesn't make sense—these symbols were present in a great many of my most valuable finds."

Adams and Rosenthal listened as they watched Dirk meander around the halo.

"But if you think about it, that should be impossible. If all of these sites were established by separate cultures over a period of centuries..." Dirk made a motion with his arms. The halo split into three parts, flattened out into clean rows, and then stacked one atop the other. "How come all these symbols are basically the same throughout each of the sites?" Dirk stretched his arms out, orienting the stacked rows into columns to form a grid with each site and its associated symbols lining up. Adams and Rosenthal stared at the holo-grid. While there were definite variations in form, order, and style, Dirk was absolutely correct. These symbols appeared in each of the sites, regardless of their location or cultural origin.

"Cultures that have any sort of language development should vary in time, place, and structure in their writings. It's a given in developing societies. Yet these are all basically the same. What do you make of that?" Dirk turned to look at Adams, a smug smile across his face.

"Amazing, Mr. Garrett. We ignored the symbols because we thought they were in the same vein as the other information and they were the least likely method of detection. I never thought...I never thought that the symbols might have some independent interest to both the Collective and the Empire."

There was the punchline. The Jade Empire and the

UWC might be after him, but these symbols held independent importance.

"I will do some homework with our contacts; we need to figure out what the UWC's and the Empire's interest is in these symbols. This could take some time, as many of these sites have been destroyed or are no longer accessible. I knew that you would be an added asset to our organization."

Dirk smirked and dropped his head to stare at the floor. There it was. *Same pawn, different team*, thought Dirk.

Dirk took it all in: the Harmonicum, the government interest in him, MESA, whoever Adams worked for, the symbols. This was insanely big. He realized that somehow he had landed in the middle of this political power play, and so far, he wasn't sure what he was doing there. "*Your* organization, huh? So what's your play then? If the Collective and the Empire can't be trusted with Harmonicum, what are you doing about it? What are you going to do with these symbols now that you know they somehow come from a common source?"

"Like I said, our organization is devoted to peace. We believe that Harmonicum has the power to change the direction of the entire human race. A single entity, regardless of who that is, should not have sole possession of that technology." Adams smiled an ironic smile, as if he thought his words were somehow funny.

"So I'm out of play, as you said. Now what? What makes you think that I can help any further? In fact, what makes you think that I am even willing to help? In other words, Mr. Former President, what's in it for ol' Dirk?"

Adams glanced at Dr. Rosenthal. The man nodded and proceeded to exit the room, closing the small door behind him. Just as the 'click' of the bolt echoed off the walls, Dirk's skin took on a whole new feeling. This was not excitement. This was apprehension.

Adams sat staring at Dirk for a long time. "Mr. Garrett..." started Adams. He sighed deeply and leaned forward towards the camera. "Dirk, I'm not going to lie to you about this."

The fact that Adams said *this* was not lost on Dirk. "I want you to help us. I've been through your file. I can offer you money, but from your history, you seem to blow through that pretty quickly. I can set you up on a nice island estate with all the things that you could ever dream of. But chances are, you would get bored very fast."

Adams took another moment, then continued. "Look, I believe that Harmonicum is more prevalent than anyone realizes. Truthfully, I am willing to go as far as saying it is probably all around us. But not all the money or land in the world could compare with what I am offering you."

Again, a moment's pause. "Dirk, what I am offering is for the name Dirk Garrett to go down in history as the greatest relic hunter that mankind has ever known. I am offering to immortalize you as the person who solves all of the world's myths of far-off places and lost civilizations. I am offering you,

Dirk, the chance to find every single hidden city and treasure that has ever been recorded as legendary: Shangri-La, El Dorado, the Garden of Eden, Valhalla, Avalon. Pardon my Gangan, but this is every relic hunter's wet dream."

Dirk eyed the man on the screen. He took a long moment. Dirk was a pawn. There was no disputing that. The question he had to ask himself was whose pawn would he be? He obviously had no love from the Empire, or the Collective for that matter. It's not like he was into this whole world peace crap either. It came down to what it always came down to—what's in it for him? Dirk wasn't sure where Adams was going with the whole lost cities mumbo jumbo, but even if he was only partially able to deliver... Dirk knew that this was a chance, the chance, of a lifetime. Adams had done his homework. The self-preservationist inside Dirk conceded defeat.

"Fine," Dirk said resolutely, "I'm in. But we talk terms now, got it?"

Adams nodded. "Of course, Mr. Garrett. I know exactly where we need to start. I believe you lost something rather important right before your imprisonment in the Empire, is that not correct?"

Dirk smiled. "You fascinate me, you know that, Adams?"

"I aim to please. Before we get down to business, I need to make one call. Please wait outside for a moment. I'll be right with you."

The door opened, and Dirk's buddies walked in and

escorted him toward the exit. Dirk heard Adams talking to someone off-screen as he walked through the door.

"Get him on comm. I have a job for him."

CHAPTER 12
UNLEASHED

Time: Early hours of the morning.
Scene: The wild sky above the Governor's Mansion in Sanzaurbi.

"You're not much of a talker, are you?" said Johnson as he moved closer to him. "I still don't know what everyone gets so worked up about when it comes to you."

"Leave the man alone, Johnson, before he decides you're expendable. Remember, none of us like you enough to try to stop him."

Aaron Johnson turned on his crewmate, Jason Roach. "You scared, Roach? He looks like a man just the same as anyone else."

"He'd smoke you, Johnson. I've seen grade school kids with better hand-to-hand skills."

Johnson sneered from the end of the chopper. "I don't

need hand-to-hand skills. I'd just take my 2x3 and shoot a plasma bolt up his—"

"Shut your pie-hole, ladies," yelled the Sergeant, "before my steel toe shuts 'em for ya."

Roach and Johnson grumbled but shut their mouths nonetheless. The other two from the extraction team, Castle and Beckett, didn't say anything but took turns shooting furtive looks at the seeming blackness at the end of their bench.

Sergeant Riker didn't so much sigh as grunt his disapproval. While he was irritated with his squad's lack of professionalism, he understood their posturing. Riker's group had done a number of clean-ups and assisted extractions with the man in black, but this was the first time they had ever been this close to him.

The Sergeant, unable to contain himself, stole a glance in his direction. Matted from head to foot in a strange black material, it was hard to believe that *the* Magician, the legendary assassin, sat in his bird like it was a Sunday afternoon joy ride.

The Magician didn't say a word. Not a single solitary comment. He just sat quietly in the corner, his face covered with the world's creepiest and featureless mask. The Sergeant had to wonder if the Magician wasn't a woman or even a person at all. He could be some sort of machine. That was a thought he did not want to consider.

"So I know you're like, stealthy and stuff," said Johnson,

apparently forgetting the Sergeant's threat about kicking in his teeth. "But why do they call you the Magician? I don't see nothing magical about you?"

The man in black ignored him.

"Hey, Mr. Magician, why don't you show me—"

The man in black stood up, surprising everyone. Riker was just about to go for his pistol; he fought the reflex. He knew the Magician had some sort of code of conduct; Adams told him as much. Code of conduct or not, Riker couldn't get the man to speak, and a man that refused to look him in the eye and speak to him... well, that wasn't someone that the Sergeant could trust.

"Easy now," Riker said, slowly moving his hand towards his sidearm, "we don't want any—what the hell?"

The men retreated, not because of fear, but something more basic, more instinctual than fear. They retreated because what they saw was so foreign to them that their flight-or-fight response kicked in before they knew what they were witnessing.

The black suit of the Magician appeared as if it were melting; literally, metallic black tar oozed out from the Magician's hands.

"Sarg, what do we do?" Johnson hollered from across the NightHawk. "If that stuff is corrosive, we're—"

Johnson went silent as a mass of black tar leapt from the Magician and covered his entire head. Johnson struggled, clawing at the semi-solid ooze. There was no way he could breathe. Roach rushed to his side and attempted to wipe at the slime. He rubbed his glove across where Johnson's left cheek would have been.

"Sarg, this thing—it's—it's hard as rock!"

Riker, who had his gun pulled and pointed right at the Magician's head, finally understood.

"Johnson, Roach, stand down. Beckett, Castle, holster those sidearms."

"What did you say, Sarg?!" asked Roach in disbelief. "Are you—"

"I ordered you to stand down!"

Roach reluctantly backed away from Johnson as Castle and Beckett holstered their weapons.

Riker addressed the Magician. "You've made your point. Now let my man go before he dies. Lord knows I don't need the paperwork."

The black ooze denatured, going limp and slimy again. Johnson's face was uncovered in no time as the metallic ooze quickly slithered back towards the Magician. It sidled up the Magician's black suit to the palms of his hands, where it disappeared, melted into the black material, like it was never there.

The men stared at the man in the black suit.

Riker sat back on the jump seat and gestured to the others to do the same. "Does that answer your question, Johnson?"

Johnson, who was still wide-eyed, answered, "Sir?"

"I said, does it answer your question."

"Which question was that, sir?"

"The one you asked before he turned your head into a cocoon?"

Johnson's face remained blank. Riker scowled. "Johnson, now you know why they call him the Magician. Now do us a favor and leave the man alone before he pulls a rabbit outta yer ass."

———

The Governor of Sanzaurbi sat in his magnificently transformed ballroom with a handful of his closest advisors, strongest supporters, and most powerful rivals. Food aplenty, representing every region of the world, and wine in abundance from every vineyard on the planet was served to the most powerful men in the Sanzaurbi region. They talked of pleasure, politics, and power, all while eating, drinking, and eagerly anticipating the night's main event.

It was the second weekend of the month, and each second weekend of each month, the slavers would come and show off their new merchandise.

Young girls, this group hailing from the southern half of the UWC, were easily recognizable because of their tanned skin and petite figures. They gathered on the far side of the ballroom as the lights dimmed. Music rolled from hidden speakers, low and hypnotic, as the girls formed up and started to walk.

The girls wore anciently-styled Persian garb, a fad that was gaining momentum in Sanzaurbi. Faces veiled, the recent acquisitions staggered with exaggerated movements, sauntering up the middle of the ballroom.

Their current owner came to a podium nestled back and away from the Governor so as not to obstruct the view of the girls he was selling. The music lowered slightly once the thirty or so girls did their initial high-fashion walk through. The power players spoke hurriedly to assistants who took notes and eyed their own counterparts distrustfully.

"Gentlemen, now that I have your attention with this month's stock, I will start, as always, with number one."

A girl, tall and deeply colored with long brown legs wearing all white, stepped forward. Her face was covered, but the veil was thin and barely masked her clear and penetrating beauty. "Now for number one, gentlemen. This little lady was taken from the mouth of the Amazon River in the Southern Collective. As you can see, she is strong and cultured. We also have confirmation that she is unsoiled and not a day older than sixteen. She was training as a Healer when we found her. An artist of sorts, she maintains the characteristic soft hands required by Shaman Healers. Shall we start the bidding—"

The lights died along with the music and anything else that ran on an electric current. The slaver continued to speak, but his voice did little to dent the open space of the massively large ballroom.

The Governor banged on his comm. "Ha-zeal, what's wrong with the power? I have guests, and it is interfering with our festivities."

"We aren't sure, your Excellency. The entire grid just overloaded. We have security and maintenance looking into it now."

"Get everything up and running immediately and then find me who's responsible. I want their entrails to litter the courtyard."

The response from the comm was immediate. "Yes, your Excellency. Right away."

The Governor gritted his teeth. This should not have happened. Not tonight. "My apologies, gentlemen. It appears there has been an issue in our power grid. My men are looking into it."

The expression of smugness was almost unbearable. The Governor wanted nothing more than to pick up his Plasma Scimitar and teach these men a lesson in humility. This was his land. His will ruled it. They should know better than to show their arrogance in front of him.

No matter. Let them laugh. He was in control here. The Governor slapped his hands together. "Bareesa, make accommodations."

An older, strict-looking woman at the far side of the ballroom rushed and came before the Governor and bowed deeply. She clapped her hands together twice. Scuffling sounds of moving bodies were heard from every recess of the now darkened ballroom, and before their eyes adjusted to the blackness of the space, servants bearing long torches topped with poles escorted their charges along the outskirts of the ballroom. Additional servants came and placed lit candelabra on the dining tables throughout the ballroom. The ambiance created from the torchlight was calming and somewhat intimate. The gentlemen sitting in their half-circle, sipping wine and hors d'oeuvres, were able to make out the general and mysterious outlines of the merchandise at the opposite side of the room. Their interest renewed and lustful hearts reignited and burned bright in the darkness.

For the first time in the many years since starting the monthly tradition, the Governor turned and addressed the slaver directly. "You may proceed with your presentation, slavemaster. Speak loud enough that we may hear you."

The Governor did not wait for an answer; he sat upright and returned his attention to the night's selections.

The slaver started again with his presentation.

———

"Two million credits, going once, going twice, sold to the Baron of Pentair. You may collect your prize upon payment, sir."

The Governor sneered. The Baron of Pentair was a complete pig, and the delicious Jadian Islander girl he just bought was extremely introverted. The expression of uncultured horror spoke more words than any soliloquy ever hoped to accomplish. This young lady, through rumor or forewarning, knew the worst possible scenario was to be sold to the Baron of Pentair. The Governor almost felt sorry for the young lady.

"That concludes the main portion of the auction, Lords and Ladies. But if you'll indulge me for a few moments more, we will get on to the special product for this month. You'll be happy you stayed, gentlemen, I assure you."

Those in attendance again spoke at length with their advisors and accountants. The slaver, Mavrik, the Governor thought his name was, always saved his best stock, his greatest find for the end. Every sixth month, the slaver would bring a girl of unsurpassed beauty. Last year it was a kidnapped princess from the province of Nihon; a gem that he himself bought. It was quite unfortunate that the girl didn't last the year.

Three massive Ganga guards holding large wooden poles carried a small decorative tent on their shoulders as musicians strummed a soft and mellow tune. Some additional torches were set in place as the Ganga neared the middle of the floor. A mere three meters from the Governor and his guests, the Ganga lowered the decorative tent and retreated once it was firmly on the ground. Mavrik made his way over to the tent, grabbed hold of the flap, and unknotted it. He grinned as he addressed the semi-circle of men.

"Gentlemen, this is the crowning achievement in my

illustrious career. As you all know, or perhaps only heard of, there lies a palace nestled in the seventh ring of the Seven Cities, right at the heart of the Jadian Empire. That palace is the personal quarters of the Emperor himself. It is a palace formed completely of gold. Yet this home of arguably the most powerful man in the world is not its greatest treasure. Look to the east of the golden palace, and you'll see the Emerald House."

Audible gasps and slightly panicked yet excited whispers broke out among the men. Who was this man, this slaver, to defy the Emperor of Jade? Was he mad?

"Yes, gentlemen, the Emerald House, where the wives and concubines of the Emperor reside. I now present to you the latest, yet unspoiled, addition to the Emperor's household, Xui Li."

The Governor, his advisors, friends, and enemies didn't realize it, didn't know, but they were on the edge of their seats in anticipatory lust. A princess from the Emerald House of the Jade Empire. It would be the crowning jewel of any man's collection. Each and every man there wanted her for his own, to dominate and force her to their will. Mavrik smiled at the looks on all their faces. He was going to make enough tonight to retire.

The slaver pulled on the cord, and the coverings on the decorative tent fell to reveal not a young Jadian beauty from the Emperor's own house, but a single individual covered in black sitting on a stool. The man appeared like a statue, looking downward as if he wanted nothing more than to stare at the floor. The semi-circle broke out once more in whispers.

"What in the—" Mavrik exclaimed. "Gremen, Bello, Afram, what is the meaning of this?"

The three Ganga looked just as shocked as their boss.

"Well, don't just stand there, seize him!"

The Ganga moved in around the man in black. They took two steps, only two, and the man in black finally unfroze. He looked up and shifted his head from side to side. He put up a hand and showed four fingers. Even in the dim torchlight, everyone clearly saw the gesture.

The first Ganga walked forward and placed a hand on the man in black's shoulder in an attempt to grab hold of him. The Ganga barely touched the black material before the audible sound of breaking bone echoed in the ballroom. The screams of the Ganga were short-lived as the black man pulled out, of seemingly nowhere, a long pointed blade. He drove the blade into the throat of the Ganga, and he dropped to the floor.

The man in black put back up his hand and showed four fingers. He slowly put down one finger.

The second Ganga, especially big, at two meters and well over 160 kilos, came in swinging. The large man was surprisingly balanced as he bobbed and weaved like an old-time boxer. He jabbed and danced, jabbed and danced, trying to find an opening. It was over in seconds. The Ganga threw a heavy body blow to the midsection of the man in black, only to step back a split second later, screeching like a banshee. The Governor saw the Ganga holding his hand, which was a crumpled bloody mess.

The man in black produced another bladed weapon, this one around 13 centimeters, and threw it into the space between him and his Ganga attacker. The Ganga took the blade in the throat and dropped just a meter away from his fallen comrade.

The man in black once more held up his hand; three fingers became two.

The last Ganga didn't see the man in black's change in tactic coming. The man in black rushed him, stepped up the Ganga's body like a ladder, wrapped his legs around the Ganga's head, and brought him to the ground. The man in black rotated his body, taking the Ganga's head with him. There was a sickening crack as the Ganga's neck broke.

Two fingers became one.

Panic set in for the remaining people. Servants and masters alike produced a wide array of weapons, from plasma pistols to antiquated lead-slinging six-shooters. Each and every weapon was leveled at the man in black.

In a strange turn of events, the weapons-wielding leaders and political power players hesitated. They hesitated ever so briefly as the man in black started to melt before their very eyes. Black tar ran down the length of his suit.

They all opened fire. The noise and debris the varying types of weapons kicked up caused the Governor to cringe and cower like a child frightened by a thunderstorm. Some of the large caliber and stronger grade weapons put out what little remaining light there was in the place, thus, despite the settling of the dust, it was hard to see anything. The Governor didn't know if the man in black was lying in a puddle of his own fluids, torn apart by the kinetic energy of the lead bullets, or melted with 1000-degree plasma bolts. The Governor had no way of knowing if the man in black was dead. Anyone near him, or within ten meters of him, probably was, but he wasn't taking any chances.

"Ha-zael, get security to the main ballroom immediately, bring flashlights, we have an intruder alert. Bring everyone!"

"Security is dead, Sir. Balzeel just died in my arms. You need to get out, it's— it's him. He's here."

"Of course he's here, I just told you—wait, who is here? You know who the man in black is?"

The answer came quickly, but Ha-zael sounded like he was running, and his accent came in thick. "The Magician, Sir. It's the Magician. You need to get out now."

Light came back on, but instead of hope of a morning sunrise, the man in black stood, unfazed among the bodies of the various servants who got caught in the crossfire of the Governor and his company. The man in black— the Magician —held a flame in the palms of his hands. He flicked his wrist to the left. A strange popping noise and a massive explosion blew a monstrous hole in an adjoining wall. The Governor and company shielded themselves from the heat and the shrapnel of the explosion. When the Governor opened his eyes, the Magician was standing less than a meter in front of him.

The Governor and company froze and were surprised when the Magician just stood in front of him. Slowly, the man in black put up his hand and showed the Governor a single finger. The Magician put that finger down. His meaning was clear. One finger became zero. Mission accomplished. The Governor closed his eyes as the Magician closed in.

CHAPTER 13
THE REPUBLICANS

Scene: A confusing one

Place: Common area ahead of the Main Tunnel of the Cheyenne Mountain Site

The man wearing the mask had a gun pointed right at her; Sam did the same but, in the confusion, totally forgot about the downed Palin. A blow to the back of her knees, then one to her lower back, threw Sam off balance and brought her to the ground. She fell in pain and bewilderment.

Palin wasn't finished with her, however. As soon as Sam hit the ground, Palin was on her, mounting her in good old jiu-jitsu fashion, locking her down with strategically placed pressure. Sam reoriented herself enough to see Palin cock back a fist and bring it fast and furiously toward her face. Sam closed her eyes and braced for the impact.

That impact did not come. Confused, Sam opened her eyes and witnessed one masked individual holding firmly onto the other.

"Enough, Palin, get up already!"

"But Teddy, she—"

He removed Palin from her sitting position on top of her, and Sam watched as the male ripped off his mask to reveal none other than Coda—perverted, goofy Coda. He stared at Sam in unadulterated, mind-boggling disbelief.

Sam took a deep breath, now that her airways weren't constricted from Palin's weight. She tried to speak but found that the words wouldn't come. She felt tears run down her face.

Coda, for once in the short time she had known him, seemed truly at a loss for words. Still, he didn't waste any time; instead of speaking, he offered her a hand, one that she took gratefully. He did not let go of her hand once she was on her feet.

Other footsteps tapped in the background, and other voices sounded. One such voice was higher-pitched and childlike.

"Teddy, do you know this girl? You look like you've seen a ghost."

Coda finally spoke. "Sam... what... what are you doing here? How... how are you here? I thought—we thought—we all thought you were dead."

"It's a long story—"

Sam was cut off as Coda pulled the hand he was still holding. He tugged her into a bone-breaking embrace and wept.

———

"Everybody, this is my friend Samantha Montgomery from Academy City 676." Coda, arm still around her, gripping her with a gentle firmness, presented her to his comrades.

There were around twenty of them, many more than Sam had anticipated when she first caught wind and hid in the main access tunnel. All of them had masks, though most were not wearing them anymore. Coda's was already off, and though he was unmistakably exhausted from whatever rigors he had experienced since their last opportunity to meet, he was the same—handsome and smiling. Always handsome and smiling, that was Coda. The little girl, Rice, once she realized that Coda and Sam were acquaintances, was also quick to remove her mask and get a better look. The mask she was wearing was of Condoleezza Rice, 48th president of the old United States of America. Sam only knew this because she had to do a report on women in the third year of her primary education. The little girl—well, "little" might be pushing it; she was probably eleven or so—was wearing a mask of a regal dark-skinned woman in her mid-forties. When "Rice" took off her mask, which was way too large for her head, it was a bit of a shock to see a beautiful, albeit incredibly pale, face looking back at her. Sam tried not to stare at the girl, not only because it was rude but because the girl gave her a funny, uneasy feeling. It didn't help that the girl was just staring at Sam as much as Sam was staring at her.

Coda introduced the rest of the group: Johnson, Franklin, Hamilton, Burr, Parks, King, Jackson, and many more. Most of the names just washed over her, all except Limbaugh, which she couldn't help but laugh at. Such a funny name, Limbaugh...

The problem was that Limbaugh caught her laughing.

"And what is so funny, young lady?" His voice was heavily accented, which was a surprise as Sam recognized the accent. He was from the Jade Empire.

Sam tried to stifle her laughter. She wasn't the only one; she noticed that many of the others were trying not to laugh. "Um... yes, I'm sorry. I wasn't laughing. I just had—um—something stuck in my throat."

"She's laughing at your name, Limbaugh," said Coda, chuckling. He squeezed Sam's shoulder. "You are so predictable, Sam. And she's right, Limbaugh, your name is hilarious."

Limbaugh was not amused. "I will have you know, Teddy, that Rush Limbaugh was an amazing American and single-handedly spearheaded the fight against liberalism in the—"

Sam giggled again. "His name was Rush? Who names their kid 'Rush?'"

"Like I said," announced Limbaugh, almost yelling it out, "he was—"

"—A propaganda machine for the ultraconservative movement of the 1980s, 90s, and early 2000s. He and his counterparts on the far left, like Rachel Maddow, were the start of the governmental conglomerate known as the UWC. If you're going to fight, you should know your history better and perhaps pick a better historical personage to emulate."

People searched for the source of the voice, which was spoken with a certain amount of chilliness. Richard materialized out of the darkness.

Chaos ensued; everyone, excluding Sam, went for either a mask or a weapon. A couple of the soldiers, including Limbaugh, tried the direct approach and attacked Richard, who melted out of the shadows like the freaking ninja that he was.

Richard was not impressed with the attack. He sneered as they neared and disposed of his first attacker with a simple yet artful sidestep. The soldier, who Sam recognized as Hamilton, had too much momentum and just kept going right past Richard, but not before Richard landed a blow to his lower back. Hamilton dropped like George W. Bush's popularity in his last term of office.

The other two soldiers watched their comrade fall and immediately halted their attack. They approached Richard cautiously, pulling out some nasty-looking blade weapons that gave off the faintest glow. Sam instantly conjured an image of a small dagger thrown at a child in the main gymnasium of Academy City 676. She felt her stomach lurch.

Sam's worry was misplaced. Richard dispatched these weapon-wielding misfits just as easily as he had Hamilton, who was still on the ground, dazed and confused from the blow Richard delivered upon him.

Richard dropped these two with a series of acrobatic kicks that should have been impossible for someone of his size and bulk. Richard dealt with them, but Sam could tell that he wasn't really trying to hurt them. He wasn't moving as fast, as sharp, or as deadly as she knew he could. Totally unfazed, Richard took a few steps back after glancing down at the two downed soldiers. He sat down on the top of one of the tables and folded his hands in his lap. The remaining soldiers retrieved their guns, and increasingly, weapon after weapon was pulled to a shoulder or held out in front of a body with two solid hands holding it—all aimed at Richard.

Boom!

A concussive wave and falling rock threw Sam slightly off balance. She almost tripped; the effect was so jarring. A booming voice replaced the explosion.

"Republicans! Stand down!"

The voice was one of authority. A large gentleman, who happened to be carrying a gun that would not have been out of place on a tank slung across his shoulders, walked briskly forward. He gestured forcefully, pointing periodically and yelling at the soldiers.

"This is our contact; stand down! STAND DOWN, I said!"

Begrudgingly, guns were re-holstered or shut down, and solid blades retracted, though masks remained on. Many went as far as to replace their masks and fidget where they stood. It was easy to see that Richard made them nervous. Sam understood the sentiment.

The leader walked to Richard and put out a hand. "I'm in charge of these miscreants. You can call me Coolidge."

Richard took his hand. "John Calvin Coolidge, Jr., born July 4, 1872, was theHYPERLINK "%22file://local-hos" 30th President of the United States from 1923 to 1929. A Republican lawyer from Vermont, Coolidge worked his way up the ladder of Massachusetts state politics, eventually becoming governor of that state, which is encompassed in Modern Day Earl Providence. Coolidge's early political career was quiet, but actions during the HYPERLINK "file://localhost/wiki/Boston_Police_Strike"Boston   Police Strike of 1919 thrust him into the national spotlight. Soon after, he was elected as the HYPERLINK "file://local-host/wiki/List_of_Vice_Presidents_of_the_United_S-tates"29th Vice President in 1920 and succeeded to the Presidency upon the sudden death of Warren G. Harding in 1923. Elected in his own right in 1924, he gained a reputation as a small-government conservative and also as a man who said very little."

Coolidge let out a roar of laughter. "You know your history, boy; I will give you that. What do they call you?"

Sam watched Richard closely. How was he going to answer this? Maybe she could glean something of Richard's motivation depending on his answer.

"Richard, sir."

"Can I assume that is a code name?"

"Yes, sir."

"What unit are you with, son?"

"Rough Riders, sir."

The older man's countenance noticeably changed from there.

"You're part of Washington's Rough Riders?"

"Yes, sir."

"I thought all of you died. You look awfully healthy for a dead man."

"That was misinformation, sir."

"Well, I will be damned. Boys and girls, listen closely because I won't be stating this again. Richard here is a marked classification part of special operations; he works completely off the books, fighting some of the nastier elements of our enemy's forces. He holds the rank of Lieutenant Colonel for all intents and purposes. This is Richard's base, and his rules. You'll answer to him for any breach of conduct. Any orders, Richard?"

"Just one: stay away from the western access tunnels."

Richard turned on his heel and left, leaving a group of utterly astonished soldiers.

"Sam..." said Coda, his voice carrying like a banshee scream on a windless night, "...is... is that who I think it is?"

Sam's answer came out a little breathy. "Yes, yes it is."

Coda looked downright shocked as Sam looked up. Their eyes met. "Sam, I think you've got some explaining to do."

———

"Okay, Sam, I think it's about time you answer some of my questions."

"Only if you answer mine, Coda; that's the deal. Stop trying to weasel stuff out of me when you aren't willing to provide the same service."

"I can't answer your questions; the answers are classified."

"OMGWB, I am so tired of you saying that."

Coda, otherwise known as Teddy, sat next to Sam in the common area's cafeteria, eating some of Sam's specially prepared entrees. Tonight was baked macaroni and cheese with a crispy breadcrumbs topping. Sam didn't make a large batch—just enough for her, Coda, and a select other few. This irritated the rest of the soldiers, and they watched Sam and Coda eat with envy emanating in waves. Sam didn't notice their irritation. She was enjoying the time with Coda a great deal more than she would have willingly admitted to anyone. He was alleviating the loneliness that was steadily drawing her inward. He was helping her fight the recluse that, until now, was eating away at her. Coda and the Republicans had been at the facility for a little more than a week now, and it was like a completely different place.

After the first few days in which they spent recovering from whatever mission they had been on, the Republicans almost instantly became an extremely lively bunch; they ate, drank, slept, and bantered into the wee hours of the night, toasting friends and loved ones lost in the good fight and swearing that justice would fall swiftly upon their enemies. The Republicans' demographic was strange; many of their soldiers weren't much older than Sam herself—around 17— with noted exceptions like Coolidge, who was obviously a seasoned soldier and commander. Everyone listened to and respected him, which probably wasn't as amazing as Sam initially thought, seeing as they were all military men and women. But even Richard was paying respects to him, and Richard didn't respect anyone. Well, the old Richard didn't respect anyone; who knew how much of that was fake and how much was real? How freaking frustrating that was? Nowadays, Sam rarely saw Richard, and when she did, he was less willing to communicate with her, which was saying something because she hardly forced anything out of him before.

Luckily, she didn't dwell on Richard's behavior. It bothered her—quite a bit, actually—but the week the Republicans had spent in the little underground base brought a smile to her face. Not to mention having Coda there was almost surreal. It was like they were back at Academy City 676. The way he laughed, ate his food, and talked—all of it was the same, so familiar. Coda acted the same—*was* the same—and yet was totally different. He was a soldier, a respected one if the actions of his fellow Republicans were any indication, and he was ranked too, apparently pretty high on the military food chain, which meant that he had been at this for a while. The knowledge that Coda was someone important made her nervous. Being someone of stature, he had obviously been sent to Academy City 676 for a reason—one that he was not willing to talk about, at least not yet. Sam was working on it, though, chipping away at his unwillingness to share little by little. Currently, the only weapon she possessed was the information on Richard, of which Coda was very curious. Richard told Coolidge on the day of the Republicans' arrival that he was part of the Rough Riders; from what Sam gleaned from Coda and his subordinates during the last week, this fact was significant and somehow shocking. Sam just didn't know how.

Sam had her questions. Coda had his, and now Coda and Sam were engaged in a battle of wills—a battle that Sam felt she was winning.

"Hey, Samantha."

"Hi, Rice, Palin," Sam and Coda looked up from their food to see Rice and Palin walking up to their table. Sam greeted them with a smile. "Welcome, you two; care to join us?"

Rice giggled; Palin scowled. Rice punched Palin in the arm. "We'd love to, Sam; I thought you'd never ask. I love your cooking, by the way. Did I mention that?"

Sam laughed. "Yeah, Rice, you've mentioned that a few dozen times in the last week."

"You know, being able to cook isn't everything." Palin glared at Sam, who forced out a smile.

"Lacey—I'm sorry, I keep doing that, don't I? You're Lacey to me. It took me so long to get used to that name that I keep forgetting that you're Palin now. Being able to cook is important—"

Sam interrupted her. "That's where I've seen you! You're Coda's girlfriend! We met at the Mega Lots Shopping Center at Academy City 676. Do you remember?"

Just then, a soldier, one whose name escaped her, came dashing over to see them. "Teddy, Coolidge wants to see you; it sounds like we've got orders."

Coda slumped down in his chair. "I was just eating my second helping. Rice, don't eat my food. I will be back."

Coda took one more wistful look at his mac and cheese and left. Silence replaced him. Palin, while reluctant initially, took a plate and started eating, her face lighting up as she took the first bite, only to be followed instantly with a sour grimace. She swallowed and angled her body, just about to speak when the soldier returned.

"Palin, Coolidge wants to see you as well."

Palin also glanced at her freshly scooped food, then reluctantly stood and accompanied the soldier. Now it was Rice and Sam eating in silence. Rice cleaned her plate with gusto, paying little attention to Sam. Sam thought she might start licking the remnants of the cheese sauce; fortunately, she did not. Instead, she set down her fork in the middle of her plate, put her hands together like she was praying, and bowed. Afterwards, Rice turned her attention to Sam. Rice smiled at her in a strange way.

"We're leaving soon."

Sam made eye contact with Rice—something she had been trying not to do. Rice was an odd one. Sam answered her. "I know, though I wish you all wouldn't."

"You mean you wish Coda wouldn't."

Sam flushed.

"It's okay; you don't have to be embarrassed. Contrary to what Lacey thinks, you aren't into Coda like that. Well, not anymore. You're just alone, and Richard isn't exactly the best of company—at least this version of Richard."

Sam felt her mouth go dry. She felt inclined to answer but couldn't.

"It's okay. I won't tell Coda. That might give him hope."

"Never mind that. How do you know about Richard?"

Rice raised an eyebrow. "You really don't know anything."

Sam mimicked the eyebrow gesture.

The small girl giggled. "Do I look that silly when I do that? Ha! That is funny."

Rice surprised Sam by standing abruptly. "I'd better go and get ready. We're going to be leaving on some urgent mission soon."

Rice started to walk away. "Wait, Rice, you didn't answer my question. How did you know about Richard?"

Rice glanced over her shoulder. "How did I know? The simple answer is I'm special, Sam; I'm special, just like you."

CHAPTER 14

BOMBS ARE REALLY EASY TO MAKE

Place: MESA Labs

Time: Shortly after the explosion.

Ms. Green stepped through the soot-covered debris, surveying the wreckage that used to be the Interface Lab. Moments after the fireball rippled out of the lab entrance, the hallway section sealed, and the Heptafluoropropane (HFP) fire suppression system kicked in, choking the atmosphere in halocarbon gas and effectively preventing the spread of the fire. Sensors showed secondary fires were extinguished in less than two seconds, and immediately thereafter, molecular ventilation vacuums vented the fire suppressant to a holding chamber while infusing the room with an increase of O_2 for the remaining occupants. MESA's in-house emergency response unit was notified and dispatched, in addition to a section security lockdown occurring throughout the entire campus. Since MESA was equipped with its own emergency room, complete with emergency technicians and rapid response practitioners, the outside world was largely unaware of the accident. Despite all these systems reacting instantaneously to prevent the fire from spreading beyond the lab and providing almost immediate medical attention to the wounded, the damage that the initial blast wreaked on the equipment and personnel was extensive.

Ms. Green looked at her interface as it scrolled through the preliminary findings. While no deaths occurred, few of the lab staff escaped injury. She reviewed the list of the injured and their associated trauma. While societal norms required her to feel compassion for those affected, Ms. Green was more interested in the short list of staff members who received no injuries and those who walked away with minor cuts, simple burns, and abrasions. She had no idea who was responsible for the act of sabotage, but she needed to rule out as many staff members as possible as quickly as possible. In her mind, if she were going to blow up her workplace, avoiding suspicion by being present at the time of the incident was a key mission objective. The act required it, but more importantly than the act of sabotage, the avoidance of serious injuries from the act had to play in there somehow. It was a fine line this traitor was walking.

She called up the blueprint of the lab and the RFID locator record of the moment right before the explosion side by side on her screen. Using the list of names, she dragged those lucky individuals from her list of casualties to the spot on the blueprint where their RFIDs indicated they last stood. After marking each of the six or seven employees, she paced around the floor, orienting herself with the locations marked on the blueprint. Swiping the side-by-side comparison off to the side, Green called up a vid still that showed the location of the lab equipment and furniture. One by one, Ms. Green went down the list of locations around the lab. At the final location, she sighed in disappointment, realizing that while there were structures or equipment blocking this set of people from the blast wave, the protection they offered seemed too flimsy and unpredictable to stake any amount of injury avoidance on them. At least initially, it appeared that these persons really were the product of dumb luck. A person smart enough to pull off this stunt would certainly not have risked so much in these variable-rich protection zones.

She returned to the casualty list and sorted the seven staff members into the preliminarily cleared status. This, of course, would have to be supported by the financial, social, and familial background checks currently underway. But Green saw these as only supplementing her instinct, not really confirming it. She checked the status indicated of the employees who had been admitted through the on-site ER. Only two had been upgraded to stable, with another ten or so being prepped for transition. The next step was to wait until she had a few more people to speak with so she didn't have to make so many trips to the medical wing.

Green called up her investigation notes compiled from the system data feeds, vid feeds, and initial reports from the first response unit. Green knew that this was an inside job. More than just the deep-seated feeling in her gut that this was the case, Green had the security team analysts calculate, out to several standard deviations, the possibility of an outside person gaining access to the lab; for all her purposes, it was statistically impossible. That left the staff, both outside and inside the lab. Staff members without security clearance to the wing were quickly reviewed and set aside—there had been no unusual activity by anyone trying to gain access where they should not have been. The analysts had reported that Thurman had gotten lost in an adjacent hallway earlier that week, but that sort of thing happened about once a month to the idiot. That left only two real possibilities: a mastermind so nefarious and intelligent that they beat every known security protocol in MESA, in addition to those not made public to the general population, or someone inside the Interface Lab. While she refused to rule out the former, the latter seemed like a more target-rich environment to conduct her investigation.

Ms. Green tapped a notification on her screen, and the initial Source and Origin report zoomed to fill the screen. She scanned through the highlights looking for anything useful. Most of the time, initial reports just rehashed what she had already gathered in her compilation report, but this one seemed to have updated information. She skipped the redundant information and started on the preliminary chemical results:

Initial chemical residue results:

- Traces of $KMnO_4$ (potassium permanganate)
- Residual traces of propylene glycol
- Ferrous oxide and aluminum particles
- Other standard trace elements normal to the environment

Preliminary theoretical source of ignition and primary combustion:

After reviewing the initial chemical and trace residues, the recorded vid, thermal, and RFID data feeds, and the molecular sampling from the vented fire suppressant holding chamber, in addition to identifying the reserve propane tanks as the primary combustion source, the series of events with the greatest probability of accuracy is thus:

The explosion was initiated by a release of propylene glycol into a concentration of potassium permanganate. This, in turn, caused an oxidation reaction with temperatures reaching in excess of 538° C. This hypergolic reaction produced sufficient heat to further start a controlled thermite reaction (produced from a mixture of iron oxide and aluminum powders most likely), increasing the burn temperature to well over 2200° C. This extremely high-temperature reaction swiftly melted through any container housing these chemicals in addition to the LPG tank hull, thereby exposing the liquefied gas to open flame. With both the loss of pressure due to the breached tank housing and the consequent escaping gas being immediately subjected to an open flame (maintained by the continuous oxidation of the thermite), the first tank exploded, thereby rupturing the adjacent tanks and causing a chain reaction that is the cause of the destructive blast wave.

Without further information from the detailed analysis of all chemical and reactive agents present, the following can only be taken as an educated guess as to the construction of the improvised incendiary device (IID). Given the ambient temperature was lower surrounding the reserve propane tanks due to their liquefied gaseous contents and their conductive metal housing, propylene glycol introduced to the potassium permanganate could have taken 60 to 90 seconds to reach critical reaction levels. These two chemicals could have been packaged in a cocoon of a mixture of iron oxide and aluminum. Once the package was breached by the initial incendiary reaction, the thermite would have taken mere seconds to reach critical temperatures sufficient to melt through the tank.

The whole reaction time from the introduction of the glycol to the breach of the tank could have lasted 90 to 120 seconds. It's estimated from extrapolation of the vid feed that the time from critical mass to explosion was 1-2 seconds. As it appears from the initial review of vid data streams and first responders' preliminary interviews with those who were conscious immediately after the event, no one noticed smoke, flames, or any noxious aromatics that would have indicated an impending explosion.

This is consistent with the package being sealed in an airtight container, thus using the oxidizing reaction contained within the container without smoke escaping into a visible area until the reaction was beyond the melting threshold of the propane tank hull. A thermite reaction consists of a self-sustaining oxidation not requiring the addition of gaseous fuel (air); thus, the HFP system did little to terminate the reaction (assuming any smoke were to escape from the airtight container prior to the tank hull breach). As the vid data streams show no personnel near the tanks immediately prior to the explosion, it is further theorized that the release of propylene glycol into the potassium permanganate must have been time-delayed or remotely triggered, with emphasis on remote activation, as exact reaction times would be very difficult to calculate.

Supplemental notes on materials used:

All materials used are available in mass quantities from a variety of sources. None are regulated to the extent of requiring personally identifiable information for their purchase. Taken separately, each has little reactivity or combustion potential. As for any timing or remote activation device, as no evidence of these materials has been recovered, it is assumed that the housing used for the IID was able to be easily consumed during the intense heat of the thermite reaction, thus erasing any usable evidence.

Ms. Green read through the report a second time. She didn't have to know that much about chemistry to understand that whoever executed this knew that the reaction would be delayed after ignition, be unstoppable by the fire suppression system, and cause extreme damage by using the propane tanks as the main explosive material. Furthermore, the chemicals used were innocuous enough that the purchase over time would not raise a single red flag anywhere on the grid. None of the elements were programmed into the molecular air samplers strewn throughout the campus, thus their introduction into a lab was unnoticed and untraceable. And using a highly explosive material that already existed in the lab allowed the perpetrator to forgo any attempt at smuggling in an explosive. Despite her mandate to investigate and punish whoever this perpetrator was, Green was completely turned on by their intelligence and serious attention to detail. She knew that was kind of creepy, seeing that he hurt a number of MESA personnel, but a girl likes what a girl likes, regardless of where it comes from.

————

Eight hours after the explosion, only 12 of the lab's staff were listed as stable. A remaining 14 were listed as pending transition while three remained critical. At the request of the old man, Green was to interview Jameson first, thus she had waited until he was transitioned out of critical care into recovery, despite a number of other staff members being kept there for observation.

Green knocked softly on the door and entered without waiting for a response. Jameson was lying in bed, nano-bandages and healing gel packs covering a large portion of his body. Green caught sight of the man's exposed leg and silently enjoyed the sight of the shaved muscular appendage. Returning almost instantly to her task, she walked over and sat next to Jameson's bed. Monitoring devices linked to every aspect of Jameson's physiology relayed his data feed to the nurses' station just down the hall. Green could see that he was awake but wasn't sure of his level of coherence.

"Charles...Charles. Are you awake?" Jameson groggily looked over at her.

"Ah, Ms. Green. How nice to see you," replied Jameson in a far-off voice.

Green called up Jameson's medical record on her interface as she spoke. "Charles, I need to ask you a few questions. Are you up for that?" Green knew fully well that regardless of Jameson's inclination to answer her questions, if the man was alert enough, she'd get her answers. A quick review of his treatment history showed a constant dose of a morphine derivative (one of MESA's own concoctions). That would probably make her life easier. She hoped the remaining interviewees were on a similar course of treatment.

"Sure," replied Jameson. "Ask away." This last part came out a little slurred.

"Charles, I need some information about what you were doing just prior to the explosion. My RFID records indicate that while you were not near the propane tanks, you did catch some of the flying debris. What were you working on this morning?"

Jameson seemed to smile happily at her as his brain processed her questions. "Working?...Yes, I was working this morning. I was working in the lab this morning."

Green pushed a little harder. "Yes, I know, Charles, that you were in your lab. What specifically were you working on?"

Jameson's brow furrowed. "I was...I was working on the latest data from the Harmonics Lab. We...we were testing... something. Yes, testing some new oscillation data that we got from the Harmonics Lab."

Green pulled up the Interface Lab's schedule for earlier that morning. There was nothing on it regarding oscillation testing. "Charles, I don't see that on your schedule. When was it added to the lab cycles?"

"Yes...we were testing cycles. Seeing which oscillations produced the best results based on Thurman's data."

"I understand you were testing it, but why wasn't it on the schedule?"

"I dunno. I don't handle the schedule. At least I think I

don't." Jameson's face screwed up as a child-like pondering expression crossed his features. "Nope, I don't."

Green sighed. Perhaps the drugs wouldn't be as helpful as she wanted. "How did you handle the schedule for that day, Charles? Who made today's cycle schedule?"

Jameson looked at her confused. "What day is it? If it's Fries-day, then it was Mike, but if it is *Fries-day*, then it was Orlando." Green highlighted both Mike Garcia and Orlando Creed on her list of staff members.

"Charles, do you recall any suspicious activity in your lab over the last few weeks? Any attempts at unauthorized access? Any misrouted deliveries? Any staff members showing abnormal behavior? Anything like that?"

"You're pretty," Jameson slurred. "Your eyes are green... Green and green. Get it?" Jameson giggled at his pun.

"Charles, focus," replied Green with more than a little sternness in her voice. "Did you notice anything unusual about your lab or staff?"

Jameson looked offended at this reprimand but thought through the question nonetheless. "Nope. Nothing to report, Capitan." With this, Jameson saluted Green with a wobbly arm.

A nurse came in just as Green stood up to leave. This wasn't proving as effective as she had hoped, and it looked like multiple visits to the recovery wing would be unavoidable. Green exited the room and started down the hall as the nurse came over to check on Jameson.

"Oh dear. Mr. Jameson, you aren't getting your pain meds. My goodness, look at this." The nurse stepped back from a puddle of clear liquid pooling from an unattached IV line flopped under Jameson's bed. "No wonder your blood pressure has been rising. You must be in a lot of pain. My goodness. Here, let me fix you, and then I'll clean this up." Jameson nodded coherently and then closed his eyes as his head rested back on his pillow.

———

Ms. Green had deliberately moved Creed to the bottom of her interview list. If she had to endure all of the barely lucid conversations she had participated in over the last two hours, she at least wanted some eye candy to round out this completely sucky day. And Creed was fine extra-dark choco-late in her book. Absolutely yummy. She, of course, would have to imagine him without all the bandages and tubes. But still, that whole nurse-patient fantasy... Green had to pull herself back to the hallway where she stood outside Creed's room. A deep breath later, and she opened the door to find the tall, dark, and still handsome man lying in bed with his leg air-casted in an osmotic cooling unit. Tubes of pink liquid circulated through an intricate web of flattened tubes, cooling Creed's recovering burns. His leg looked slick from all the reparative gel that was accelerating his skin regrowth. At another medical facility in the world, slight scarring was almost a certainty for Creed's leg. But with MESA's access to its own product line of medicinal wonders, only a full-body scan would reveal any noticeable difference in appearance.

"Orlando," Green cooed in a sweet voice, "So good to see that you weren't hurt more extensively." And she meant that. Who would she fantasize about if his face had been marred?

"Ms. Green. I suppose you are here to interview me," Creed replied politely. It was his total act of playing hard to get combined with his physique that just seemed to melt Green to the core. *Dark chocolate indeed*, she thought.

"Yes, Orlando, I am. You've been through a lot today, so I'll make this easy and brief. I've already interviewed Jameson and everyone else in recovery. I've also reviewed the prelim and secondary reports from the incident and have constructed an initial timeline of events."

Creed nodded as she rattled her list off.

"So really what I need from you is any insight into the days and weeks leading up to today. Jameson, while understandably under the influence slightly, indicated that he had not noticed any unusual activity at all. Can you confirm that?"

Creed let out a single mirthless chuckle while shaking his head. He looked out the window of his room for a moment before responding to Green. "Look...I need...I..." Creed rubbed his forehead as he tried to collect his thoughts. "Green, you and I have always had an amicable relationship, right?"

Green had no idea where he was going with this. "Of course, Orlando."

Creed stared at her, then turned again to look out the window. Green was absolutely baffled at his reluctance. Did he know something about the explosion...or even better, did this near-death experience finally soften those exterior defensive walls? She licked her lips at the possibility of chocolate-dipped strawberries.

Creed returned his gaze to her. "I need to know that you are committed to MESA. I know the old man and Kingston put you in charge of this investigation, but I need to know that your loyalty lies with the company. Can you assure me that?"

Company loyalty? Not deeply hidden feelings of desire? Green's dark-chocolate-filled balloon popped with a rather unsatisfying return to reality. "Yes, Orlando. I am loyal to MESA. What are you on about? Why all the cryptic questions?"

Creed evaluated her response for a long moment. "I know who is responsible for the explosion."

CHAPTER 15

ANSWERS

Scene: A week and a half after the arrival of the Republicans.

Place: Samantha's bedroom

There was a knock at her door.

"Samantha, can I talk to you?"

Sam jumped off her bed, the knock startling her. She recognized the voice. It was Coda.

Sam hesitated. Coda wanted to enter her room. She had never had a boy in her room before—well, besides Richard, but he didn't really count.

I need to stop thinking like that, she thought. Richard wasn't her Richard anymore. Why couldn't she remember that?

Sam stood, checked her reflection in a mirror on the wall, and answered

, "Just a second, Coda." She scrambled a bit frantically to open the door. A grime-faced Coda greeted her. Sam looked him up and down, lingering on his face and mouth. He really was a handsome devil. This thought soured her disposition. Pathetic. It was pathetic to think that the only boy she had ever had in her room was fat Richard. He walked into her room with a nod. There was a Cloud Tablet in his hand.

"Won't you come in?" said Sam sarcastically. Coda seemed not to notice, but Sam didn't care. The Cloud Tablet was much more interesting. Sam eyed the piece of technology. Richard continued to fervently deny her use of anything connected to the Cloud. If it was connected to the Cloud and she borrowed it from Coda, then perhaps she could find out about her mom and Cammie...Adam.

Coda glanced around the room; he appeared as if he was looking for something. There was none of his usual jovial self. He was all business, a business that was almost certainly unpleasant. He searched for a moment more, then turned to face Sam.

"We're leaving tomorrow."

Sam's face remained passive. She figured Rice told her as much. She knew they were leaving, but she didn't have to like it and didn't have to show Coda that she didn't like it. "I know."

Coda's expression changed. "Surprising. How did you know?"

"Rice," said Sam simply.

"I swear I'm going to beat that girl within an inch of her life. She knows she's not supposed to ignore the change of command like that."

"I wouldn't be too hard on her, though I'm not really sure how she knew either."

Awkwardness settled upon them—something Sam thought impossible a few weeks ago, before all the craziness happened.

Sam waited for Coda to speak. When he didn't, she took the initiative.

"What did you come here for, Coda? What is it you want?"

Coda walked casually to Sam's bed and sat upon it. "You know why I'm here, Sam. I want answers."

"You know the deal—"

"I get it," interrupted Coda sharply. "I know. I'm ready to answer your questions if you answer mine."

"What happened to clearance and rank and rules and all that nonsense?"

"I'm going to have to risk it."

"Why?"

Coda ran a hand through his dirty blond hair. "Rice."

"What does this have to do with Rice?"

"There was another incident at an Academy City. The one that Rice was attending."

"Which one?"

"679."

Sam gasped a little. "Oh my George W. Bush. That is just south of 676. Do your people know why?"

"No."

"But you think it has something to do with Rice?"

"Not exactly."

"You're not making any sense."

Coda squirmed uncomfortably. "You see, the thing is, well, Rice...she likes you."

"And that's a bad thing?"

"No, but Rice doesn't like anyone."

"Should I be insulted?"

"Damn," said Coda, shaking his head. "I'm not explaining myself very well."

"No, no, you're not."

"Rice is intuitive to a fault. She's drawn to you, and that is saying something. But it's not just her. I must admit—I mean, I have to confess that I was also drawn to you. I thought that there might be more to you than you were letting on or something that you didn't know about yourself. I don't mean anything by that; I am just trying to understand how you play into all this. Academy Cities 676 and 679 aren't the only schools that MESA has been poking around. They've been in almost every Academy City within the Sigler Province. We have no idea what they are after. Fortunately, so far, Academy City 676 was the only one that got super violent, and from what I've heard, that wasn't sanctioned. Ms. Green took some license in that ops."

Sam felt her blood boil a bit, remembering the leather-clad psycho who enjoyed throwing knives at kids.

Coda ran a hand through his hair. "The events at Academy 676 were strange. It was a random and seemingly unnecessary escalation of a fight that we don't quite understand. I need to know why MESA, and more importantly, why a Jadin Special Ops unit attacked the school. I mean, it must have taken months to get that unit and equipment into the country, and for what? To shoot up the school and some security guards? I don't think so. I've been trying to work this all out since the day of the attack while I was grieving about you and Richard's death. Your and Richie's involvement baffles me, and while learning that Richard was a part of the Rough Riders answers some questions, it adds another layer of mystery. Richard was undercover for so long when all the Rough Riders were supposed to be dead a long time ago. It makes sense that he's part of that unit. The fact that Richard had not been recruited and everyone refused to listen to me about him was even stranger than my being drawn to you. Ultimately, I don't have the answers I need, and it's foolish to move on with a confrontation with MESA, the UWC, and potentially the Jade Empire without more information."

"And you think I can provide you with that information?"

Coda shrugged. "Not necessarily, but I want to hear your tale. I am hoping that your story will add to the image that I am already painting in my head. At some point, the picture will develop into an understandable illustration. So this is my proposal: in return for your story, I will describe mine. I've answered some of your questions already and given you some details of my life. I am willing to follow through with that. Be straight with me; I will answer any other questions that you have."

Sam considered this arrangement. "That seems fair, but you'd better deliver."

"I will do my best."

Sam sat down next to Coda on the bed and started to speak. "Do you remember the last time that Richard got in a fight with Dyson? I think that's really where it started."

Sam told Coda everything—the strange change she had been feeling over the last year or so, Adam, Richard, the slavers, the attack on the school, Richard's change from pincushion to ninja, and the miraculous escape. She told him about the box, spending the bulk of her story describing the increasingly weird effect it was having on her, how she had found it, and what she knew about it so far. She rounded off her story with her life here. She also gave him a few choice observations about Richard. He listened quietly but interjected with things like "really" and "fascinating" every so often. Sam talked until her throat was dry and then stopped. They remained quiet for the better part of five minutes while Coda considered things.

"I can't believe all that was going on right in front of my face and I missed it."

"It wasn't your fault," said Sam. "How could you have

known? You were gone for a big chunk of that time. Cammie complained about it constantly; we thought you were ditching with Lacey. Now that I know that was a front, I've got to ask: what were you doing?"

Coda leaned back on Sam's bed. "Funny you should say that. Remember the slavers that you were talking about?"

Sam nodded her head. "Yeah, what about them?"

"Believe it or not, we were trying to track them down."

"Not that that isn't honorable or anything, but why were you trying to do that? What does that have to do with your revolution?"

Coda glared at her. "You make our cause sound like some virtual gaming tagline."

Sam chewed on the side of her lip. "You didn't answer my question; why would your rebel alliance be after a group of two-bit traders?"

Coda's hand found his face, and again he rubbed his chin and cheek as if he had a beard. Sam wasn't even sure if he realized he was doing it.

"We thought the slavers were just your everyday human traffickers. The warlords of the Burning Plains and some of the more unsavory parts of the UWC and Jade Empire will pay big money for girls from the Academy Cities. They are young, clean, and for the most part, disease-free. Anyway, as you know, this isn't totally uncommon. Well, about six months ago, more and more of these kidnapping incidents occurred, and we aren't talking about the dangerous Academy

Cities like 871 and 431; I mean ultra-elite cities like 2121 and 64. Adams and Washington thought it would be prudent to—"

"Wait," interjected Sam, "Who are Adams and Washington? I didn't meet them."

"No, you didn't. They're the leaders, Sam. So a little American history for ya. George Washington was the leader of the Continental Army that led the British colonists to revolution in the 1700s. Apparently, he was honest to a fault and very much beloved and influential at the time. In our little band of misfits, he's the big boss man. He calls the shots."

"And Adams?"

"Now that is where it gets interesting. The second president of the United States of America, John Adams, was the brains behind the American Revolutionary operation. While Washington had the heart to lead the Continental Army to victory, John Adams had the brains. Now Adams is our information officer and the most brilliant hacker in existence. The Cloud Net is basically his. He essentially owns it."

Sam went over the information in her head. It all made logical sense, but there was a piece of data that should have been obvious. She was missing a vital part, and she couldn't place her finger on it. Sam decided to redirect.

"So why were Washington and Adams so concerned about the slavers?"

"They were concerned about the rate and amount of abductions. There were dozens and dozens of kidnappings in the last six months or so. The slave trade depends a lot on a certain amount of obscurity. Border security has improved immensely since the end of the last Great War. The traders attempting to move that many girls without being noticed is stupidly impossible and is essentially suicide. Border Patrol isn't exactly the forgiving kind. So with that many girls gone missing, Adams came to the conclusion that—"

"The girls were still in the UWC."

Coda pulled up his hand and pointed his finger at her like a gun. He shot an imaginary bullet. "Bingo."

"But what a stupid risk! Why do that, especially on such a large scale?"

"That's what we asked."

"So what happened to the girls?"

Coda shrugged. "We don't know. We tracked at least some of the missing girls to a medical center north of Academy City 676, but before we could do anything, it was destroyed."

"The Obama Center for Hope Ever After!" said Sam abruptly. She knew that had to be it. She remembered the story vividly. "So it wasn't destroyed by the Republicans?"

"No."

"Do you think the kidnapped girls had anything to do with the destruction of the facility?"

Coda shook his head. "I don't think so, but it's hard to tell as we don't know who did it."

"Wait a moment," said Sam, straining her memory of a

school's poolside conversation. The name—if Sam could remember the name... "Coda, do you know someone named Mackie? Kind of a goofy kid, used to sit with a group of friends at lunchtime with a holo-project board. He used to bother Richard every once in a while."

Coda considered Sam's words. "The name doesn't ring any bells off the top of my head. Why?"

"Because I just thought of something. Do you remember the day we had that big lockdown at school? It was the same day that Richard got in his 'fight' with Dyson, and you came to his rescue."

Coda made a weird straining face. "I think I do remember that day. Adam—that's right, Richard got in a fight with Dyson, and Adam told me to go and help him. Freaking Richard, ya drug-addled ganga. I want my concern for your safety back."

Sam tried to hold back a laugh and ignore the pang in her heart. Just hearing Adam's name stirred something within her. "Good, you remember. That will make this easier to explain. So on that same day we had that lockdown, Mackie and a group of his friends approached me and Richard because the authorities supposedly caught an assassin named—"

"The Magician," finished Coda. "Oh, I know all about the Magician. You know, now that I think about it, we should use Richard. He, being the genius that he is, should be able to—"

It was Sam who interrupted this time. "That's not necessarily true, Coda. I don't think we can make any assumptions about Richard."

Sam leaned against the headboard of her bed. "Richard might have been faking the whole genius thing, though he did sort of indicate otherwise."

Coda shook his head. "No, he's the real deal, Sam. You can't fake the stuff he pulled off. Richard is one smart cookie. We can't deny that."

"Ignoring for a moment that 'one smart cookie' is a stupid saying and doesn't make any sense, why don't you finish your thought? Richard is a genius and?"

"And he should help us with the Magician."

"How does Richard being a genius help you with the Magician? Scratch that; instead, answer me this: why did Richard tell me that the Magician doesn't exist?"

Coda laughed. "He would say that, but no, Samantha, the Magician is very real and very dangerous."

"You are so not making any sense. Is there some sort of connection between Richard and the Magician?"

"Think about it; you can probably put it together."

Sam closed her eyes, chewing on her lower lip. "Okay, so this is what I know about Richard. According to you, he has a beyond-genius-level intellect, has the ability to take out Jadian Death Squad members like they're schoolchildren playing World War Four, and can make nice with most electronic devices. Oh, let's not forget that he walks around with 60 kilograms of biomechanical weight as if he were some sort of science fiction experiment. He was at Academy City 676 for a reason, and whatever that reason was, it kept him there long enough for us to almost finish our under-school education. Knowing all that, I have to think that he was placed under-cover at Academy City 676 for something more than just a simple cover or base of operations. Perhaps he was hiding something or hiding from someone."

Coda sat up a little. "Interesting theory. Why would he be hiding? There doesn't seem much out there that's a threat to him, assuming, of course, he's as dangerous as you claim."

"He is; trust me. You should see his training facility." Sam's eyes ward skyward and met only the ceiling. "Maybe it has something to do with the Rough Riders organization you were talking about. Maybe he was hiding from them."

"You wouldn't know," answered Coda. "But the Rough Riders organization was wiped out, and Richard was a part of that organization. If they were still around, why hide from them?"

Sam let out a puff of air. "I've just got the feeling that I'm looking at this all wrong. I think I need to go back over it."

Sam tried to piece the puzzle that was Richard into a congruent picture. Slowly, as she considered the pieces, an image formed. It was barely recognizable, and then it struck her. That was it. That was her answer. "Coda, I get it now. I know the answer. It makes sense! All of it makes perfect sense."

"Sam, are you going to share with the rest of the class?"

"Richard was in hiding because it was him they were looking for; don't you get it, Coda? It was Richard; it was Richard all the time."

"Sam, I'm sorry, you lost me—"

"Richard, Coda, Richard is the Magician!"

———

"Wait a second, Samantha, you've got it all wrong. Richard can't be the Magician."

"Why? It all makes sense—the weapon skills, hacking skills, the strange ability to stay calm in volatile situations. It seriously all makes sense. Richard is the Magician. He has to be."

Coda raised an eyebrow. "Sam, how much do you actually know about the Magician?"

"Not much really, only that he has a huge fan base on VII space. Why?"

"Sam, the Magician is a really bad guy. He's absolutely brutal. No mercy. No one has ever seen his face and lived to tell about it. The guy has destroyed entire military facilities by himself—women, children, non-combatants, everyone, Sam. He is an assassin in every sense of the word. Do you really think that Richard is capable of all that? Not to mention the Magician only kills using some sort of magic. We can safely assume those are parlor tricks, but regardless, from what you told me, Richard likes to play with 20th-century .45 caliber pistols. That's hardly magical."

Sam shook her head. "No, that's true. Those things were anything but magic. And you're right; I don't think Richard is so brutal as to be killing kids."

"There is also something critical you are missing in your theory."

"What's that?"

"Timing. Sam, the man known as the Magician has been around for at least the better part of two decades."

Sam's jaw dropped a little. "But I've only recently heard of him."

"You're not as plugged in as you should be, and he has only gotten really public in the last, say, three or four years."

Sam harrumphed. "Well, that kills my theory, doesn't it? But if Richard isn't the Magician, we are back to where we originally started, and it begs the question: who the heck is he?"

"He's a Rough Rider, Sam. That tells us everything we need to know about him. The Rough Riders were an elite group, formed in secret by Washington several years ago, and it was their mission to find and kill a single individual. Sam, Richard was raised to be a weapon, a bullet, if you may; a bullet that's got a name inscribed on it. I would tell you whose name, but from the look on your face, you already know, don't you?"

Sam nodded. Now it made sense. The final piece fell into place.

Coda continued, "And that's the other part wrong with your theory. If Richard is a Rough Rider, then he couldn't be the Magician because his sole mission is to go and find the Magician, to find and kill him."

CHAPTER 16

INQUIRIES

Scene: The day of the Republicans' departure.
Place: The main exit of the Cheyenne Mountain Facility.

Sam, Coda, and Lacey stood at the exit of the underground facility. The Republicans were heading out, and Sam came, reluctantly, to see them off.

"You've got to promise me that you're going to be careful," said Coda as he shouldered a large, wicked-looking assault weapon.

"I'm always careful, Coda. You have nothing to worry about."

"Says the girl who landed herself in the middle of a governmental resistance partnered with a should-be-dead black operative."

"But I was totally careful the whole time I was with him. I even wore a Jaidan magic bullet blocker thing."

Lacey, sounding slightly bitter, piped in, "You have a Jaidan Oscillation Shield?"

Sam snapped her fingers. "That's what Richard called it. Yes, I do. Richard took it off one of the soldiers that he—ah—killed during our escape from Academy City 676."

"How did he get past the security protocol?" asked Coda, sounding amazed. "Those things are impossible to hack."

"Uh?"

Coda laughed. "No, I don't suppose you'd know that. Richard is just full of mysteries, isn't he?"

Sam shrugged. "An understatement if I've ever heard one."

Coda's composure changed; it was slight but enough. "All joking aside, Sam, I... I'd be disappointed if something happened to you."

"That goes for you too."

Coda threw his arms around Sam and hugged her tightly. Taken aback, Sam barely heard what Coda whispered in her ear. "Under your pillow, a gift that I think you might find useful."

He gave her another squeeze. "Goodbye, Sam."

Coda let go of her, picked up his backpack, turned on his heel, and walked out the door. Sam listened as his boots echoed in retreat. He walked away, and she choked up; the farewell remained firmly in her throat. Lacey nodded and followed Coda. Soon they were swallowed by the blackness of the tunnel.

The melancholy was instantaneous. Sam hesitated as desire rose within her. She wanted to go; she wanted to leave with Coda and the Republicans. Coda's footsteps were getting more distant, nothing more than tapping echoes on her eardrums. Sam continued to hesitate but stepped forward. She took another step and then another. She was just about to break into a run when—

"I know what you're about to do, and you can't."

The jarring interruption of the silence almost caused her to fall flat on her face as she simultaneously tried to stay and leave. She stopped before falling, righted herself, and spotted a single person sitting on a metal box.

"Rice?"

The girl smiled in a sad sort of way. "Yeah, Samantha. It's me."

"Rice, what are you doing? They are going to leave you."

The girl shook her head. "They aren't going to leave me. I told them to wait."

"You told them to wait?" said Samantha, flabbergasted. "And you just expect them to do so?"

"Yes," answered Rice sweetly, "because what I have to tell you is important."

"And what is that?"

"You can't leave Richard."

Sam paused, swearing she heard wrong. "I'm sorry, Rice. What did you say?"

"I said you cannot leave Richard."

"Umm... okay... and why can't I leave?"

"Because you need to stay."

"Oh well, that clears it up. Thank you."

Rice neared Sam, and in that instant, Sam felt a strange, compelling fear and then unadulterated calm. The switch in emotions was so extreme that when Rice took her by the hand, she didn't know what to feel. "I know you're scared, Samantha. But you're needed here; your place is here. Richard needs you."

"Rice, you've got to stop being so cryptic. Why do I need to stay? And why on earth would you ever think that Richard needed anyone, most of all me?"

Rice smiled, and Sam felt her warmth shimmy up her hand and into her chest.

"Sam, you need to use less of this."

Rice pointed at her head "and more of this."

Rice reached out and touched directly over her heart. She smiled again. "You do more of that, and you'll figure it out."

Confusion, once again, assaulted Sam, but with no clear direction as to where she should attempt her next inquiry. She let the moments squander.

Rice let go of her hand; immediately, the warmth drained from her hand. Rice took a deep, labored breath. "I don't suspect that you and I will see each other again. So I have two things to tell you. Don't ask me what they mean because I don't know."

Sam nodded. Rice's eyes brightened.

"The first, and far less cryptic as you say, is this: Something very dangerous resides close to us. Even now, I can feel it. If you are not careful, it will rain hell's fury down upon you. Be vigilant."

"I thought you said the first wasn't cryptic."

"No, I said far less cryptic. Now hush; we are running out of time."

Sam sighed.

"The second is a simple admonition. The answers you seek, Samantha, can only be found," Rice reached up a second time, again touching her heart. "The answers can only be found within."

Sam rubbed at her eyes. What the flip kind of warning was that? How could any of that sort of talk help? Stupid. This wasn't a virtual theater; tell her what the hell was going on or shut up about it!

"Listen, Rice, I know that you are trying to help," Sam removed her hand from her face. "But—"

Sam didn't finish the question, as Rice was nowhere to be seen.

————

While the evidence is extensive that the Magician is actually some sort of black ops team, there are still many who believe that he is a single individual working within a network completely loyal to him. Magi, or experts in Magician folklore, generally fall into the highlighted categories of belief concerning the fabled assassin. The first theory, known as the Magician Singularity, represents the proposition that the Magician is and always has been a single genetically enhanced individual. The second school of thought, Magician Group Theory, takes the opposite position that the Magician isn't a single individual but a group of people working with a point man who is interchangeable within the construct of the organization. The historical and scientific communities are deeply divided on not only the two theories but on the simple existence of both the man and organization. Many feel that the Magician is a fabrication and propaganda machine for deep cover elements of the UWC and Jade Empire. There is a large amount of evidence to support all sides of the controversy.

The development of the legend surrounding the Magician started shortly after the Internment Camps of 2101. The followers of the Magician Singularity Theory state that if there ever was a single individual that held the title, he was probably a contractor and survivor of the Cerberus Virus (the Cerberus Virus being named as such after a priest of the Neo-Olympian Church discovered his dog had the strange disease). Singularity theorists state that this hypothesis seems consistent with the most common attributes traditionally associated with the Magician's unusual skill set, including a rabid tendency towards increased physical attributes such as strength, speed, reflexes, and general extrasensory perception.

Experts supporting Magician Group Theory disagree with

this, stating that mission data that have been traditionally attributed to the Magician's handiwork has shown, over the years, clear deviations in style, planning, and outcomes. These experts believe that there is a demarcation between the early missions of the Magician and his latter career, and that difference is especially noticeable within the last five years of the Magician's supposed operations.

Sam scrolled down the page of the tablet, picking up on the Wikipedia entry. The secure line to the Ex-site took forever to load, but Sam didn't mind as it gave her time to think. She ran her fingers along the edge of the tablet and thought of Coda. It had already been a week since the Republicans' departure, and still, she wondered if what she did was the right thing in staying. After her conversation with Rice and the girl's little vanishing act, Sam ran down the Cheyenne Mountain Site's main tunnel looking for Rice and the rest. Despite Rice's warning, Sam made the choice to follow; she wanted to follow. Rice's urgings nagged at her, but she was going to convince the Republicans to take her with them, even if she had to beg.

It was to no avail. Coda and his comrades were gone, long gone. Sam ran out into the woods surrounding the entrance of the base, only to see a breathtaking view of trees and prairies all around. Beautiful, but there was no one and nothing else in sight.

Sam sat on a rock and thought. At one point in time, this

valley had been home to more than 500,000 people. It was amazing what a world war could do.

Depressed and in tears, Sam retreated back to the safety of her quarters. She stripped her clothes off, flinging them to the side of her room. She got into bed, fully intending to sleep for the next week. She flopped onto her pillow and... pain erupted in the back of her head. She hit something hard. Rubbing her head, she pulled out a thin, heavy object that was wrapped in decorative paper. She wasted no time ripping it open. She found a tablet and a note written on yellow paper that stuck to the front of the tablet. "Post it" was written on the back of the little paper. The note simply said:

"A gift, something to keep you occupied until we meet again. Tell Richard that he still owes me one."

Sam recalled the note, which was sitting in the top drawer of her nightstand, and smiled. It did that each time she thought about it. Sam was initially reluctant to use the tablet. Richard told her that logging on to the Cloud or Vii Space allowed anyone to track them, and that was something to avoid. For the first day or so, the tablet just sat under her bed, the temptation calling her like Beelzebub himself had made the piece of equipment. She wanted desperately to log on to the tablet and look for news of Academy City 676, her mom, Cammie, and Adam. Finally, on the morning of the second day after the Republicans' departure from the mountain facility, she broke down, pulled the tablet out from under her bed, and powered it up. She figured that it would be a big deal if she used it only sparingly. She had to know, and with Richard MIA, it was a chance she was willing to take. Her concerns were for naught. Upon powering up, a video started to play. It was Coda.

"Sam, I left this for you with the intention of giving you some way to communicate with me if something were to happen. That is my personal tablet, modified by Adam himself when I left for Academy City 676. It is untraceable. Not even Richard should be able to track the signal. Just stay away from certain Cloud sites, and you should be able to use it freely. If you ever need me, use the ICE button in the top left corner. I've already programmed my information into it. Be safe. I will hopefully see you soon."

The tablet was like manna from heaven. Sam wasted no time looking up news on the attack on Academy City 676. Sure enough, she found ample reading material on the subject, though the events relayed by the official networks were far different than those on the social networking sites and Sam's own recollection. The only group that was mentioned in the news report was the Republicans, and they were blamed for the entire fiasco. Sam's conversation with Richard, Mackie, and Mackie's lackeys came back to her. Mackie warned her about the State and their information manipulation. It had seemed funny when Mackie talked about it. Sam was not laughing anymore.

Then there was Richard. For some funny reason, that poolside day and conversation stuck out in her mind—the discussion of the Obama Center for Hope Ever After, a medical facility with highly advanced security. At the time of that broadcast, Sam remembered feeling that something about the official story wasn't right. That was another attack blamed on the Republicans; she never had the chance to ask Coda if his people attacked the center. Something she needed to remedy if she wanted to come to an observable conclusion on this topic. Regardless, she possessed enough information to make at least one assumption: the medical center probably wasn't a medical center at all, and she couldn't trust official sources of information. It was a hard lesson to learn.

This lesson wasn't what really bothered her. What really bothered her was Richard's insistence that the official sources were accurate. He had to have known that was untrue, but he told her otherwise. The most obvious answer was that Richard was playing a part, being the fat Richard she had grown to know and love, but was his declaration of the non-existence of the Magician lumped into that category as well? From what Coda said, the Magician not only exists, but Richard, as a Republican Rough Rider, was specifically trained to take out the Magician, and many of his comrades died unexpectedly in pursuit of that mission. All of this was connected; that much she felt. The question was how.

The facts bounced around her head and simply deepened

Sam's curiosity. The weeks confined to the Cheyenne Mountain Facility had already given her copious opportunities to ponder Richard and his apparent mystery and contradictions. Coda and the Republicans' sudden appearance and the subsequent revelations added much light to a darkened topic but also fueled that fire—a fire that could only be quenched through discovery.

The strangest thing of all, now with the dust of the Republicans' visit finally settling, was that her mind continued to wander to the Magician. She kept moving back to him. She didn't know why that was the case, but she did just the same; it was as if the Magician was some sort of pleasant childhood memory just wanting to burst forth. This was the reason that she was up at the dead of the night reading about him. She was hoping, just hoping, that a picture of this man or organization would reemerge from all the hype and controversy.

Sam went back to her reading.

Former UWC's Czar of Defense Elisha Graham, terrorism expert, military tactician, and former confidant of Chancellor Himms, proffers an official position in his book "A Blind Eye." Mr. Graham states: "The perpetuation of the mythology surrounding the so-called 'Magician' is less about the truth or falsity of the existence of said Magician and really more about what he represents. The Magician represents a dramatized ideological version of freedom—freedom that extreme political naysayers and drug-using upper-education students claim is lacking in modern society. If one takes an unbiased look at actual evidence of generally accepted acts of the Magician, there is an absolute lack of uniformity in M.O., weapon choice, and even targets. Sometimes the so-called Magician is targeting political proponents of the Labor Party, and others Bollywood starlets. Some actions are full-scale assaults on highly fortified military facilities, and others are data manipulation in the international banking community. There are times when the military actions are executed with such stealth and brilliance that there is absolutely no record that there was any involvement at all by an outsider. On other occasions, the Magician is pictured or seen with the data or witnesses being left alive. And then there is the sheer magnitude of the needed influence and network that the Magician would have to have access to; this individual or organization would have to have almost unlimited connections and resources—a network of completely loyal agents and security hardware to match. There is no way that an organization and/or individual like that exists without the government having an idea of who they are and what they are trying to accomplish."

A noise grated right across Sam's concentration. It was incredibly jarring. Sam looked at her clock. It was already 2:00 in the morning. She needed to sleep. No wonder she was hearing things.

The noise sounded again. Sam felt the hairs on the back of her neck stand high, and her arms developed goosebumps the size of moose. Sam felt her breathing deepen and a black cloud settle upon her.

What was happening? She didn't understand. A faint glowing light, a light that was growing bright, stretched out from under her bed. Suddenly, Sam knew what was going on—

Tap, tap, tap.

Sam looked to the door as her concentration was once again jarred. The distinct sounds of someone knocking on hard metal pinged in her ears, blocking all else. For some reason, the noise was much louder than it should be.

Sam reflexively closed her eyes and put her fingers to her ears as the sound assaulted her. The discomfort lasted only a moment, as if it weren't real to begin with. When Sam opened her eyes, the room was totally normal—no magnified noise or eerie light—but there was no time to contemplate the development as there was more rapping at the door.

Sam walked to the door and cracked it open.

It was Richard.

"Samantha," said Richard, barely visible in the dark of the hallway. What she could see of Richard wasn't encouraging. He looked exhausted.

"Hi, Richard. What's going on? Are you okay?"

"Nothing, I was just checking on you, and I'm perfectly alright."

Sam forced herself to mask surprise and minor delight.

"You're checking on me? Okay... well, where have you been? I haven't seen you since Coda and the others showed up."

Richard showed no emotion but stubbornly refused to look her in the eye. "Where've I always been, Sam? The western access tunnels. Does it surprise you that I retreated from the others? You understand, with all the social graces I possess."

"Yes, you've made your point."

"It pleased me when you didn't attempt to bring the others there." Sam heard it. She swore she did. Richard's voice softened.

"You're welcome, but truth be told, I didn't know what you'd do to them. You being a Rough Rider and all."

Richard scowled. "Yes, you heard that, didn't you? Well, that was a long time ago, and—"

Richard spoke with a slight increase in volume. "I don't want to talk about it."

"Okay..." said Sam, disappointed. "I will be going to bed then."

"Goodnight, Sam."

Sam closed her door and leaned against the metal—quite the reunion; same old stubborn, scary Richard. Why did he come? And so late at night? Sam banged her head against the metal harder than she meant. He avoided her eye, and his voice softened when he spoke to her. She smiled to herself. *He* was the one that came to her, and he refused to look her in the eye, seeming embarrassed. The last time they spoke was when she flashed and punched him. Maybe Richard was more of a boy than she thought.

She couldn't ponder that right now, though; she had other things to attend to. Sam looked to her bed, where she knew the tin box was sitting. She started towards it. She had ignored it too long.

CHAPTER 17
A GOLDEN SWORD

Time: Early morning
Place: A Republican Nighthawk

Dirk Garrent was screwed. Again. And this was the last straw; Fate was totally getting the ax from the Christmas list. Sanzurbi. It had to be Sanzurbi. He was going back to the one place, the single place on good old mother earth where people knew him by name, face, and occupation, and where the price on his head was the equivalent to the UWC's GDP. He was so very, very screwed.

The Nighthawk chopper cut through the air like a stingray in water. They were flying in Sanzurbi airspace now, so close to the ground that anyone below was probably freaking out because of the random sandstorms. Soon they would enter the Providence of Egypt and the territorial airspace of the Governor of Sanzurbi. Luckily, the automated flak cannons and SAM anti-aircraft missile launchers left over from the last war wouldn't detect their heat signature, and they would coast right past them. The defenses shouldn't detect them. The Nighthawk was a tenth-generation stealth craft. The thing was freaking invisible to everything, including the naked eye. Then again, Dirk learned a long time ago that Fate's influence was much more—well, *influential* than any electronic system ever hoped to be.

Dirk stared at the group of soldiers sitting next to him; the men brooded in silence. They were the same group that picked him up after the man in black broke him out of jail. The man in black... it had been a while since Dirk thought of him. He wondered what that bloody magician was up to.

One of the soldiers, Johnson, Dirk thought his name was, played absentmindedly with a light shiv.

"Aren't you ex-UWC special forces?"

Johnson stared at Dirk like a housewife might look at soap scum on her shower. "Yeah, what about it?"

"I'm not a military man myself, but I know enough about the Jadin and UWC's militaries—occupational hazard, you see. Anyway, I know enough to know that UWC soldiers don't use light shivs."

Johnson narrowed his eyes. "You talk too much."

Dirk shrugged. "I talk when I get nervous, and flying into Sanzurbi to explore makes me nervous."

Johnson gave Dirk a patronizing look. "Aren't you some

sort of relic hunter? A tome-raiding badass? Sounding pretty pusillanimous there, *Dirk.*"

The soldier on the other side of Johnson leaned forward. "*Pusillanimous,* Johnson, what did I tell you about playing word games on the Cloud? Don't use those words, ya Ganga. You sound like an idiot."

Johnson twisted. "Shut up, Roach. I'll talk how I damn well please."

Dirk sighed. He had been to funerals that were more cheerful. He found that he was suddenly missing The Chair.

John Adams seemed like a smart guy. He was the freaking president of the United States, for Pete's sake, or taking on the persona of the second President of the United States. The original John Adams was a smart cat. If the new John was half as smart as good old President Adams, they wouldn't be flying into a place where "impaling" was still in style as an execution method.

"You appear nervous, Mr. Garrent. Haven't you been here before?"

Dirk jumped. It was an uncontrollable response. Where in the George W. Bush did that voice come from? "I'm sorry, I didn't mean to scare you."

A woman sat down next to Dirk, appearing from seemingly nowhere. It wasn't out of nowhere, of course. A trapdoor from the belly of the chopper was closing even as the question popped out. Still, he was surprised.

Dirk studied the woman. She was a foxy one, Jadian by

the looks of her, from the western side of the north of the Empire, near the North Atlantic probably. Her English was good but had a thick accent. She really was an attractive thing —thick brown hair, full lips, and huge brown eyes, no more than 20. It had been a while since he'd been with someone that young. Dirk's skin instantly started to tingle. He smiled. He was already on it. Skin. He was already on it.

"The State of Wallace, most likely the upper highlands towards the northern part of the island," said Dirk conclusively, "and you didn't leave until very recently."

The young lady laughed. "Very good, Mr. Garrent. You're as good as they say."

Dirk smiled wickedly. "You've no idea, my dear. I can show you just how good I can be."

She laughed again and raised an eyebrow. "Charming."

Dirk shrugged. "Sorry, I've been in prison for over a year. I'll try to control myself."

Dirk's curiosity overcame the lack of oxygen to his brain. "So what's a pretty young thing from the highlands of old Scotland doing with a group of former UWC Special Forces on a Nighthawk chopper heading to one of the most dangerous provinces among the rogue states? You an adrenaline junkie?"

She smiled, her grin almost as wicked as his had been. "And ruin the surprise, Mr. Garrent—"

"Please call me Dirk."

She nodded in acknowledgment. "Rona."

"Ahh, nice and Gallic. Beautiful."

Rona's eyes went a little wide, obviously impressed.

Dirk leaned a little closer. "So, Rona, tell me, are you really a *wise ruler*?"

Rona pushed back her mousey brown hair. "You know the meaning of my name; now isn't that a development? Your reputation befits you, Dirk."

Dirk winked at her. "It's all true, Rona. All of it."

The sergeant's voice interrupted the moment. "ETA 90 minutes, ladies—equipment check, then lock and load. We aren't expecting any surprises, but move with caution. Mr. Garrent over here is priority one."

"Sergeant, where exactly are we touching down? There are a couple of smaller villages we could—"

"We're heading right into the capital, Dirk. Ain't gonna waste time on the outer villages. We've got a schedule to keep."

"Sergeant, do you realize what—"

The sergeant was already out of earshot, disappearing back into the cockpit.

Dirk's sudden joy at the appearance of the young, beautiful Scot evaporated. They were going to fly right into the capital??? Were they insane?

"Are you okay, Dirk?"

Dirk tried not to look at Rona. "I've just got some very *unpleasant* memories of Sanzurbi. The fact that John Adams wants to go here—did you know that the Governor actually idolizes Vlad the Impaler so much that he implements Vlad's favorite forms of execution?"

"Impaling, burning, skinning, roasting, and boiling people alive. Yes, I'm familiar."

Dirk's skin tingling kicked it up a notch. "Impressive."

Rona leaned down. "You've no idea."

Dirk smiled back. Now look at that; she brought it right back on him. Nice.

Rona adjusted herself in her seat. "You need not worry about the Governor, Dirk. When Mr. Adams does something, he takes every precaution."

Dirk answered skeptically. "What's that supposed to mean?"

Rona beamed and winked. "You'll see. Like I said, I wouldn't want to spoil the surprise."

———

"Hello? Yes? Hello? This is Dirk Garrent, and I would really like to set an appointment with Fate's Supervisor. Yes, I understand that your office is busy, but I need to speak with him immediately. No, I can't leave a message; this is very, very important. Listen—I understand, but I have to inform him that I'm concerned with the way that Fate is doing his job."

The Nighthawk was taking the direct approach. The DIRECT approach—flying directly into the capital city, right at twilight, into the face of gun platforms, flak cannons, and

SAM anti-air missiles. They were flying into the capital city, and Adams thought that the soldiers were gonna be just okay with that. Everyone knew that Nighthawk's active camouflage was temperamental in rapidly adjusting light. So what does the genius do? They fly into a gaggle of anti-air weaponry right when the active camouflage is most vulnerable. Brilliant. Dirk wondered idly what The Chair was up to right now. Probably being an inanimate object. If he were dead, then he would be an inanimate object. Maybe he should start trying to practice.

"Dirk, is something wrong?"

Dirk opened his eyes to Rona's face a few inches from his. She was prettier up close. He blinked, pushing the girl from his mind. "Rona, would you marry me?"

Rona blinked. "I'm sorry?"

"Nighthawk's active camouflage systems are sort of fickle in changing light. We are approaching the capital in the dawning hours, changing light. If those flak cannons see us, we are as good as dead. I was just wondering what it would be like to be married, settle down, buy a house with a white picket fence."

Rona blinked again. "Why a white picket fence?"

Dirk shrugged. "People in the 1950s, 60s, and 70s loved them. I figured they knew something I didn't. So what do you say? Want to be my pretend wife for the next 40 minutes or so, or until the Governor of this godforsaken country blows us out of the sky? I won't even make you sign a prenup."

Rona touched his leg. The gesture surprised him. He was only kidding about the marriage thing. Actually, marriage scared him more than death.

"You don't need to hastily propose quite yet, Dirk."

Rona pulled out a tablet. "Perhaps this will make you feel better."

It was the capital city as seen through the pilot's Extra Sensory Goggles. A few hundred feet in front of them was the capital's anti-air weaponry in all its wonderful glory. It was difficult to see because of the rising sun in the east. They were approaching from the worst possible direction at the worst possible time.

They were all dead.

Dirk, dignity out the window, closed his eyes and prayed. He went with Zeus this time; he seemed as good a god as any. Minutes passed with nothing happening. Dirk chanced it and opened an eye. Rona sat close to him. She was trying really hard not to laugh.

"For a world-famous relic hunter, you're awfully jumpy." Rona touched several buttons on the screen of the tablet. The Nighthawk was so close to the gun platforms now that Dirk had to fight an impulse to leap from the Nighthawk and take his chances on the ground. It was an impossibility, he knew, so instead, Dirk closed his eyes a second time and waited.

Again, nothing happened.

Rona shoved him slightly. "Dirk, you look silly; open your eyes."

Dirk did so, and he watched as they flew right over all the defenses. No one fired upon them; for that matter, there weren't any visible signs of patrol. Where were all the guards?

It was then that Dirk noticed the smoke. He touched the screen.

"That's the Governor's palace."

Rona nodded. "Yes, it is."

Dirk brought the tablet closer to his face. "You wanna tell me why it's smoking like a Ganga fire pit?"

Rona pushed back a lock of her thick dark hair. "You aren't the only one that has been to this particular province, Dirk. Mr. Adams is well aware of how dangerous this section of the world is. He didn't want to be interrupted. He took out a little extra insurance."

"That's quite cryptic, Rona. What does it mean?"

Rona flipped the switch of the tablet; the image of the capital faded into black. "It means, Mr. Garrent, that you do not have to worry about the Governor of Sanzurbi, not now, not ever again."

———

The body of the Nighthawk touched down right in the middle of the capital city on a makeshift landing pad created within the grounds of the governor's mansion. The soldiers formed up around Dirk and Rona, masks covering their faces and plasma weaponry at the ready.

The sergeant was in the lead. "Alright, boys, form up and keep your butt holes puckered; Mr. Garrent here has an appointment to keep, and we wouldn't want him to be late. Move on my signal."

The bell doors of the Nighthawk opened, and they were greeted with a blast of hot, dusty air. The sergeant waved them on, and they all exited the Nighthawk.

The journey to the Governor's mansion was swift and uneventful. Not that there weren't interesting details to take in. There were. Many, actually. The most notable was how the city continued to bustle. Shop owners took their latest doohickey or thingamabob to the massive central market under the watchful eye of the Sanzurbi security forces. The first encounter Dirk's party had with the backwater cops made him so nervous it almost caused him to run. His paranoia was misplaced. The soldiers not only acknowledged them but actively aided in their navigating the city. Strange. Very strange indeed.

"Dirk, relax. You're going to give yourself an aneurysm, and I'm getting dizzy just watching your head go back and forth."

Dirk watched the sergeant nod at one of the security forces in passing. Now isn't that interesting.

"Yeah," replied Dirk, doing his best to multitask, "like I said, I have unpleasant memories of this place."

Closer to the governor's palace, the capital was less—

normal. There were clear signs of combat: blown-up build-ings, destroyed cars, leveled walls, and blood—lots of blood.

"What on earth happened here?" said Dirk as he and his honor guard streamed up the street like they owned it.

Rona flipped on an electric fan and pointed at her face. "I told you, when Adams does something, he does it right. When you informed us of your—issues with the Governor, Adams ordered a little extra help."

A man in black, last seen on a mountaintop in some obscure corner of the Jadian Empire. "The man in black, he did this, didn't he?"

None of them answered.

Dirk smiled internally. This was really starting to get interesting.

———

The last occasion Dirk Garrent had the pleasure of working in Sanzurbi, he had almost died. Twice. The Governor wasn't exactly a forgiving man, and Dirk had gotten to *know* his eldest daughter. Twice. Now that he thought about it, there was a certain amount of symmetry to the whole affair. The Governor's daughter's supposed honor, or lack thereof, aside, there was also a find—an incredible one—that the Governor's men caught Dirk, umm—*borrowing* from the royal vault, and deprived him of his newly acquired find. In Dirk's defense, he had originally found the piece in a cliffside some years back. Hopefully, if all went according to plan, an opportunity to correct that particular misfortune would present itself.

So the last time he had almost died. Twice. And now he was walking up the street to the Governor's mansion completely unmolested. Now isn't that karma for you?

Dirk, Rona, and his honor guard walked straight through the front gate and were greeted by some of the security forces. Curious.

"Sergeant." The man saluted.

The Sarge returned the salute. "Now what's the status here, Corporal?"

The light bulb went on in Dirk's head. This was a soldier in disguise. Now it made sense. Ahh... clever. "It's clear of all hostiles, sir, and the propaganda Trojan software program is working like a charm. I don't know which team the boss sent in last night, but they're a group of bad-asses. I've never seen such a clean job."

"You've no idea, Corporal."

Dirk leaned in, hoping the Sarge would divulge some-thing. He did not, but instead pointed towards a main cobble-stone walkway. "This way to ground zero?"

"Yes, sir."

The Sarge didn't say another word but led his team up the walkway and into the main palace of the Governor's mansion.

Everywhere Dirk looked, there were signs of a struggle.

Yet it seemed very calm. Dirk had difficulty putting his finger on it.

The procession entered a massive ballroom through a doorframe with no door. The door was disintegrated and strewn across the floor. The group passed the threshold, and what Dirk saw made him want to throw up.

Death, death in all its ugly glory, littered the place like dog crap in Giuliani City's central park. The analogy may be lost in translation; there is a lot of dog crap in that park.

On the far side of the room, two or three workers labored, digging mounds of dirt out of a peeled-back wood floor. To the left of the giant hole, a group of scantily clad, very attractive young ladies sat on the floor as an older woman spoke to them. Many of them looked a strange mix of fear and awe. Directly across from them, from the lovely sight of beautiful ladies, was the not-so-lovely sight of dead bodies. It was quite unpleasant.

"Do I even want to know what happened?" asked Dirk to Rona as they made their way to the giant hole in the ground. "Who could have done this?"

"Like I said," answered Rona, "Mr. Adams takes every precaution. He hired someone very special and very expensive for this job."

"The man in black."

Rona smiled. "That title works as well as any."

"Is there another one?"

Rona's eyes narrowed suspiciously. "Are you serious?"

"Do I sound like I'm not?"

"Now isn't that interesting; you can rattle off Gallic names and meanings like a game show host, but you don't have any idea who 'the man in black' is."

Just then, a man who appeared to be in charge greeted them. In an odd twist of events, the man was wearing a rubber mask. Now that wasn't something you saw every day.

"General," said the Sarge, saluting as he neared the man.

There was joy in the "General's" voice. "Ricker! You arrived safely, package in tow—excellent. Any problems on your way in?"

"No, sir, it was clear sailing. Your boy did his job."

The General laughed; the mask muffled it. "Not mine, Sergeant. Adams is the one with the connections. I sure wish he were, though. Unbelievable what he can accomplish in a night."

"General," Rona interrupted. "I'm sorry to intrude, but we don't have a great deal of time, and I would hate for all the Magician's work to go to—"

Dirk burst out into laughter. "Rona, don't tell me you believe in fairy tales? The Magician? You actually believe the..."

His voice trailed off. The man in black... the way he seemed to melt in and out of the darkness, the miraculous ability to manipulate metal, air, and explosives—a man on contract for a specific time and for a specific service. The gods in the heavens... Dirk had met the legendary assassin.

"The Magician is very real, Mr. Garrent," said the Sarge. "You're looking at his handiwork. He gave us a window; we shouldn't waste it. Adams brought us here. Why, Mr. Garrent?"

Dirk's mouth went a little dry. He didn't get the chance to savor the mystery. He pushed it out of his mind. There was another mystery to solve.

"We're looking for a sword."

Silence fell upon the crowd in an anticlimactic way.

"A sword? That's why Adams forced you to the other side of the world?" one of the soldiers from his honor guard said—Roach, Dirk thought his name was.

Dirk shook his head. "Not just any sword. This is a very special one. It's a sword from the early Dynastic period of Egypt."

Rona interrupted. "So we're looking for a tin bronze approximately 30 centimeters."

Dirk smiled. Rona would appreciate this. "Actually, we're looking for a sword blade that's more than a meter long, with the hilt close to 15 centimeters."

Rona was the only one who reacted. "Dirk, that isn't possible. That sounds like a medieval longsword, and those were introduced until the 13th century—more than 4,000 years later."

"Exactly." Dirk gave Rona a little wink. "We are going to retrieve an artifact that people have been looking for for

5,000 years, ladies and gentlemen. The Golden Sword from the vault of Gilgamesh."

CHAPTER 18
LIES, LIES, AND MORE LIES

Place: MESA Labs
Time: Current

Ms. Green sat in her darkened office, pacing back and forth behind her desk. After a few more laps, there was a knock on her door. Her desk interface immediately illuminated the door vid, showing a tall, dark, and handsome Creed standing outside her office, complete with a walking cast and cane. Green quickly launched the mirror app on the interface, checked her hair, and then opened the door. Creed hobbled in with a slight limp but looked remarkably well otherwise. Green indicated for him to sit down.

"Thanks fo—" started Creed until Green quickly put a hand up to silence him. She sat at her interface and called up the security matrix. While her office was not on the main record feeds to begin with, she and a few of the top executives were given security codes to not only suspend all recording activities in their offices but, at the behest of MESA's legal division, could also employ countermeasures to prevent any unintended discoverable material.

Green finished loading the countermeasures and then spoke to Creed. "Okay, let's get down to business. What do you know about the explosion?"

"Sally Hammond. Sally Hammond is responsible for the explosion, and I think Jameson helped her carry it out."

Green reeled at this information. She assumed Creed had some juicy details from their earlier conversation, but nothing like this. "You mean Charles Jameson? The director of the Interface Lab, Charles Jameson? He and this Sally blew up the lab."

Creed nodded. "Orlando... that's... well, I can certainly see why you needed to discuss this in my office. You do realize that what you are insinuating is paramount to career suicide, right?"

Orlando harrumphed and started to get up. "I knew this was a mistake. Please forgive me, but I'll be going now."

"No, Orlando, wait." Green walked around to him and put her hand on his arm. "It's not that I don't want to hear you out... it's just, well, I need to know that what you have evidence-wise will protect you from any backlash if this proves to be false. That's all." She put on her sweetest, most empathetic smile. The truth was, if Creed was right, Kingston would owe her big time. No more babysitting ugly Warrick, no more "I want you to handle this personally" assignments, and maybe, just perhaps, some extracurricular activities as well. It worked, and Orlando smiled reluctantly back and sat down again.

"You told me that Jameson said there was nothing unusual leading up to the explosion, correct?" asked Creed. Green nodded. "I mean, he was a little out of it, but even in my follow-up interviews, he hasn't mentioned anything. Why?"

Orlando pursed his lips as he shook his head. "Earlier this month, I requested a staff change. In my opinion, Sally represented a security risk, so I asked Jameson to rotate her out of the lab. He gave me his song and dance about how good her work was and how we were at a critical time, and losing an asset like Sally would hinder our progress. I agreed with that but felt that her incessant inquiries into matters beyond the scope of her assignments far outweighed any contribution she could make. Long story short, Sally left, but not without considerable resistance from Jameson and a reprimanding from the guys upstairs."

"Wait, what do you mean by her incessant inquiries?" asked Green. Orlando relayed his entire conversation with Jameson and the response he got when he delivered his report to the board. He confirmed that Sally was indeed reassigned outside of the Interface Lab, but that Jameson's abnormal defense and reluctance to get rid of her stuck in his mind.

"As soon as I was coherent enough to realize that the lab

had been sabotaged, Sally and Jameson were the first two names that popped into my mind," finished Creed.

"So an inside job was your first thought?" asked Green. Creed nodded. She sat drumming her fingers against her lips. "I came to the same conclusion but have no indication of Jameson's involvement. Orlando, I have to ask again. You realize that we'll need solid proof of this before I can take anything to the board. Anything short of that, and you and I are finished."

Creed nodded. "I do. And I have all the evidence you need." Green felt her stomach do a little flip as she sensed the confidence that this man exuded. She reached down and picked up a glass dish from her desk, offering it to Creed. "Chocolate?"

It had been a full month of updated reports, background checks, chemical analysis, vid and data stream review, and full staff interviews. The old man sat at the boardroom table as Kingston manipulated reports and charts on the projected image.

"That's all of it?" the old man asked Kingston as he slid the last report out to the side of the screen.

"That's all of the official reports. There have been some slight successes in our underground efforts, but..." Kingston hesitated.

"But *what*, Kingston?" replied the old man irritably.

"Sir, Ms. Green and Orlando Creed have been working closely to piece together information about a rather unorthodox suspect." Kingston stared at the old man.

"Unorthodox or not, someone came into our house and left their mark. What is it, Kingston?" The old man looked intensely solemn.

"Do you remember in one of Creed's reports where he indicated that he was concerned that Jameson's focus had wavered a bit?"

"Kingston, I do not like where this is going..." The old man sat impassively as Kingston continued.

"I agree with you, and like you, did not want to entertain any further discussion on the matter. But Ms. Green required me to review their evidence. While certainly far from a smoking gun, and as much as I hate to admit it, the evidence is extremely compelling."

The old man looked up at the ceiling, staring off into nowhere. He got up and walked over to his standard spot, looking out of the full-length windows of the boardroom. It was many minutes before he spoke. "Kingston, you understand the weight of what you are saying. Further, you understand that the repercussions of either a false or an accurate accusation will have far-reaching effects. This will effectively close the file on the explosion and... well, I fear what will happen after that. You have weighed all of this and the so-called evidence, correct?"

Kingston walked towards the window and stopped a few meters short of the old man. "Yes, I have." His voice became very quiet and deadly serious. "And if my loyalty is to this company, then despite the implications or any other personal feelings you or I have..." Kingston paused and took a deep breath. "I would be derelict in my duties if I did not insist that Jameson be moved to the top of the suspect list."

The old man continued to look out the window for a number of silent minutes. Finally, without turning around, he replied to Kingston. "Fine. But I will not approach this as some covert op. I want Green, Creed, *and* Jameson in this room together. If their evidence is as good as they claim, then they should have no problem presenting it directly to the man they are accusing."

Kingston nodded and walked over to the table interface.

———

Twenty minutes later, Jameson, Kingston, and the old man were seated at the boardroom table, chatting pleasantly, with no indication from any of them about the impending conversation. The elevator doors opened, and Creed and Green stepped into the room. If Green was surprised to see Jameson, she didn't show it, but Creed's face betrayed an ever-so-slight hesitation as he approached the table.

"Good morning, Mr. Creed, Ms. Green. I understand you

have a final report on the Interface Lab incident," said Kingston.

"We do," replied Green. "In fact, I think we can confidently assume that we know who is responsible."

Creed did all he could not to look directly at Jameson as he and Green presented all of their investigative notes, reports, and conclusions. They were very careful to leave out any names and only referred to suspects and perpetrators. The amount of surveillance feeds they had collected, which showed at least two persons meeting in off-campus sites, personal communications that, taken in the right context, showed the cooperation of the two in planning something, and the other circumstantial yet supportive evidence that these two were indeed responsible was very compelling, just as Kingston had said. At the end of their presentation of the evidence, the old man asked them one simple question. "And who are these two individuals?"

Creed looked at Green, who did not return the gaze but rather stared directly at Jameson. "All of our evidence points to Charles Jameson and Sally Hammond."

All eyes were focused on Charles Jameson. Each of the remaining four people expected shock, confusion, denial, outrage, anger, or worry. None of them expected Jameson to smile, yet that is exactly what he was doing.

"Very well done, both of you," replied Jameson cordially, without a hint of sarcasm or malice. "I, for one, can rest easier tonight knowing we have such capable minds working for our company."

The old man's expression was unreadable. He sat watching his friend of many years as he waited for his explanation. Kingston, on the other hand, had not remained so impassive. Apparently, the rehashing of the evidence and Jameson's lack of a reaction had done a number on Kingston's temper. He stood slowly from the desk. Just as slowly, Jameson turned to look up at him.

"You prick! We sat through the last 45 minutes of evidence that shows you and that woman were responsible for an attack on this company, and all you can say is 'well done'?" Kingston's temper seemed to boil just a bit more with every sentence that came out of his mouth. "You have the audacity to sit here with your smug smile and your holier-than-thou attitude after all this? You are completely crazy, Jameson. Completely messed up in the head."

Jameson sat calmly as Kingston continued his rant. When it was evident that all in the room expected him to say something, Jameson stood. He placed a calm hand on Kingston's shoulder. "You are one of the greatest men I know." Kingston just about lost it. Before he was sure that he was going to have to dodge a strong haymaker from Kingston, Jameson tapped the comm on the table. "Mike, please upload those files I asked you for to the boardroom interface." Moments later, dozens of documents streamed onto the boardroom screen. Call logs, hyperfeed logs, vid and data feeds... all of them filled the boardroom screen. "Kingston, you are my friend, and I am not at all upset that you reacted the way you did. But let me set your mind at ease about my actions."

Jameson walked over to the holo-board and opened an affidavit dated three months ago. "This affidavit was filed in a secured cloud server off the MESA nets and identifies my intentions of pursuing a lab employee who I believed was stealing information from the Interface Lab."

Everyone looked at the digital file and saw the Secured Encrypted Digital Certificate showing its time and date stamp. SEDCs were based on a combination algorithm that combined genetic DNA sequencing with an encryption method proven to be statistically impossible to forge. It was the absolute guarantee the document was original and not replicated or produced in any other facsimile fashion.

"I had to store this off-site under a one-time use anony-mous client as I did not know what access this employee had to information stored at MESA, and it was imperative that she was not alerted to my actions."

"She?" asked the old man.

"Yes, Ms. Green and Mr. Creed were right to implicate Sally Hammond as the person responsible behind the sabo-tage." Jameson continued as he opened some of the reports and files so that everyone could see their contents.

"Additionally, my actions, taken out of the context of conducting my own investigation, match perfectly with their conclusions that I was cooperating with Sally. However, as these updated reports show," Jameson strung a line of documents across the screen, each with a date stamp covering the three-month period at regular intervals.

"I was, in fact, attempting to find out who Sally was working for and, more importantly, why they were having her feed information to me."

Jameson slid the reports off to the side and pulled up vid and data streams. These were almost identical to those that were presented by Creed and Green, only they were taken from a different perspective. "I knew that whoever had placed her was watching my interactions with her. They would have seen the vid feeds from these public places and would use them to confirm her reports of our interaction. I took the additional precaution of having a private vid stream captured anytime we met off-site."

Again, these were slid off. Just as he was about to continue, Creed interrupted. "But none of this proves that you didn't plan this whole thing out. You and Sally were working together, and that is why you were so reluctant to have her removed from the lab."

Jameson smiled. "I was indeed reluctant to have her removed, but not for the reasons you assume." He expanded another document to fill the screen. "Days before you and I had our conversation, I spoke with Sally about some ideas I wanted to put into practice over the next few cycles. She, of course, was delighted to hear that and asked what she could do to help. I explained that these tests were not exactly on the books. I wanted to really see what Harmonicum could do. She tried hard not to become overly enthused, but she was completely giddy about the whole idea."

"But—" Creed started but was cut off by a cold voice at the head of the table.

"Let. Him. Finish." said the old man calmly, but with an unmistakable tone of caution to Creed and anyone else who next chose to speak out of turn.

"I told her I would set the cycle up but have Mike leave it off the schedule so that we wouldn't be hindered. My hope was to provide her with information that I could trace to her source. I had our Blackwire team cook up some tracer files that could be followed through any lines of communication." Jameson pulled up the confidential requisition form showing the details of his request. "I marked the file as declassified just this morning, thus it didn't show up in any primary level search results."

Creed squirmed uncomfortably in his seat. Green stared at the holo-board as if no one else was in the room.

"I purposely scheduled Sally for times when I would also be on the lab floor. We were a few days away from my planned sting when Mr. Creed came into my office to discuss Sally."

Creed shifted again in his chair. "I can't blame him for bringing my behavior to you and Kingston," Jameson said to the old man. "I expect nothing less from my head of operations. It was during our conversation that I realized that my reluctance to let Sally leave the lab raised too many questions. I knew that she would still try to obtain the information she was looking for, so I agreed to the staffing change with intentions to keep tabs on her in her new assignment." Jameson pulled up the staffing change request in addition to a memo to recommend Sally be placed in the nano-biology lab across from the Interface Lab, as they were in need of a team lead.

Jameson appeared to be at a resting spot. Heeding the old man's last comment, Kingston waited a few moments to ensure he would not interrupt Jameson.

"Help me understand why, if Sally was looking for information, she would destroy the lab in which the information resided?"

Jameson smiled at this and grabbed a second document similar to the one he had filed for Sally's reassignment. "I believe that also can be attributed to Mr. Creed." Jameson blew up the document, which showed Creed's request that Sally be moved completely out of the wing and reassigned to a menial post in one of the basic medical research labs. The document was also cc'd to the head of that lab.

"Again, I could not be sure how much access Sally had gained into the MESA servers, but I believe this proves she was at least keeping tabs on Orlando and myself. It was no secret that Orlando did not care for Sally, and despite his efforts to be polite and cordial, I am sure Sally was aware of it. I believe that she accessed this secondary reassignment request after reviewing mine. Further, I believe that she also put together that Arturo Dominguez and Orlando Creed both came to MESA upon graduating from UWC Western University... in the same year. If Sally was crafty enough to infiltrate the lab, then she certainly was intelligent enough to know that Orlando wanted his old school buddy to keep an eye on her and report any activity back to Orlando."

Creed had been rubbing his forehead for a while now. This seemed not to change that.

"Now, I can't prove that this was her thinking, but I believe that Sally figured it would be impossible for her to regain access to the Interface Lab without Orlando knowing about it. Further, I believe that her handlers, in light of her no longer having access to the information they needed, advised her that she needed to set our efforts back significantly. This is when I believe they concocted the sabotage plan. Leaving before the explosion is a surefire way to draw significant attention to herself, but the move should allow some ability to fade into the background. In fact, I am sure Ms. Green did a thorough investigation into any recently dismissed employees to rule out any revenge motives."

Green nodded silently to this assumption.

"Thus, Sally had to be present the day the explosion happened in order not to draw suspicion to herself. In fact, I believe she has taken her assignment one step further."

Jameson opened a mail from Sally to him dated just a few days ago.

"Here, Sally sent me a note wondering if I was recovering

well from my injuries. She continues to go on about her new position in the medical lab and other benign topics. Yet right at the end, she offers this: I understand that you will be short-staffed for a while as your lab employees recover from their injuries. I know how accelerated your timetable was to produce results and want to offer my services as temporary help while you get the lab back online. I've cleared it with Mr. Dominguez, who has agreed as long as it is temporary."

Jameson turned to face the room. "Sally is still attempting to gain access to the lab despite her efforts to set us back. I believe there is still an opportunity to find out who is ultimately pulling her strings."

Kingston looked around the room. "Jameson... CJ, why didn't you come to us with this sooner?"

Jameson sighed. "I see that I made a mistake in waiting this long to present all of this information. But please understand... It was unacceptable to allow the lab to be compromised again. I rebuilt it once. And this time I still have all the data and results from our work, so it's merely replacing equipment and perhaps some staff. But I simply could not bear the thought of a repeat of the event at the desert facility... all that work lost. That was the reason for my paranoia and my secretive actions. I knew, eventually, an accounting should be made for them, which is why I documented this history so thoroughly. With all of the aftermath of the explosion, I knew that if I came forward with any of this, we would lose the connection to Sally. My deepest regret is that my staff was injured because of my oversight. It won't happen again."

The old man stood and walked over to Jameson. He put his hands on his shoulders and nodded. "Thank you, Jameson, for all that you do." He affectionately squeezed Jameson's shoulders and turned to look at Creed and Green.

"As for you two, while you *were* up against the most intelligent man in this company, I expect that in the future we refrain from fitting the facts to fit theories. I will take this up with the board, but for now, you both are excused."

Without a word, both of them stood from the table and walked to the elevator. "Oh, and Ms. Green," called the old man. She turned around to face him. "Please see that all of these files are erased from the MESA history logs." Green nodded, and she and Creed exited the boardroom.

Jameson told the old man he was heading down to see the progress on the repairs to the lab and invited him to come with. The old man happily obliged. "Kingston, aren't you coming?" he asked.

"No, go ahead. I'm going to just clean up a few things here. I'll meet you down there."

Kingston watched as the elevator doors closed on the two men. *I don't care what precautions you took, Jameson,* thought Kingston. *That was one helluva story.*

CHAPTER 19
ROB'S GOT A HEADACHE

Place: Somewhere within the borders of the UWC

Scene: An unpleasant one.

Rob awoke, and his head was killing him. He was having problems remembering what happened, and he didn't know where he was. He tried to remember.

The last job—it was a weird one. They had just been trying to make a pickup when...

"The security guard," Rob blurted out. His wits came fully back to him. He searched his surroundings: a dark room, large mirrored surfaces, and him tied to a chair. Perfect. Just perfect.

"Rob, you awake?"

Rob looked to his left, but the darkness was fairly encompassing. He wasn't able to see much. He did recognize the voice, however.

"Samuel, where are we?"

"I was just about to ask you the same thing. All I remember is we were at that shopping center outside Academy City 676, and we got jumped by a security guard."

Rob sneered. "That was no security guard. I've never seen hand-to-hand combat skills like that. Not even in the Masters in the Empire were that brutally efficient. Whoever he was, he had some serious training."

Samuel didn't sound impressed. "That's not super comforting. Do you think that's why we're here?"

"I don't know why we're here. Just keep your mouth shut and let me do the talking. I'm sure we'll find out soon enough."

"You two sure are chatty," said a digitally altered voice.

Lights flipped on, flooding the space with overly bright illumination. Not surprising at all. Rob knew this was a common interrogation technique. It was a way to make the prisoners uncomfortable without actually doing anything to them.

"Who are you?" yelled Samuel, coming across more confident than Rob knew he was. Samuel was the newest to their little group and really not cut out for the cutthroat business of slaving. "Show yourselves."

Samuel instantly started to scream; Rob couldn't see him, didn't know what they were doing to him, but he knew whatever it was, it must be painful.

"You shall not speak unless spoken to," said the digitally

altered voice. "You're only alive because my colleague thinks you know more than regular hired grunts should. I need information concerning your activities. Answer my questions, and we'll see about letting you live. Don't answer my questions, and…"

More screaming, this time it was Tony. Though he was unable to see him, Rob could distinguish that scream anywhere. Tony and he went way back. This wasn't their first time being caught by enemy forces.

Tony finished screaming, allowing Rob to determine his location. He was behind him, far enough that he couldn't see them. Heavy panting over his right enabled Rob to fix his exact location. He was approximately a meter and a half behind him.

Moments of silence where no one spoke dragged on. Rob knew this game all too well. He waited.

"Now that we understand each other," said the digitally altered voice, "why don't you start at the beginning? How about Jackel Mickleson? Why don't you tell us about your businesses?"

The lights in the room shifted, some going out and darkening while others brightened. The brightened lights focused on a point, again behind Rob. The way the screams carried and the reverb told Rob that the five of them, if all five of them were there, were staggered, one behind another in a triangular shape. Rob didn't know why they were doing this. Seeing one another would make much more sense. They could play off each other; you get some of the same effect by having them in the same room, but in most cases with people in their profession, out of sight, out of mind.

"I've got nothing to tell you," said Jack, sounding really funny as he spoke, labored far more than Rob felt.

The voice sounded amused when it answered. "Wrong answer, Mr. Mickleson."

Screams—penetrating, gut-wrenching screams—pounded against Rob's eardrums. Whatever form of torture they were pulling on Jack, it was horrible. Alternating current, maybe? Or a fine plasma drip on the bearskin? Those were pretty horrible torture techniques, Rob knew, having employed them himself. The problem with those techniques was they didn't keep the victim intact long enough to get any real information out of them. It was just for the fun of the interrogator.

If this is just for fun, we might as well be dead, thought Rob. There was going to be no negotiating out of this one.

"Jack," whispered Rob, "just answer his questions; you know the drill."

No answer and no breathing.

"Jack?"

Again, nothing.

"Jack's not moving, Rob."

It was Samuel.

"I think...I think he's dead."

Rob tried not to lash out. Jack is dead. These bastards just killed him like he was nothing.

"Antoine Meyer. Were you listening?" The voice held no hint of remorse.

"Yes," like Jack, Tony sounded funny as he answered.

"Same question."

Tony didn't answer briefly but quietly said, "We're slavers."

Tony was never a man of many words. Tony got a hit of whatever delightful pain-inducing mechanism that just finished off Jack. It didn't seem as bad—Tony's pain.

"Good, now we are getting somewhere. Describe your operations."

"We kidnap kids, mostly girls, from the UWC and the Jade Empire and sell them." Tony's voice was as emotionless as their keepers.

"How does it operate? Details—how do you get the girls out of the country?"

"We have the port authority in Los Angel, the one in the province of Schwarzenegger. From there, we'd attend auctions in the Burning Planes or in some of the other rogue states. That's generally how we operate."

The voice answered. "Generally? What do you mean, generally? Has that changed?"

Tony hesitated and then screamed, a real one this time, one that was eerily similar to Jack's.

"Mitch Bateman, same question. Answer quickly, please."

Mitch didn't hesitate. "Things changed some months ago when Rob took on a different—"

"Mitch, what are you doing? Are you trying to get us—"

Mitch started screaming, just like the others, and Rob didn't have to ask. He knew that Mitch was dead.

"You dirty sons of a—"

"Samuel Knight, how have things changed within your organization? What have you been doing differently?"

Samuel didn't answer right away; Rob prepared for the screaming.

The screaming didn't come. Rob opened his eyes, just realizing that he had closed them.

"I've got something special for you, Samuel. I need your leader here to understand how important this is."

"But—"

Sound indicated movement from overhead, drowning out anything Samuel said. Unable to see, Rob didn't know what they were doing. There were some strange sounds—the grind of shifting metal and the click of moving gears—but nothing else. Rob waited, listening for any clue. He wasn't sure how long he waited.

Rob grew hungry and really had to take a piss. He wasn't going to say anything, though—not to these people; they were looking for that weakness, wanting to dull his wits for their own purposes. He wasn't going to play that game. Still, Rob waited, waited so long that he started to doze off.

Suddenly, Samuel appeared in front of him. This time it

was Rob who screamed. Samuel's eyes were rolled back into his head, and he was foaming at the mouth. He fell in front of Rob.

"What the hell did you do to him? You sick bastards. When I get out of this chair, I'm going to—"

Energy ravaged Rob's body; the electric current streaming through his frame made him lose control of his extremities. He pissed all over himself.

"Roberto Shoemaker," said the voice, "we've been watching you for a long time. You're a busy man. A captain in the Jadian Horde, you left seven years ago after—now isn't this interesting—you left after your own sister was taken by slavers."

The voice sounded amused. "Is that why you got into it, Rob? Were you trying to find your sister?"

Rob spat blood out of his mouth; he had to take control of the interrogation. He had to answer in a way that would make them want to keep him talking. If he did that, then maybe he could get out of this alive. "What'd you do to Samuel?"

Again, the voice sounded amused. "There's an interesting phenomenon they discovered in the 21st century having to do with audio sounds and dopamine in the brain. They discovered that your brain can only decipher a certain range of sound. Anything outside that range, and your brain gets confused, and in that confusion inadvertently releases copious dopamine."

There was a slight change in inflection. When the voice

spoke again, he sounded a little unstable. "Copious amounts of dopamine, in a sleep-deprived state, will cause insanity in the victim."

Rob looked at Samuel, who was in the corner of the room, muttering incoherently. Something about that explanation didn't sound right, but Rob believed the voice. He couldn't help himself.

"Rob, can I call you Rob? In the interest of time, why don't I go ahead and ask you my question? Then we'll see if you can even answer."

Rob didn't respond.

"You've been slaving for the better part of five years now, but the past year, according to your data, you stopped leaving the country. My question is why?"

Rob answered. "We came under contract; same job, different employer."

"Who was the employer, Rob? Who hired you?"

Rob stared into the light, trying to see anything. "MESA Corporation, a man named Warrick was...is our contact point."

When the voice next spoke, it was cold; the difference was obvious even with the digital voice scrambler.

"MESA had you capturing girls. Why?"

Rob gave a half-shrug through his restraints. "They were looking for something very specific."

"What were they looking for?"

"How the hell should I know? They paid me a great deal

of money to do it. What do I care what they wanted them for?"

"Your last target right before we picked you up, the two at the MegaLots Shopping Center outside of Academy City 676; what made you pick them?"

"A cross-section. We'd already captured all other age groups from that area, and we needed to fill a quota," said Rob. "Around that time, MESA became more demanding, having made some kind of breakthrough. We weren't the only group working in the area. Also, know that these weren't the normal slaver jobs. These girls weren't sold, at least not that I know of."

"You weren't the only slaver."

"No. MESA was building some sort of database with these girls. They were also placing devices in their bodies. Whatever it was they were looking for, they were close to finding it, or at least close to figuring out a way to find it. But then something happened, and they lost all their data, and the backup system was corrupted. I was never briefed on what happened, but our operations base for that province was changed after that, so I assume that had something to do with it."

"Your base of operations was destroyed."

"Exactly—wait, how could you know that?"

"Because I destroyed it."

Rob whistled. "You're an interesting individual, Mr. Voice."

"Back to MESA, Rob. What was it they wanted? How close are they to finding it?"

Rob narrowed his eyes. "If you destroyed our base—"

"The Obama Center for Hope Ever After. Yes."

"Okay, if you destroyed it, shouldn't you know what MESA was looking for?"

"We have an idea; we were interrupted before all pertinent information was gathered. Hence why you are alive."

Rob scowled at the reminder. He knew he was in the voice's hands. It annoyed him. "If you're going to just kill me anyway, then why should I tell you anymore?"

The lights flared up and focused on Samuel, who was still whimpering in the corner, foam and spittle falling from his mouth.

"Because there are worse things than death. Now, you said that they were experimenting on the girls. How exactly were they experimenting on them?"

Rob again looked at Samuel, who was curled up in a fetal position now. "Blood. MESA wanted samples of the girls' blood."

"You know this for a fact?"

"Yes, but it wasn't the blood, at least initially, that was special. They were attempting to create some sort of bio-sensory feedback system. One that was almost purely biological in nature."

"How could you possibly know that?"

"They invited me into the lab on more than one occasion.

One thing you should know: Jadin Special Forces all have engineering degrees, Mr. Voice. Warfare is more than just swinging a light shiv these days. Soldiers need to know stuff. I, myself, have a PhD in biological mechanics, and I saw the signs. Though this was far more advanced than anything I've seen. MESA was using the blood to form biofeedback products that they tracked remotely and integrated with computer-human interfaces. The blood testing was to develop a profile of compatibility with the products. They took the girls' blood type, did gene mapping, among other things. The cross-section of the many girls would create a database that would eventually become a system of data feedback posts. MESA was developing a way to categorize the living and gain intel on pretty much the entire physical world. Just like spiderbots have been doing on the Interweb for over a hundred years. Pretty amazing, actually.

It was during this process that someone from a different branch of MESA came. I just happened to be there dropping off a load, so I know. Anyway, this one big-shot gal—I mean, a high up, so high up and secretive that she wore a mask around the facility—made some kind of breakthrough that was supposedly going to change everything within her own project."

"Change everything...isn't that a little vague?"

"Can't tell you what I don't know. The facility was destroyed—you destroyed the facility before I found out what she did exactly. It was a big deal, though; apparently, she's working on some project that's detrimental to MESA's future, blah blah blah, and somehow this new breakthrough was going to jump her light-years ahead in whatever her field is. I never found out what the project was and only heard the code name once."

"What was the code name?"

"Beta 1. That's all I know."

"I believe you," said the voice. Rob looked up; the voice didn't sound like the voice. It sounded like—a man was standing next to him. Rob squinted and stared at the man's face.

"I know you."

The man smiled. "Yes, I'm sure you do."

"Are you going to kill me?"

"Yes, I am. I can't let you go free. You've seen too much. You know too much, and you're a slaver."

Rob nodded. "Yes, 'tis the life of the slaver. What about Samuel and the others?"

"Ahh..." The man clicked a notch at the bottom of Rob's chair and swung him around. There was nothing there.

"How—how can that be? I heard—"

"You heard copies of their interrogations. They've been dead for hours."

"And Samuel?"

The man spun on his feet. "Oh yes, Samuel, that's enough; you can get up now."

Samuel did just that. He smiled at Rob.

"You made a deal?"

Samuel nodded. "Just like you taught me."

"Good man."

The man nodded at Samuel, and Samuel left the room.

Rob watched him go. "You're going to kill him, aren't you?"

"Yes, yes, I am."

"Could you spare me a request; say as payment for all the information. Could you make it quick?"

The man pulled out a gun and pointed it at Rob's head. "Don't worry, Rob. He won't feel a thing."

CHAPTER 20

A FINE PIECE OF EQUIPMENT

Scene: Sam is very frustrated
Place: Sam's room

"Why won't you do anything now?" Sam said in frustration, almost yelling at the box. "There are times you flare up like a freaking torch, but I can't get a dull glow out of you when I'm looking for it."

Okay, she needed to calm down. She was yelling at the box, talking to it like they were married. A hazy, reeling image jumped into Sam's head of her standing at the altar, wearing a wedding dress while she herself sported a tux. Why was she dressed like a guy? She wasn't sure, but apparently, the box was female, and she was a dude. Now that was messed up.

Sam slumped onto her bed. She looked toward the place where she kept Coda's tablet. She was tempted—oh, was she tempted—to take it out just to have some connection to the outside world. She knew that Richard could pop up at any time. It had been almost three weeks since the Republicans had left, and since Richard made his first appearance in her bedroom two weeks ago, he had been popping in on her ever since. He was like a flipping shadow. One moment all was quiet, and she was alone; the next, poof, he was there, doing his best to say as little as possible and not look her in the eye. She didn't know what was going on with him.

Richard's random visits were inconvenient. She knew that Richard wouldn't approve of her using Coda's tablet. It didn't matter how supposedly secure it was; Richard would not let it slide. She also couldn't fight with him to keep it. He would incapacitate her so quickly it would make her head spin. Then she would be without the tablet, and Richard would probably stop coming around her so much. He might even throw her in jail, or the paramilitary equivalent. She needed to remember that Richard was a big shot. No one would or could come to her aid. She was breaking his rules, in his base, and doing so blatantly. If she was going to take such a risk, she needed to be careful.

So she was—careful, that is. But it was getting really old. The tablet was sitting in its hiding spot, collecting dust. Now she was simply bored. She tried to cook, read some of the old books she found while exploring the tunnels; she tried to sleep her day away. She could only sleep, and the books were mostly old textbooks from the time when the United States military occupied this space. None of these activities kept her attention, so Sam turned to the only thing left that she had of interest: the box. Over the last three or four days, she had taken to studying it. She didn't glean much in the way of answers, just minor deductive conclusions and a lot more questions.

Even before all the madness with Richard, the Republicans, and MESA, Sam had come to the conclusion that the box was special. On more than one occasion, the box had acted out in fairly dramatic ways, like sticking to her hands like a magnet sticks to metal or lighting up like a light post. These overt displays by the box were few and far between, but Sam was starting to realize more and more that the influence of the box was far deeper than she had originally thought.

When Sam was in her room, she thought about the box. She knew, she just knew, that Richard and those people who attacked the school—specifically MESA—were connected to the box. It was a feeling that, at some point during this crazy journey, became lodged, entrenched in her mind or psyche or whatever. If she could only figure out what the box did, then maybe she could understand what MESA's, Richard's, and the Republicans' interest was in it.

Why didn't I ask Coda?

The question blindsided her. *Why didn't she ask Coda about the box?* Thinking back, the box had not once crossed her mind. It simply didn't occur to her.

I was just caught in the surprise, the moment, the excitement. It doesn't mean anything, does it?

Still, it was another one of those feelings that she couldn't shake—the feeling that she was missing something obvious but exceedingly important. It was doubtful, however, that she would figure out what that was.

Sam retrieved the box from its hiding place and set it down on the nightstand next to her bed. She pulled the thick dark cloth wrapping she had placed on it after the last encounter with Richard. She didn't know what the box was really capable of, so determining how dangerous it was was close to impossible. It was doubtful that the cloth wrapping would amount to much in the way of precaution, but surprisingly, it made Sam feel better. Silly? Probably, but it was just her debating the implications of the choice and the possible endings, so in the end, her logic won out.

Sam watched the cloth-covered box for a few minutes from the foot of her bed. Nothing happened. Sam sighed—not that she really expected something to. If she was being honest—and it was hard not to be honest when the only person you could lie to was yourself—this whole tin box mystical artifact thing seemed idiotic. What could this box possibly provide for MESA, Richard, or the Republicans? Was this really what they wanted? If they didn't want the box, what could they want? Richard? That would explain the Republicans' behavior, but not MESA or the Jade Empire. She also couldn't rule out the idea that each group had some sort of independent objective. An obvious problem jumped out the moment Sam thought this. If each group's objective was independent and unrelated to each other, then each group's attack was mere circumstance, and the actuality that all three groups descended upon the school at the same time was total coincidence. That seemed unlikely.

Sam moved back toward the box. She worked at the knot binding the cloth and revealed the tin within. Sam studied the box. She didn't know much, but she did know that the odds of the Jade Empire, MESA, and the Republicans attacking Academy City 676 at the same time while pursuing completely independent objectives was totally insane. The attacks had to be connected. She just had to figure out what that connection was.

Sam touched the corner of the box and felt a shock of energy run up her arm. A flame of pain ravaged up her arm, completely jarring her. Sam pulled back as she understood. The box was acting up again. It was going to do...something. Sam rubbed the length of her forearm, the burn of pain lingering. She didn't know what, but she had to take the chance that she might finally glean some detail as to its origins.

Sam placed the whole of her hand on the top of the box. Instantly, a flash of pain, for a second time, shot up through her fingers into her wrist, then her elbow and shoulder. Sam endured, focusing her mind on maintaining her concentration and purpose. The pain diminished and was replaced with a distinct thump. The throbbing pulsed against her hand; it was almost as if...as if the box...had a heartbeat.

The beating pulse grew louder in her ears, and Sam's vision grew cloudy. Her body grew weak. Sam tried to remove her hand but was unsuccessful. It wouldn't budge. The beating in her ears grew louder and louder. Sam closed her eyes.

The beat of this box was very much like the beat of a heart—constant, unwavering, doing what needed to be done involuntarily and without concentration or consideration. Sam listened to the ba-dump, ba-dump, ba-du-dump.

What was that? she thought, as the beating of the tin's heart skipped a beat. Instinct answered her question.

The sound...the sound of the beating heart was irregular. The beating was off. The beating of the heart was sick.

It was all wrong. The beating heart was trying to get back on rhythm but couldn't get to where it was going. It was broken and would stay that way until someone fixed it—but who?

Once again, instinct answered, and Sam found herself whispering without meaning to move her lips.

I can.

Light flared behind her closed eyes, and moving parts appeared. Sam did not know what the parts really were—whether organic or inorganic, human or animal. She did not know. She did know that that which could fit, that which should work in perfect clarity and cog, did not. The parts ground against themselves, knowing there was a problem but not knowing the solution. Sam, however, knew. She felt like she had always known. That was the part, the changing enigma, the mystery of which she didn't know if it was a blood vessel or a wire or a tube. The part was not connected to the whole. The part was not doing its job. Sam could not allow that to remain as such.

She concentrated. She focused with anything and everything within her heart. The part had to be moved. The whole had to be fixed. She focused. She yearned. She called upon all deities, both real and fictional, to lend her the strength to complete her task.

She grabbed hold of the part by will alone. She knew— she didn't know how she knew, but she knew what must be done to fix that which was broken. She had to move it. She had to reconnect that part.

Ethereal images taken directly out of a dream world drew Sam in as she threw all her strength of mind into what she felt had to be done. She didn't know; she couldn't possibly know what she was attempting to correct. She only knew that it, whatever it may be, was broken, and she wouldn't feel right until she fixed it.

The bend and blur of smoky apparitions twisted and taunted her as powerfully familiar emotions welled up from unseen space within her. The sensation of crude leather clasping her skin did its best to desensitize and demoralize as a jolt of purposeful anarchy raged through her body.

Restriction. The feelings of fear pressed only to be assaulted from left and right by comprehension and discovery. A breakthrough—the breakthrough of the seemingly impossible—now discovered and understood radiated from within. This discovery, this discovery would...change. The. World.

Sam almost lost track of her goal; the feelings, the adulation, the dreams and possibilities rolled over her like the wake of a run-off river. She pushed. Her goal was just ahead, floating serenely in colorless animation. It lingered just in front of her, waiting for the salvation that Sam's hand would bring it. Sam's hand, only to the wrist, appeared before her, disembodied like images formed of wispy smoke. Sam reached forth her hand and took hold of her goal.

Information in the form of complex algorithms, supported by convoluted algebraic equations, began streaming from her goal in the moment of contact. It was flooding toward her, wanting to balance and inundate. Sam threw up her other hand, which miraculously appeared before her, to stop the onslaught. The equations pushed against her. Sam could see that her goal needed only to be adjusted—pushed or placed, shoved or forced into its rightful position for all to be well...for all to be well.

Sam fought. She fought like she had never fought before. She pushed forward, ignoring feelings, images, smoky apparitions, and projected mathematical equations. Sam pushed forward, clenching her goal with all her might. She made the final push and watched her goal descend into its place. The correction was made. All was right again.

Sam opened her eyes, with the revelation that they were actually close. The images and flooding emotions were gone as well. It was as if nothing had happened; like the whole experience had been a dream.

The outside of the box grew hot—hot enough to cause some level of discomfort for Sam. She looked down at the tin box, marveling. She knew it wasn't a dream, but if it wasn't a dream, what on earth just happened?

Sam tried to move her body and felt only weakness. She hit the ground, the whole of her weight folding in on itself with absolutely no strength left in it. A loud clack followed, only to have her world go black.

"Sam, you need to get up now."

The voice came from a distance. It made her head hurt.

"Sam, you brought this upon yourself."

Sam felt a bone-chilling splash of water streak across her face. The ruddiest of awakenings, Sam sat up, not really knowing where she was. It wasn't until a pair of incredibly strong hands grabbed and pulled her up that she grasped some semblance of where she was.

"Sam, I need you to focus. Now."

Richard's face, blurry at first, came into view and made her jump as he was really close.

"Geez, Rich, water? Seriously? There couldn't be a better—"

Richard brought his hands up quickly, slamming them together less than an inch from Sam's face. She went silent—not from this clapping but from the look on his face. She knew that look. It was the same one he made right before he turned into super Richard back at school. He was about to shift into battle mode. She spoke as soon as she shut up. "Sam, where the hell did you get this?"

He pointed to the tin box. Sam looked at the box, confused. "I got it from the lake in T. Tracks, but I thought you knew that. Why are you only asking that now?"

Richard let out a stream of swear words and a show of emotion way beyond Sam's comprehension of him. "Richard, why are you so—"

He rushed and picked up the box, turning it over in his hands a few times, touching and tapping it with his pointer and pinky fingers. In a smooth, soundless motion, the box opened, revealing wires and a data readout screen. Richard followed the screen momentarily. He swore, closed the box, and threw it on the bed.

Richard pulled up his ancient 20th-century pistols, his face growing cold, calculating, and emotionless. Sam's throat went dry as she eyed the guns; she just noticed he was wearing them. And that wasn't all. He was dressed to the hilt with weapons, wearing a black mesh outfit, complete with an external earpiece and mini-eye display. Something was not right with this scenario.

Richard opened a chamber on his belt and removed two

cylindrical tubes, maybe five inches in length, and threaded them into the barrels of his two guns. He tightened them and replaced them in his holsters.

"Sam, listen to me very carefully. Can you do that?"

The tone of his voice scared her—low, quiet, and tense, so tense that it was almost tangible falling from his mouth. Sam nodded her acknowledgment to his question.

"I noticed some suspicious traffic earlier around the base of Monument hill; it's an old landmark just north of our location. I have some tracking assets there. I spotted a large-scale mobilization. We've got incoming enemies ETA; they are probably knocking on our door as we speak. We need to evacuate. I can't have you asking to many questions and I can't be worried about you following my orders. They are coming. I can get us out but I need to know that you'll listen to me."

Sam nodded again.

"Good," he said, sounding pleased. "Gather your stuff; you've got two minutes."

"Why only two minutes? Can you—"

Richard yelled, "Because they'll probably be on us in five. Now get moving!"

Sam did as she was told, packing everything that had become hers in their short stay at the Cheyenne Mountain Site. She packed what little clothes and hygiene products she had, a number of trinkets hidden in the bedside table, and when Richard wasn't looking, she shoved Coda's tablet into her bag. She was just about to grab the tin box when Richard caught her arm.

"No, leave it."

"But—"

"Leave it, Sam!"

He didn't wait for her answer; he pulled her out the door, and they rushed down the hall.

Richard didn't speak as they scurried like rats from a fire. He didn't move as fast as Sam knew he could—primarily because he was carrying a rather large pack on his back and still scanning each room, hallway, and hiding place for bad guys. He still covered a lot of ground, though, moving fast enough that Sam was nearly running to keep up with him. This kept Sam from asking questions.

They made it to the western access tunnels, where Richard placed his pack and Sam's stuff into a crazy-looking car. Six wheels with a very wide frame, the car appeared completely transparent but was not—only covered in incredibly clear glass. A massive triple-barrel gun sat on a swivel pod on top of the car. It was one of the more intimidating things Sam had ever seen.

Richard finished placing the gear in the car, and Sam got a quick glance of a pile of other weaponry before he closed the hatch.

"Are we going to war?"

"A war is defined as an armed conflict between nation-states, Samantha, and I'm pretty sure you and I and MESA don't qualify as nation-states. Granted, MESA has the GDP to pull it off."

"I could do without the sarcasm," said Sam, sounding irritated.

"I could do with you not giving away our position."

"What's that supposed to mean?"

"Never mind, just get in the car."

Sam did so with some grumbling; since he was already annoyed with her, she figured there was no harm in asking another question.

"Why didn't you take the box?"

"Because it might give us a chance to escape, and I can't stop the transfer now that MESA knows where we are."

Sam felt her own patience waver. "Richard, that doesn't make any sense; don't we want to keep the box out of MESA's hands? Isn't that the whole reason for this whole freaking circumstance?"

"Sam, what are you talking about? What would have given you the idea that MESA was after that box? MESA made that box. They've made thousands of them. Why would they go through so much trouble just to retrieve it?"

"But isn't—isn't that why they came to Academy City 676? Weren't they after the box? I thought you said—"

Richard turned on the car; it roared to life. He flipped it into drive. "Sam, MESA was never after the box. MESA came to Academy City 676 for one reason and one reason alone. MESA came to our school to find and capture you."

CHAPTER 21
CONTAINMENT

Place: Mountain Facility
Scene: A hot one.

Their discussion was interrupted by gunfire. Plasma bolts slammed into the side of their dune buggy, taking off chunks of the armor. Soldiers—lots of them—wearing glittering blue and black camo filed into Richard's underground lair, lighting up the place like a disco with their multicolored energy blasters. Richard slammed his foot on the accelerator and touched his palm to a large, bulbous button on the dashboard. The soldiers moved quickly and in a coordinated manner. They pounded the car, but to Sam's disbelief, they weren't actually hitting it; the bolts stopped mere inches from impact, absorbed by a sort of blue light. Richard kicked up the gear on the car, and they sped down the tunnel, plasma fire trailing after them.

"We should be dead," said Sam, looking over her shoulder at the soldiers, who were being left farther and farther behind. "How are we not dead?"

Richard took a sharp left, speeding down a tunnel that Sam had never seen before. It was dark and eerily quiet; irritated that Richard was ignoring her, Sam was just about to ask another question when additional explosions ripped from either side of them.

Sam looked behind her. Mini one-person buggies that looked like rockets on wheels were speeding behind them, easily keeping up with Richard's and Sam's larger vehicle. On either side of the rocket cars were sentry guns on robotic arms. The arms were firing free electron rounds in machine-gun bursts. This was not looking good.

"Get in the gun pod, Sam."

"Excuse me?"

Richard turned his head briefly and gave her a withering look. "You heard me."

Sam glared at him. "Why do you want me to get into the gun pod?"

Richard glared back. "Why do you think?"

"You want me to shoot people??"

"Sam, the shield is already at 50%. If you don't get on that pod and start exchanging fire, we are both dead."

"Richard, I can't—"

Richard took another sharp turn to their left. She bumped her head against the window and almost bit off her tongue.

Rubbing the spot on her head, she noticed two of the rocket cars took the turn a little too fast and crashed into the tunnel wall. The bright light momentarily lit the underground passage like a New Year's celebration.

Richard pounded the accelerator, and again they sped up the tunnel, three more rocket cars on their tails.

"Sam, get on the gun pod now."

"Richard, I told you I can—"

"Sam, in 90 seconds this tunnel is going to open up into a massive cavern. If you aren't on that gun pod by then, returning fire, they will surround us, and we are both dead. Now get on the gun pod."

Richard turned his head again, and for the briefest moment, Sam saw Richard's concern. He looked at her like he used to; like he cared.

Sam threw away her hesitation and jumped into the pod. She called back to Richard, "Now what, Richard?"

"The start-up code is 0214. You have three different weapons on the pod. The first is a 20th-century GAU-17/A mini-gun that I took off an old United States helicopter. It's the first trigger; it can put out some lead, but it runs through ammo like you wouldn't believe. Use it in bursts. The second is a large-beamed assault free-electron laser. Be careful where you aim that thing; it will cut through anything without a disbursement shield in seconds. The last is a multiple-core launch filled with thermobaric explosives that fire and release after a designated amount of time—"

A large blast from one of the bikes hit the ceiling just in front of and above their transport. Richard swerved to avoid it and slammed into the wall to the left. At their high speeds, Richard almost lost control; fortunately, the tunnel opened up right then, and Richard was able to regain direction over the vehicle. Energy bolts from the rocket cars continued to fly at them, most hitting nothing but walls, ground, and air. The rocket cars' fast speeds and lightweight appeared to throw off their firing mechanisms, making their targeting incredibly inaccurate.

Ninety seconds were up, and the already expanding tunnel opened up into a full-on cavern. The subterranean grotto was huge, stretching for miles. Unexpectedly, Sam could see fully despite being deep underground; the cave seemed to glow like a brighter, closer version of a starry night sky. No time to marvel. Sam punched in the gun pod's code. The weapon instantly came to life, weapons rising out of hidden panels in the vehicle. A holo-screen right in front of her face flared as well. The screen held a single crosshair that responded to Sam's hand gestures on the control stick.

"Remember," called out Richard, "when using the mini-gun, short—"

Sam let loose a torrent of bullet fire, holding the trigger for a solid ten seconds before letting go. She focused her fire on one of the rocket cars; most of her bullets missed. The ones that did hit bounced off harmlessly. The rocket cars returned fire, forcing Richard to do some fancy maneuvering to avoid the blasts. Sam returned fire and finally found her mark, hitting the rocket car to their right with two three-second bursts. More of the bullets hit this one, though they didn't get through its pursuer's shields. This second rocket car didn't return fire, thankfully, but decelerated, dropping back considerably.

"The bullets aren't doing anything, Richard," Sam called out. "What do I do?"

Richard swore again. "MESA's improved their shield technology again. Hit the cars with a three-second burst and then use the laser to finish them off. Don't hold it for too long, and try very hard not to hit the ground."

Sam did as she was told, pointing her crosshairs at the car directly behind them. She hit it with the three-shot burst and was just about to fire the laser when a noise distracted her.

"Warning! Warning! Missile lock found. Evasive maneuvers advisable."

The rest of the warning fell upon deaf ears as Richard yanked the steering wheel to the right, and a Wasp Class anti-vehicle missile shot right past them. Sam swiveled to return fire. She took aim at the rocket car closest to them and, to her horror, saw the missile take a turn and fly directly at them. The missile moved in slow motion. Sam could see it—the burn of the jet propulsion, the dark black and bright yellow of the body, and the wicked-looking tip. Sam slowly started to close her eyes when Richard punched another button on his dash.

"Close your eyes, Sam!"

Sam got a single look at another hidden panel pulling away and the discharge of projectiles that burst into flame the moment they left the barrel. Sam pressed her eyes shut tight and instinctively covered her ears.

She could see the bright light through her eyelids. She wasn't sure what happened next. Explosion after explosion sounded one after another, accompanied by a display of bright lights. With her eyes closed, Sam couldn't tell what was going on, but she kept waiting for the pain to come. The surroundings went quiet, and the lights faded away. Reluctant to open her eyes for fear of what she might see, Sam peeked only slightly through her eyelid. She saw Richard driving at breakneck pace through the remainder of the cavern. No one was following them.

Sam slipped out of the gun pod and back into the front seat. She turned to Richard. "The rocket cars?"

"Destroyed," said Richard nonchalantly. "The anti-missile flares brought down the Wasp missile that missed us and two more they fired after the fact. The explosion blinded them, and one of them hit a pillar; the other two ran into mini-proximity mines I let out right before I sent up the flares."

"So we're safe?"

Richard looked at Sam. "Safe? No, not even close."

———

Sam didn't know how long they drove in the cavern. It seemed a little too big to be completely real. After what seemed like hours, the cavern tapered off into more tunnels, though in stark contrast to the underground facility, these ones appeared to be real. After a series of twists and turns, Richard took another sharp left into a larger tunnel that was lit up by ceiling lights placed at even intervals on the wall and floor. He cruised up another 50 feet or so and slammed on the brakes. He looked at Sam.

"Get out."

Sam felt her frustration rise. "I hate it when you talk to me like that. Why don't you try being nice?"

Richard rubbed at his temples. "Samantha Montgomery, would you be so kind as to exit the vehicle? Pretty please with sugar on top?"

Sam glared at him and whispered to herself under her breath, "Stupid smartass. I will give him an... if he's going to insult me, at least use a phrase that isn't a billion years old."

She did what she was told, nevertheless. Richard hopped out too. He ran behind the buggy, pulled open the back door, and pulled out his giant duffle bag.

"What are you doing, Richard? Aren't we supposed to be making our escape?"

Richard pulled out giant metal rods and began setting them up on either side of the wall. "We don't know what's at the end of the yellow brick road, Dorothy. Who knows what's waiting for us at the exit of this tunnel? I'm setting a trap for anyone coming this way just in case we have to make a hasty retreat into the mountains. I think we can safely assume that S&D are on their way. Containment Section 1 and possibly 2 —we can handle as long as we get to checkpoint Omega. If S&D gets here, I'm not sure what we are going to do."

Okay, now she was worried. Richard sounded concerned. Sam wasn't sure what she should do, so she did the only thing she really knew how to do well: she talked.

"Richard," she said, trying to sound calm and collected, "who are S&D?"

Richard continued to work, putting up whatever contraption he was erecting. He did level a beady eye at her. "Is that really the question you want to be asking? You're not going to bombard me with questions about MESA, the box, and whatever cockamamie story conclusion you've already worked out?"

Sam threw a rock at him. It wasn't a big one, but it hit square in the back and probably hurt. She threw it hard enough for it to sting. Richard turned on her.

"What are you doing—"

"What I am doing? What are you doing? Who the hell do you think you are? You rip me from my home, treat me like I'm an idiot, and then insult me over the flipping questions I ask. Everything I understood about this whole freaking situation had to do with that box. If it isn't the box, I don't know how else I am involved. I get it, Richard. I'm not that stupid. I know that they are after me. What I don't know is why or if I am ready to hear the answer. So if you ever, EVER cared about me, ever in the whole time we were pretend friends, you'll stop treating me like that."

Sam felt the tears well up. She didn't know where that outburst came from, but she was tired, scared, and just watched more people die. Worse than that, however, was that it was all because of her. If MESA or whoever was following them wasn't after the box, then they had to be after her. It was the only thing that made sense.

There was a moment of silence. Not total silence, as Sam's low sobs carried slightly, but enough silence that the loneliness of the space bore down upon them.

"Search and Destroy," said Richard, interrupting Sam's growing despair. "MESA's primary tactical battle force is called Search and Destroy, or S&D for short."

Sam wiped at her eyes. "That's not very original."

"What they lack in title, they make up for in equipment. Samantha, MESA is the top weapons manufacturer in the world. Their weapons are so advanced you'd only recognize most of their stuff from a science fiction novel. That is why we need to get out of here. S&D recon is surely on their way to capture you; S&D armored division can't be far behind. I can stop them as I am. If recon finds us and tracks us, it's only a matter of time until the armored division brings us in."

"So the big bad wolf waiting at Grandma's house is S&D."

Richard looked at her in mild shock.

Sam smiled. "It is really that shocking? I took 20th-century fairy tales too, you know. I got in the top 10 percentile right after you."

Richard rolled his eyes. "Now that you understand, can we go?"

"Yes." Sam climbed back into the car, followed closely by Richard.

"In the gun pod, Sam," Richard's tone was serious. "I need you in the gun pod and ready to shoot."

Sam gulped but said nothing as she moved toward the gun pod.

Richard turned the car back on, and Sam re-inputted the code for the gun's targeting computer. They sat in silence for a minute or two. Richard broke the silence.

"Are you sure you don't want to ask?"

She was out of sight. She knew this. She shook her head anyway and whispered, "No."

"There may not be another chance." Richard put the car into gear. "We may die; you may never know."

"Well," said Sam as the buggy's weapons popped out of their hiding spots, "if we die, then it isn't going to matter anyway."

Richard nodded and hit the accelerator.

————

Richard and Sam's buggy exited the underground passage at breakneck speed, expecting to see MESA's containment force converging upon them. They found nothing but a gorgeous day and the low hum of wind-swept trees.

"I don't understand. After all the fuss, it ends just like this?"

Richard scanned from side to side, checking both electronic monitoring equipment and his own eyesight. "You sound like you're disappointed."

Sam shrugged. "It was all awfully exciting, wasn't it?"

Richard turned to look at her, appearing genuinely speechless. "You know I've developed groundbreaking technology and theories in almost every scientific field there is. I'm also probably the smartest person who's ever lived, and even with an IQ of 240, education by some of the most well-learned people in the world, I can't understand you."

"I could flash you again; would that make you feel better?"

Richard raised his eyebrows.

"Richard... are you blushing?"

Richard adjusted himself in his seat. "You wish."

"Oh my George W. Bush, you can act like a teenager. Who would have thought?"

Richard was looking at his instruments again. He pointed at a sharp blip on his screen. "We aren't alone."

A single animal perched on a rock a few hundred feet away. The sun glinted slightly off it, making it hard to see.

The animal adjusted its position on the rock. It was a fox—a red-tailed one. It was an incredibly rare breed. Sam was just about to ask Richard what they should do next when Richard flipped on his targeting computer and zeroed in on the fox.

"Richard!" said Sam incredulously. "What on earth are you doing? Red foxes are on the endangered species list! Why on earth would you choose now, of all times, to shoot at one?"

Richard adjusted the optical zoom on the targeting module's screen display. He adjusted the locking mechanism and crosshairs. "Sam, you're wrong, you know."

It was Sam's turn to roll her eyes. "And what am I wrong about this time?"

Richard narrowed his eyes as he got a lock on the red fox. "You're wrong about the American red fox. They aren't endangered. They're extinct."

Richard fired the free-electron laser, and Sam watched as the fox melted—not into a pile of blood, guts, and bones, but into a pile of metal and wiring.

It was already too late. They were spotted. Soldiers popped out of nowhere—some coming from the woods, others from the sky, and others from the dirt paths that at one point were probably roads in and out of these mountains. There were vehicles too: hover tanks, larger versions of the rocket cars, helicopters, and floating gunnery pads. Sam swiveled in the gun pod.

"Richard, not good, really *really* not good."

"You still have that captivating grasp of the obvious, Samantha."

Sam reached down and slapped the back of Richard's head. "So not in the mood, Richard. So do you have a plan to get us out of here or what?"

"Yes, I do. You shoot anything that moves, and I will do the rest."

Richard touched a button on his dashboard. "Doughboy to Big Daddy, follow-up sit rep as follows: now outside home base and two clicks away from extraction point, containment on the scene with S&D ETA unknown. Where are those fast movers? Request for Alpha Protocol submitted."

The answer came swiftly. It was the same voice Sam heard back at school and in Richard's lair. "Number two to Doughboy, Big Daddy is detained. Fast movers are incoming. Hightail it to the extraction point. Alpha Protocol under review."

"Richard," said Sam, taking aim at the soldiers closing in on them, "what's Alpha Protocol?"

"Something very dangerous," said Richard as he cracked his knuckles. "Something that just might save our lives if they okay it in time."

"Oh good," said Sam sarcastically. "More surprises."

Richard wasn't listening; instead, he slammed on the accelerator as Sam took aim. She really hoped that these guys had shields. Sam opened fire on the MESA containment soldiers.

CHAPTER 22

WHAT IS THE MEANING OF S AND D?

Place: Somewhere in the Rocky Mountains.

Time: Really, at this point, does it matter?

"Doughboy to Number Two, Doughboy and the Package are under heavy attack. Containment Sections One and Two are on our six and closing in fast. Shielding is less than 15%. Where are the fast movers?"

"Number Two to Doughboy, faster movers are engaged with unknown assailants. Big Daddy just scrambled secondary ships. Keep it under control until help arrives."

Sam called out as she took aim at a hovercraft with the free electron laser. "Does that mean we are on our own?"

Richard swore, "At least for the time being; it's a good thing I'm prepared. Hold on, Sam. Things are going to get bumpy."

Richard veered suddenly, pulling onto a dried-out riverbed.

The land vehicles, the ones that were equipped, came after them as MESA's air support shot skyward over the treetops. The ride was bumpy, making Sam and MESA's shooting go all over the place. They would have been sitting ducks for the airships, but fortunately, the tree cover was thick enough that MESA couldn't see through it to get a clear shot. Still, this was not going well.

"Richard, where are we going?"

"Clearing up ahead. Three minutes, Sam. Keep them off of us for three minutes."

Discharge missiles, plasma bolts, and electron shots rattled off from Sam's gun pod and the pursuing MESA vehicles, hitting everything except the opposing target. She didn't know what Richard was doing, but she hoped he had a plan.

"Sam, on my mark, I want you to use the mortars on the riverbank. We've got one shot at this."

"Richard, I don't know how to—"

"Now, Sam!"

Sam didn't think twice; she pointed the crosshairs of her display directly behind them, fired, and held all three triggers. Sam felt the discharge of bullets, the pulse of the laser, and saw groupings of small black mortars streak back toward the way they came.

The buggy flew over the bank of the dried-out riverbed. The explosion was much bigger than she anticipated. The shockwave and flying debris destroyed not only the river path and everything within a hundred meters but were strong enough to pick up the back end of the buggy. Richard regained control only to find that the buggy wouldn't move anymore.

"Move!" Richard jumped out of the buggy and kicked open a side panel. He disappeared briefly to re-emerge with the biggest gun Sam had ever seen. "Hurry, Sam. We've got to get to that tree; run!"

Sam struggled to extract herself from the car. Overhead, the air support of MESA's ground vehicles was already above the clearing. Some were letting soldiers down by zip lines while the attack planes circled.

Why aren't they firing?

No time to contemplate. She and Richard were running full out, Richard periodically firing from the hip, toward a tree at the center of the clearing. Sam felt the hope drain away as the conclusion seemed inevitable. They were outmanned, outgunned, and out of time.

"We aren't done yet, Sam," Richard called to her. "Just follow me."

Then Richard did something crazy. He threw away his gun.

"Richard, what are you—Ahh!"

Pain pierced her body, the pain of a thousand fire-heated needles scurrying along her flesh like steroidal fire ants. The pain pushed out everything—noise, thought, and concern. She would have hoped for death if she could have thought clearly enough to offer the suggestion. Sam's knees went out, and the blackness started to envelop her.

Good, she thought. *At least the pain will stop.*

As quickly as the pain had come, it stopped, only to be replaced by something else. Sam opened her eyes to find a blurry confusion of darkness and tears blocking her vision. She did a quick body scan. Hearing was intact, and she didn't feel like she was dying. The explosions had not stopped, but they seemed to be more distant, farther away. Sam lifted her arm, which felt like it was going to fall off, and wiped at her eyes. The room came into focus.

She was lying on a leather couch, an old one from the looks of it, in a room with no windows and a single iron door. Richard was standing toward the front of the space in the middle of a holo interface, wearing conductor's gloves, surrounded by screens and images that scurried to and fro in different directions. Richard was calling out commands and moving his fingers like a piano player on drugs. His fingers moved so fast that Sam had trouble following them.

Richard's dance lasted a few more minutes. Sam didn't really know what was happening until Richard was at her side again. He touched her with warm hands.

"Here. Sit up." Richard pulled her gently into a sitting position. Sam felt like her head was about to fall off. A cool bottle touched her face, the opening of which was right next to her mouth. She drank as the bottle was tipped. The water rushed down her throat and felt better almost instantly.

"What happened?"

Richard screwed the cap on the bottle. "You were hit by a pulse round."

The word stirred something within Sam's memory. The school and MESA opening fire on a group of schoolchildren; this was the type of round they used. She suddenly felt very sorry for her classmates.

"What's happening, Richard? Why aren't we dead?"

Richard set the bottle down on the ground. "We aren't dead because MESA wants you alive, and I just happen to be with you."

"Shooting missiles at us seems like a bad way to keep us alive," said Sam, thinking back to their flight to—well, to wherever they were. That question seemed more important. "Richard, where are we? The last thing I remember is running toward a giant tree in a clearing, and then I got hit and..."

She trailed off.

"Yes," said Richard, "you seem to be forming a habit of making me carry you for long periods of time. This makes three if I remember correctly."

Sam thought about that. "I count only two: this time and when I got hit with the debris at school when we escaped. What was the third?"

"Number Two to Doughboy, come in Doughboy."

Richard touched the side of his ear. "Doughboy here, go ahead, Number Two."

"Doughboy, we've got a lot of activity going on in your vicinity. Two different groups are converging on your area. The fast movers have been completely wiped out. We've got Chameleon One inbound to your area, ETA 2 minutes—get the package out and wait for further instructions."

"Understood, Number Two. Doughboy out."

"Okay," said Richard, picking Sam up like a child. "Time to go."

Despite all that had happened that day, and to her total chagrin, Sam's face lit up like a torch. She kept her head down. Richard walked through the one doorway that was in the room with the holo board and monitors. He then proceeded up a wide metal staircase two steps at a time. They came through another door a few moments later. Sam gawked. The door led outside and popped right out of the tree. Sam gawked—again. Richard had built a fortress out of the massive tree. It was so like him.

"Who are you, Peter Pan?" Sam's voice said weakly.

"Because of the lair in the tree; you're hilarious."

"I have my moments."

Wind kicked up, and the whirl of blades cutting through the air sounded like a helicopter, but Sam searched skyward and didn't see anything.

"Listen carefully, Sam. The people I am sending you with will get you somewhere safe, but don't trust anyone. At some point, there will be one who can answer all your questions. Until then, keep your head down."

"Geez, Richard, if I didn't know any better, I would have thought you were worried about me."

"Just be careful, Sam. I don't want to have to come and save you again."

Sam tried to reply, but the wind and chopper noise were overpowering now. She, for a second time, attempted to ascertain the source of all the commotion but again couldn't see anything. Where was all this coming from? As soon as she thought this, a distinct shape formed in an outline in the sky. Sam couldn't believe her eyes, but as she attempted to rationalize the shape's abrupt appearance, it became more distinct and visible. A few seconds more, and a large transport chopper blinked into existence, hovering 30 meters from the ground. A door slid open on the side of the chopper, and a man stepped into the picture. He motioned to what Sam could only assume was the pilot, and then he hooked a line on his belt to some unseen anchor on the top of the plane. The man started to rappel down the line.

Richard put Sam down on the ground and pulled her close, putting his lips right by her ear.

"Good luck, Sam. I'll—"

Sam couldn't hear the rest as another sound joined the party. Sam wasn't sure what this one was.

Richard, apparently finishing whatever he wanted to say, turned from Sam and started to walk back toward the tree, making it obvious that Richard was not going with them.

Involuntarily, Sam took a step toward Richard. She—she didn't want him to go. She didn't want to face this alone.

Sam glanced over her shoulder. The man rappelling from the chopper just touched ground. He reached toward Sam, and—an explosion ripped from above. Sam watched as the chopper burst into flames and fell. The man who had descended to collect her didn't stand a chance. Sam threw herself back and barely missed being crushed. A second explosion sounded as the remnants of the chopper collided with the ground. Sam covered her head as a burst of heat racked up her body.

"Samantha, are you okay?" Richard's voice sounded in her ear.

"I think so."

"Good. We need to leave."

Richard tried to get her to stand, but her legs wouldn't hold. He kept her from crumpling to the ground. "Richard, wait, what—what on earth just happened?"

"The chopper was hit by something. I'm not sure what; I didn't see. Whatever it was…"

Richard trailed off.

The crackling of the firebombed wreckage smoldered as the burning blare of jet propulsion filled the air. Sam searched for the source and this time clearly saw what was making such noise.

Robotic humanoid-looking suits landed one after another in the clearing of the large oak. The suits formed around them, encircling the enclosure one by one. She was flabbergasted, speechless at the current events. Sam was hypersensitive to Richard's next movement. Slowly, he reached his hand to his ear.

"Doughboy to Big Daddy. Come in, Big Daddy."

"Doughboy, this is Big Daddy. Go ahead."

"Big Daddy, this is Doughboy. Sit Rep as follows: Package not secure. I repeat, Package is not secure. And S&D are on the scene. I repeat, S and D are here."

———

Sam had never seen anything like it. The foes that appeared before them were something straight out of an old twenty-century comic book or a virtual theater experience.

"The XR Strategic Thermodynamic Exo Aerobatic Lining, or for short—Steel Man," whispered Richard, "one of MESA's most advanced projects, pilots wrapped in a damn near impenetrable wall of technology. The Jadians and UWC don't even have this stuff. MESA keeps the best of their weapons for themselves."

Sam whispered back, "So what are we going to do?"

"We are going to run; there are only a few weapons that are going to hurt those things. These Steel Men are going to follow. We still have the advantage as they are trying to keep you alive. I'm going to buy us some time. Get back to the tree, but run to the opposite side. You understand?"

Sam gave half a nod. "But what do I do once I get to the other side of the tree?"

"You'll know once we get there." Richard scanned their surroundings. "We need to move on three, two, one...NOW!"

Sam and Richard took off at a sprint at the same time that Richard touched the side of his head and yelled, "Engage."

The clearing came alive. Weapon turrets poured out of the ground while large panels from the great oak tree peeled back to reveal additional gun ports and rocket pods. A cacophony of gunfire and explosions lit the clearing up as Richard's automatic defenses engaged MESA. Sam heard and felt the zip bolts, probably pulse rounds, whiz by her body. She did her best not to seize up and cower. Those pulse rounds really hurt.

Over the din, Sam heard Richard yell again as he touched his ear. The words were lost to the noise all around her.

Sam and Richard cleared the front side of the tree without harm, but she didn't know what to look for, and it was not as obvious as Richard seemed to think. The ground beneath rumbled at that precise time, and Sam came to a shuddering halt, almost tripping over her own feet. A space, perhaps 12 feet across, shook violently, and a small crack in the ground appeared, lengthening and widening with every shake. The ground rose and flipped outward to reveal hydraulic arms connected to a steel frame. This area was obviously part of the little hideout inside the tree.

Explosions barely drowned out the sounds of grinding

gears, but Sam didn't need to wonder what the grinding gears meant as a jet cycle, not totally unlike the rocket cars that attacked them in the caverns, came into view. Sam didn't need to be told. She opened the hatch and jumped on right after Richard. A verbal command and touch from Richard's hand in the biometric reader, and the bike flared to life. Richard kicked into gear, and they were off.

Sam laughed at the irony; this was the second time in six months she was making an escape from a dangerously violent situation. The irony didn't stop it from being really scary either.

They were not more than 15 meters from the bike platform before a missile hit, which caused some sort of reaction within the system. A massive explosion, not unlike the one that Sam unleashed with the black mortars, utterly decimated the tree and anything hiding under it.

Richard rode the bike to the edge of the clearing and jumped onto a dirt path that was unconventionally smooth. Sam tried to call to Richard.

"Where are we going?"

Sam couldn't hear the response. What she did hear was the buzz of flight. To her right, left, and just behind, Steel Men were coming up fast.

"We've got company!" yelled Sam, trying to make herself heard. "Steel Men are right on our tail. What do we do?"

"Introduce them to plan B," said Richard.

"What?" yelled Sam.

Richard flipped two switches on the bike. The first didn't seem to change anything, though Sam could feel a slight tingle in her hands when she touched their protective shell. The second, however, let loose a discharge like she had never seen.

A cloud of electricity stretched skyward, mushrooming dozens of feet in the air, lighting up the forest and path with a glorious conflagration of color. The three Steel Men flew skyward as soon as the discharge detonated but were too late. The electric cloud of light overtook and enveloped them. The light show lasted but moments in which Sam thought it was over for all of them. She kept her eyes peeled this time. She was surprised to see the Steel Men right on their tails.

One of the Steel Men flew close, pulling within a few meters of Sam and Richard's transportation. Sam could see the shifting of the armor. She watched as the plating moved at the forearm; a blaster rose from within the confines of the suit. The Steel Man pointed the weapon at Sam and Richard.

"Richard...."

"I know, Sam. Wait for it."

The Steel Man pointed the weapon and—he dropped out of the sky. But not just the single Steel Man; his comrades too. They dropped out of the sky like airplanes rumbling. The crashes were rather spectacular.

"What was that?" called out Sam, moving close to his ear.

"Electromagnetic Pulse Land Mine," answered Richard. "When they are in flight, the countermeasures in the Steel

Man for the EMP mess up the flight software data. EMP mines are a great countermeasure if you've got followers like them."

"You knew they would come?"

"Of course I knew; it's my job to know."

That seemed like the obvious answer, but still. How could he be this well-informed and prepared for a weapon that doesn't exist anywhere but MESA?

"Sam, watch for the EXP."

"What's that?"

"It's a heavy suit transporter. You don't want to see it. We've got to get you out of here before they arrive."

Sam glanced over her shoulder. "Richard, what exactly does the EXP look like?"

"It's a giant transportation hover…"

Richard glanced over his shoulder to see what Sam had already noticed. A giant craft was coasting across the air, probably 1000 meters back.

Richard didn't say anything but punched the speed, literally getting up to a pace that Sam had to bury her face into his back because of how fast they were going. The EXP lost distance, but was fast enough that they didn't completely lose sight of it. It didn't help that Richard had to slow a couple of times to take some unusually perilous turns. Sam thought they were out of the woods, figuratively, when Richard attempted a second round of the EMP mines. He must have set off more of them. The arc of the electric cloud was bigger, much bigger than the ones that took out the Steel Men. The EXP looked totally unaffected, flying through the clouds like an old-school jetliner on any old commercial flight. Sam gulped. Was there no way to stop this thing?

"Sam," yelled Richard, "listen very carefully."

Sam squeezed him from behind to indicate her attention. "When we get to this next clearing, I am going to stop. I need you to run to the rock as fast as you can. Do you understand?"

"No," yelled Sam back. "Rock? What freaking rock?"

"You'll know when you see it."

"What do I do when I get to the rock?"

Richard turned slightly so she could see one eye. She heard him clearly, even though she could have sworn he did not move his lips. "You'll know that too."

The clearing came into view, and the EXP was right on their tail. The thing could move when it needed to. This second clearing wasn't completely unlike the first one. It was large, ringed with trees, but instead of having a giant oak tree, there was a series of boulders laid out in a sort of natural fortress with a mini mountain in the middle. Richard pulled the bike over as the path turned to grass. He stopped almost as fast as he started, making Sam queasy. She prayed she didn't throw up.

"Now, Sam." Richard hopped off his bike, turning in the direction of the EXP, now less than a hundred yards from the clearing. Sam got a fleeting glimpse of him touching his ear.

"This is Doughboy! Where the hell are we on that Alpha

Protocol? S&D are hot and heavy. I repeat, S&D are hot and heavy; the package is compromised."

Sam didn't hear the rest as she was running at a dead sprint through the twists and turns of the boulder-like fortress. Sam figured Richard probably had another secret base under this landmark, though she wasn't sure how much it was going to hold against S&D. They destroyed the last one with little to no effort. Sam could only assume this one had better armor or something because if not, Richard was dead, and MESA would have her. She didn't like the prospect.

Sam tripped as an earthquake shook the ground under her feet. She tried to get up, but then it happened again. Then a third time, and a fourth. The time delay earthquakes continued for the next 20 to 30 seconds; certainty at this point was impossible. Next, suddenly, the shaking stopped, and Sam was able to stand. She did just that. She gawked at what she saw. Smoking crates littered the area, each of the craters filled with a giant steel ball-like EXP, and Richard's medieval fortifications were playing an over-scaled game of marbles. No time for inquiry was given as the answer to the purpose of the giant steel balls revealed itself once the balls cracked open and divulged their contents.

Armor walkers. Each ball revealed giant, monstrous energy shields and metal-clad, two-story tall walkers.

Sam felt her knees go weak; they just needed to kill her already. She couldn't handle it anymore.

Blasters, missiles, and other types of explosions rained down, giving the illusion of an ignited sky.

Still, Sam didn't stop running. The path up the rocks was twisted, doubling back on itself over and over again until it came to the crest of the mountainous boulder she had seen from the bike. At the top of the mountain, she ran to one of the larger rocks and jumped on top of it. Careful to keep her body as low as possible, Sam peeked down to look for Richard.

From this height, Sam could easily see the progress of the battle; automated defenses were slowing down the walkers but doing depressingly little damage. The defense grid, similar to the one at the giant oak, would change little in this fight. Their only chance was to escape. Sam searched for Richard in the mayhem. No such luck. What she did see were Steel Men flying directly at her.

Sam threw herself off the top of the rock and rolled right as two Steel Men flew low at her. She popped back up and cast her eyes about. She was in a bottleneck. There was no place to go.

The two Steel Men landed at the opening of the entrance. Up close, they were eerie like metal zombies. One of the Steel Men gestured. Sam didn't catch his meaning. He might have spoken, but hearing was impossible in the exchange of fire all around them. The Steel Man gestured again, and this time his meaning was clear.

Come.

Sam smiled. "I don't think so."

Bursts of sparks and multiple colored lights bounced off the Steel Men as something and someone hit them from behind. One of the Steel Men received a blow to the lower leg, and the other just above the hip. They didn't stagger from the blow but from surprise, as the shields and armor protected them. The attack clearly spooked them, as both flipped on their burners and chimed backward, settling a good 20 feet from where they were.

Richard stood at the mouth of the bottleneck, a light shiv in either hand. He was covered in a thin nimbus of light.

He nodded at Sam and then attacked.

Richard darted forward even as the Steel Men opened fire from arm cannons. They missed. How Richard wasn't hit was a total enigma. The balls of rapidly firing light struck everything around them but their intended target. Richard's approach was less than direct. He closed the distance, moving at impossibly inhuman speeds until they opened fire. He pivoted at the last possible moment, then ran at the wall of the mountain top enclosure. He literally ran on the side of the enclosure, taking several long strides until he had closed the distance between them. He jumped as he neared the Steel Men and raised one of the light shivs in a cleaving ax motion while the other dangled at his side. The Steel Men raised their blasters and fired off a couple of energy rounds. Richard miraculously cut or dissipated them with several quick swipes of the energized blade. Sam bet that if she could have seen the faces of those pilots in the Steel Men suits, they would have been quite astonished. Richard landed right in between them and had to roll as soon as he hit the ground, as the first Steel Man tried to stomp on him and the other attempted to blow him into the 28th century. Richard instantly countered. He did a weird spin move on the ground that made him look like an upside-down propeller. The Steel Men took a couple of quick steps back, and Richard pressed them.

Richard fought the two Steel Men with the light shivs. Richard was obviously faster, but the Steel Men had the advantage in technology and numbers. It didn't help the situation that the few times Richard landed a solid hit on the two Steel Men, the laser blades just bounced off. It appeared they needed more firepower.

Sam caught Richard's eyes in the speed of attack and counter, defense and reverse. She didn't know how, but she could see him see the progression of the fight, and she knew he was in trouble. What did she do?

Sam took another unsure step back. She didn't know...she just didn't know anymore. Sam touched her hand to the far side of the wall. The place where she touched grew warm. She pushed her hand into it more, and...it disappeared.

Her astonishment almost trumped her worried belief. It came back in full force. Sam pushed through the seemingly solid rock and found—another secret room. It was large and full of sorts of gadgets that Sam may have been curious about given any other circumstance. She did wonder: how many of these did Richard have?

Sam looked for anything—something that would help her help Richard: a gun, a sword, a rock, a pair of scissors. She was about to give up hope when a hand caught hers, and she turned to punch, only to have it dodged. Richard spoke. "Remind me if I can get you out of here to give you some proper defense training."

"Okay, sensei."

"Funny."

"Are the Steel Men..."

"Let's just say they won't be bothering you again; now get in."

Richard led her to a pod-looking thing. He pushed a button to open the door. "Get in."

"But—"

"NOW, SAM!"

Sam scrambled to jump in the pod and strapped herself into a seat. She really hoped that Richard knew how to fly.

Richard, however, didn't enter after her. Instead, he closed the door and sealed it after her.

"Richard, aren't you coming with me? What about S&D? They're out there; you aren't going to try to fight them, are you?"

Richard wrenched on the pod door, tightening the seal. "This will get you out of here. I will cover your escape."

Sam screamed. "Are you mental? That's suicide. You'll

die for sure this time. You aren't invincible. Get in this pod, or so help me—"

Richard yelled over her; she barely heard him through the door. "Remember, Sam. Trust, but verify."

"What's that supposed to mean?"

Richard hit another button, which caused all sorts of lights and sirens to go off. Richard looked at her; she looked back. She put up her hand and touched the window. He put up a hand and waved. His hand slowly dropped to his side, and he ran away, swallowed by the rock wall.

It was goodbye, goodbye, and maybe...just maybe even a good luck. Sam felt the corners of her eyes. They were wet.

The sirens got louder, and the floor shook. Sam searched the enclosed space, spotting a chair with straps. She jumped into it, and the restraints automatically kicked into place. More shaking occurred, and the room inside the rock sort of melted away. Sam was once again able to witness the battle.

The walkers destroyed most of the automated defenses, as the greater part of them was a sparking mess sending up smoke along the perimeter of the pasture. The walkers were not advancing, however, as they were unable to maintain footing on the rocks surrounding the mountain. There were already two or three of the walkers down from trying to scale the outer walls. Most of the remaining walkers' pilots, S&D ground forces, and Steel Men were milling around the base, evidently now having to deal with some nasty surprises from

Richard in the rock structure. Richard really did think of everything.

Slowly, the nature of the boulder's structure revealed itself to the sieging force, and while the deceptive nature of the boulders threw S&D off, both they and Sam could now comprehend the contraption Sam was sitting in. It was a sort of rocket transport. Richard was sending her away while he held the ground. Sam tried to get out of the seat. She couldn't move.

The shock of the mini-rocket port appearing out of almost nowhere was being quickly overcome by the S&D forces, who tried an assault on the established pathway Sam used during her climb of the boulder structure. Again, the soldiers ran headlong into some downright cruel booby traps, compliments of Richard. Sam closed her eyes after the first one went off. It was an image she would soon forget.

A loud voice within the cockpit of the structure sounded. *"We have takeoff in T-minus 10 seconds. 10, 9, 8, 7, 6, 5,"*

The Steel Men backed off and took to the air, streaking above and stopping to hover right in front of Sam's rocket pod. They remained only for a moment. Gun and laser fire mixed in with the sounds of sirens and flashing lights distracted the Steel Men long enough for the cacophony of firepower to find its mark and down its target. Some twenty meters away, sitting in a monstrous gun turret, Richard pounded on the S&D forces, sending down showers of small explosive devices, bullets, plasma rounds, and free electron shots.

It was then that she saw it. One of the S&D walkers, standing back a ways, separated from the fighting. A cannon nestled on top of the walker was pointing right at the boulder... No, not at the boulder... at Richard. Sam screamed.

"3, 2, 1..."

The rocket under Sam ignited, sending waves of devastating heat over the body of the boulder base. Sam was thrown back into her seat as her transport shot her skyward. The rocket rose to an altitude of probably around several hundred meters, quickly leaving the Steel Men following in the dust. After about a minute of shooting straight up in the air, the thrust forced upon Sam lessened dramatically, and the flight evened out. Sam was able to move. She struggled but was able to finally get her restraints off. She ran to the window of the rocket, feeling nauseous as she did. She looked out of the window and saw nothing but unrecognizable landscape. Sam swore as the realization sunk in. It was over. She was safe.

Sam's tears ran freely. She was out of harm's way, ushered to safety away from MESA and their S&D. But at what cost? She didn't want to think about it... She didn't want to think about Richard.

Sam slouched back into her chair. Richard was fighting alone on that boulder, outnumbered and outgunned. People don't survive encounters like that in real life. Odds are she was never going to see Richard again. She never really had the chance to tell him—well, anything. She knew she was going to regret that.

Sam's arm hit an unnoticed button on the side of the chair. Instantly, a holo-screen appeared; Sam recognized it immediately. It was the launch pad. She was seeing the launch pad.

Sam didn't care if it didn't make sense. She just thanked the gods in the sky that it was true. Sam searched for Richard.

Sam could not tell, had no way of knowing if the holo-video feed was in real time or not. What she witnessed next dropped her into the depths of despair.

A beam of energy, fired from somewhere off-screen, leveled the entirety of the boulder area. The whole platform... it was gone—completely and totally incinerated.

"Richard..." was all that Sam could say as she broke down into gut-wrenching sobs.

A ping, like the sound of a chat request on VII space or product notification for World Bay, resounded around the room. Sam looked back up at the holo-screen to boldly written words that said:

Alpha Protocol engaged: 5 minutes duration and counting.

EPILOGUE

Time: Mid-afternoon, 6 months after the attack on Academy City 676
Scene: Capital of the UWC – somewhere in the middle of the Rocky Mountains.

"You have a 12:15 with the Zealand Minister of Finance; he wants to discuss a rate change for their bailout loan. At 1:25, you have the Mothers Against Jadian Immigrants; they're trying to make the Romney Providence a percentile zone, where no one with less than 75% UWC blood is permitted to take up residency within the providence, with mandatory testing every 12 months. At 2:25, you have lunch with the providential governor of the British Isles; he has another proposal concerning cessation..."

Patty, chief executive assistant to the Chancellor, walked just behind Chancellor Himms and about a half dozen people, all trying to get his attention. Patty walked quietly, monitoring the Chancellor's personal tablet. The Chancellor was waiting for a specific message today, and she was not going to miss it; other aides and minor executive assistants fought for his words and notice.

"Chancellor, the Continental Congress needs your approval for the amended budget considerations."

"Chief Justice Rehnquist the Fifth called and wants to know the status of Chief Mark Day O'Connor's impeachment process?"

"Your wife is on the secure vid line and wants to know why you haven't been picking up the regular vid line."

"Your mistress is on the second secure vid line and wants to know if you broke up with your wife."

The entourage continued to fight for the Chancellor's attention until they reached the Ground Force Zero conference room. Once there, the Chancellor put up a hand. "You all know what to do. Sync up with Patty and schedule your concerns—consolidate foreign, domestic, and private affairs and line them up in that order. I will attend to them after my meeting. Patricia, come along."

The Chancellor entered the conference room with Patty at his side. The name "Ground Force Zero" Conference Room was deceptive. The space wasn't just a conference room in the traditional sense but a massive, fully interfaced room built in the last five years to be a central brain for the entire UWC. Here, the Chancellor could holo-conference with every branch of his government, from the Council of Governors and Continental Congress to the leagues of Southern Mayors, whose headquarters were in the southern half of the Collective. The space was a technological marvel if there ever was one.

The Chancellor proceeded to a throne-like chair in the very middle of the room. "Patty, can you get me a—"

"Starbucks Mocha Latte? Yes, sir, you were always one for the classics."

"And that notification I've been waiting—"

"Nothing yet, sir. I will inform you immediately."

"Perfect."

The Chancellor sat in his throne. The room came to life as soon as he sat. Patty was always flabbergasted by how advanced the biometrics of Ground Force Zero were. It was another thing the MESA Corporation built, and they always made the coolest stuff.

Holographic projections of six men, from the waist up, floated in a half-circle in front of the Chancellor. "Gentlemen. Do you have conclusions for me?"

The man on the far left, a bald, bulky man named Mason Rank, who looked way too big for the space, spoke up. "There is nothing conclusive, sir. There are signs that more than one combatant was involved."

The Chancellor interlocked his fingers and leaned forward into them. "Explain, Mason. What does that mean?"

The bald man looked downward, and Patty could only

assume he was looking at a tablet. "We found evidence of different breach points, Your Excellency, and Military Scene Investigation thinks the battle signs are inconsistent with the school's coded defenses, but at this point, it's impossible to tell with any amount of certainty."

The Chancellor's eyes narrowed. "What do you mean it's impossible to tell?"

Another man spoke up, the Continental Security Force Chief Computer Officer; Steve Jobs was a tall, dark, and handsome smooth talker—not your normal computer nerd. He sounded nervous at the moment. "The system's black box was compromised, Chancellor; the hacker spiked the system, completely corrupting the data."

"I thought that was impossible."

"It usually is; it's completely impossible remotely, but if you have access to the physical interface, knowledge of binary code from the very basics, and the ability to do high-level calculations in your head while battling the defense programming, then it's possible."

"Who could have done all that?"

"Currently unknown, sir. I probably could, but only with a 15% probability of success, though not under the similar circumstances found in the Academy City incident."

Patty brought the Chancellor his latte. "Go on, Jobs."

"My analysts speculate that there were at least two more military-grade hackers within the system at the time of the spike; I've seen the data read trails on them before. The two hackers in the system are two of the best we've ever encountered."

"Data read trails? Explain."

"Think of it as a digital fingerprint, sir. Computer experts all have very distinct styles of attack. The fingerprint can tell us a lot about their school of thought and educational influence. It helps us develop a profile. I've seen these two fingerprints before. The first is an old-school expert UWC who works for the Jadian Empire. He defected about ten years ago. The second is a freelancer who is up-and-coming; the second hacker is especially concerning to my organization and one that needs to be found if at all possible."

"What's got you so worried, Jobs?" asked Mason.

Jobs sounded annoyed when he answered. "The second hacker we think is an apprentice. His skill, in the times that we've seen him, has progressed in an amazing fashion. There is no way that one can advance that quickly without some sort of tutor. That leads me to believe that we've got a master hacker out there who is literally so good at what he does that he leaves no trace."

Chancellor Himms nodded. "Keep me posted on this development, Jobs. If there is an expert of this magnitude, I want him dead or working for us. No exceptions, do you understand?"

Jobs indicated his understanding.

"Now tell me, Jobs, Mason, explain to me how Jadian forces penetrated this far into our borders?"

Mason answered. "They used the slavers' route, Chancellor, appearing to have taken in their equipment piecemeal. That made it damn near impossible for our border security to detect them."

"But that must have taken months; what on earth could the Emperor want so badly that he spent millions of credits to sneak one of his squads in? Or better yet, what could they want at a mediocre Academy City in the middle of nowhere?"

No one answered.

"After six months, this is all you have for me? What about the other team? The supposed other group that attacked the school?"

Mason replied again. "We believe it was the Republicans, sir. The weaponry was consistent with their known arms, and we got a few IDs off the bodies. The Republicans weren't as good at cleaning up after themselves."

The Chancellor rubbed at his temple. "It's like a bad joke, gentlemen: MESA, the Republicans, and the Jade Empire walk into a bar, but where is the punchline?"

Chancellor Himms addressed the rest of the cabinet. "So tell me, gentlemen, I've heard reports of MESA's involvement in the incident in Academy City 676. What did the investigation turn up?"

A third man, a small, timid-looking one, answered. "MESA was definitely there the day of the incident. No question about that."

The man paused to the obvious annoyance of the Chancellor. "Well, Simon, continue your report."

The man fidgeted uncomfortably. "That's just it, sir; there isn't much else to report. MESA was there conducting regular medical research, they said; something about a new blood product that is a self-contained clinic. They wanted blood samples for the continuation of their research. It all looks on the up and up. All the paperwork is filed with the proper Providential Authority."

The Chancellor did not look happy. "You're telling me that is the best that you—"

Patty didn't want to interrupt, but it was here. Finally. "Um... sir, your next appointment just confirmed. He'll be here within the hour."

The Chancellor's grimace instantly vanished. "Good, it's about time. For what I'm paying him, he should have been here weeks ago."

The Chancellor stood up sharply, obviously surprising the floating holo-men. "Gentlemen, I'm going to get some answers as we speak. File your appropriate reports and keep me abreast of the goings-on, and Jobs."

"Yes, sir."

"Find that hacker."

"I'm on it, sir."

"Then you're all dismissed."

The holo-images faded away. The Chancellor stood without another word and started to walk out of the room,

Patty on his tail. "Patty, send out an update via the interface to cancel all my appointments for the day."

"Understood, sir." Patty faltered slightly. She pushed forward, wanting to ask the Chancellor. "Sir, are you sure this is wise?"

"You're referring to our informant?"

"Yes, sir. I just wonder if it is wise to trust a man such as him."

The Chancellor smiled at his assistant as he opened the door for her. "Don't worry, Patty; he has his uses, and I am well aware of his nature."

The Chancellor stopped walking abruptly just inside his own office. There was a man sitting opposite the Chancellor's desk. The man was tapping casually at a tablet. "Patty, will you go to the wine cellar and bring up the Th.J 1787 Chateau Lafitte? I think we have something to celebrate."

Patty's mouth dropped. The 1787 Chateau Lafitte was from the cellar of Thomas Jefferson and hundreds of years old. Patty didn't say anything. She just bowed slightly and walked towards the door, hearing the tail end of the Chancellor's greeting to his guest.

"Well, Mr. Warrick, how are MESA and the old man doing these days?"

ABOUT THE AUTHOR

Collin Earl is a trial lawyer, entrepreneur, and lifelong storyteller. Known for blending sharp dialogue, layered world-building, and emotional depth, he's the mind behind The House of Grey and co-creator of the Harmonics series. When he's not in court or at the keyboard, Collin is running his firm, raising kids, or losing sleep to whatever creative rabbit hole he's fallen into.

Chris Snelgrove is a writer, producer, and corporate strategist with a background in psychology. He's best known for his collaborative work with Collin Earl on The House of Grey and Harmonics, where his character-driven storytelling adds a distinct voice to the narrative. He lives outside Denver with his wife and four boys, finding time to write between bedtime stories and business meetings.

Thank you for reading.

To explore more of their work, get exclusive content, and stay updated on upcoming releases, visit SilverstoneBooks.com. Whether you are looking for fantasy, sci-fi, or something in between—your next favorite story is waiting.

www.ingramcontent.com/pod-product-compliance
Lightning Source LLC
Chambersburg PA
CBHW050922030726
47503CB00007BB/2417